I0818087

PARADOX TRILOGY: BOOK THREE

ASCENDANCE

JAMIE RIPP

INK STREET PRESS

ISBN: 978-1-7336261-4-9 (eBook)
ISBN:978-1-7336261-5-6 (paperback)
ISBN: 978-1-7336261-9-4 (hardback)

Published by Ink Street Press
support@inkstreetpress.com
Edited by Alan Brown and Blair Thornburgh
Cover Design by Alexandra Purtan and Amber Ripp.
Formatted by Lorna Reid

BOOKS BY JAMIE:

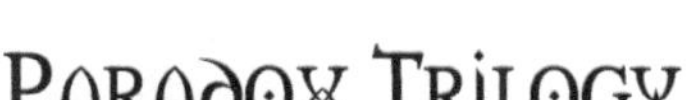

Paradox Trilogy

Paradox
Revelation
Ascendance

Exclusive Bonus Chapter:

Forgotten Journal

www.jamieripp.com

I dedicate this book to my fans and my family, all of whom have supported and inspired me. Thank you.

ONE

"I didn't come for you. I came to seek an audience with Arri." While my mind stumbled to process his request, he looked pointedly at me. I could feel his frostbitten glare as if it were something tangible. His eyes appraised me with contempt. His lips were still curled into a knowing grin, and his fingers twitched as he awaited my response.

Then, the coward smirked, "To negotiate your surrender, of course." Was he insane?

As I sat at the table, frozen, it felt like I was in the *Twilight Zone*. The dull conversation of other patrons coming from the other side of the shaded glass doors started to fade.

The ancient brick walls of the restaurant seemed to pale and dim against the man standing in the center of the banquet room. For a moment, I was paralyzed, and speechless, but I wasn't the only one. My parents, Phoenix, Ash, and Catherine all seemed to be just as stunned. The silence and tension that filled the room was palpable and thick.

Gavin! The man responsible for stabbing me and leaving me for dead was now here, proposing that I surrender!

Before I could react, Michael crossed the room and attacked Gavin, making no effort to hide his anger. Wasting no time, he took Gavin by the collar and threw him against the wall. The deafening and thunderous crash as Gavin landed against the brick resounded throughout the room and into the conjoined dining area. A gasp left Gavin's lungs as Michael cradled Gavin's throat in a crushing grip. As Michael pressed a steak knife against his neck, Gavin let out a painful whimper. Michael, more than anyone, usually handled things with decorum and civility. Today, propriety and formality flew out the window.

"Surrender!" Michael growled. The sound vibrated in his throat. With the six of us looking on, and the crowds murmuring from the other side of the shaded glass doors, Gavin had the good sense to submit. His face fell as he realized his impending death.

"You have a lot of nerve showing your face after what you did, and now you dare come back here and ask for her surrender?" Michael's voice turned acidic as he held Gavin in mid-air.

"Nicholas sent me personally to retrieve the child." Gavin's voice was forced and raspy as Michael's knife dug further into his neck.

"Sent you? Or did you volunteer to rectify your failure?" Michael asked, as he pressed harder yet.

"Look," Gavin lifted a shaky hand and pointed toward me, "even now you protect her while she hides behind you." Gavin's strained voice broke as he struggled against Michael's relentless hold. My mind was still trying to wrap around the fact that he was actually here.

Michael's muscles tensed and the knuckles holding the knife in place paled as Michael fought to control himself. I could sense Michael's emotions and knew that he barely restrained his fury. Gavin suddenly seemed rather small as he looked at me in fear. His superficial bravery was losing strength by the second. His eyes widened with horror as Michael pressed the knife harder against his skin. Gavin's scared and panicked emotions were palpable, as was the terror in his eyes.

My dad's words broke in as he addressed Michael. "Michael, please. Let us sit and discuss this without making a scene. I'm sure there is an obvious reason for Gavin to be here and assume she is willing to surrender." His voice rang with clarity as he spoke.

"Give me one good reason that I should let you live," Michael said.

"If I die, there will be nothing to stop the horde of vampires outside from feeding." Gavin threw a meaningful glance at the door, indicating the humans occupying the dining room. He looked to Michael, waiting to be released. There was a look of pure hope and relief on Gavin's face as Michael's hold loosened, but Michael's lips turned into a slow, knowing grin.

"Yes, of course," Michael said, narrowing his eyes. With a simple shove, Michael sent Gavin to the floor and scrambling to his feet. Michael stood steadfast, blocking Gavin from his only exit.

Gavin fixed his shirt, smoothed the wrinkles from his collar, and took a seat. He schooled his face, hiding his menacing thoughts behind a mask of indifference.

I made sure I showed no sign that this whole thing scared the wits out of me. I understood why Michael had reacted so aggressively, but for me to feel so furious made me wonder what I would have done if Michael hadn't beaten me to the punch.

As Gavin sat, a smug look crossed his face, as though he had a secret. I knew he said he was here to accept my surrender, but I also knew that wasn't all he came here for.

"As I was saying." He cleared his throat, squared his shoulders and repeated, "I am here to accept your surrender."

I mustered all the bravery I could and forced a straight and impervious expression. "I heard you the first time. Unfortunately, I must respectfully decline your asinine request. I suggest you leave immediately."

"Ah, she has spunk," Gavin said, folding his arms and leaning back into his chair. "I always hated that side of you. Acting like a glorified Girl Scout when I know you are nothing but an unworthy cur. I wonder what you'd do if given the opportunity to show your true colors in a real fight."

My dad shook his head. "You will never know."

"Oh, but I will. That is, if you want to leave here tonight."

"Are you planning on fighting all seven of us alone?" Michael asked.

"No, I'm not dumb enough to think I could beat the likes of you. I am merely here as a courtesy."

"What would the courtesy be?" Michael asked.

"To give you fair warning. Nicholas has pulled out all the stops to gain her capture. He has assembled his troops and is waging a war. I am here to offer you a choice."

"To offer me a choice? To what, give up, wash my hands of my responsibilities, and let him win? Or is my death the option you are offering?"

"As for dying, if necessary, yes, but to let him win, no. He has already won."

"So, is that how you plan on gaining her surrender? By making her fight?" Michael scoffed.

"I have come to accept her surrender with whatever means possible. If that means through force, then so be it." Gavin had really stepped it up. He didn't fidget, run his hands through his hair with hesitance; he didn't even blanch when threatened. Gavin merely stared at us, undaunted and uncaring. He honestly thought he had won.

"Arri has no intention of surrendering," Michael said.

"Yes, well I wasn't asking you. I was addressing her. Is Arri unworthy and unable to speak for herself?"

"You're rather cocky when you're outnumbered seven to one and considering the fact you were just under Michael's blade." My dad stood from the table and slowly made his way around to stand in front of Gavin. Gavin appeared egotistical, brash, and arrogant, but he was shaking with fear. My dad's presence alone had Gavin trembling, but when my dad stood over him and glared down at the worthless man, dread and terror shown in his eyes as Gavin's courage wavered and he cowered in my dad's shadow.

"I told you. I'm not alone." His shaky and quivering voice betrayed his outer confidence. "I came with a few friends." Gavin gestured outside. "This fight will happen. It's only a matter of whether she going to sacrifice all of you to save her own hide." With that, Gavin stood, taking careful measures not to move too quickly or too close to my dad. "I'll be outside waiting." Fastening the top button of his dinner jacket, he turned to leave with a devilish grin on his face. His snide smile faltered as he saw Michael blocking the door. Michael's unyielding and rigid posture gave no indication he was moving.

"Now that I have you here, and I know of your men, why would I let you leave?" Michael folded his arms and stared at Gavin with an uncompromising expression. "You still have to pay for what you did. I think your head would be sufficient." Michael's tone had Gavin faltering even more.

"I will pay no such price. My men are outside waiting to hear of Arri's decision. If I don't deliver, then I'm afraid the humans in the other room will pay for your insolence."

Michael tossed a fleeting glance in my direction, as if asking permission to kill Gavin. I knew Michael wanted to kill him, regardless of the price. I could feel it. The way his heart yearned to take Gavin's life. The way the fury pulsed through his veins. Michael wanted blood for Gavin's wrongdoing, and I knew he would settle for nothing less. The anger that flowed through him had me shivering in angst.

"You think that a few measly human beings are going to stop me from getting what is rightfully due to me?" I could hear in Michael's voice that he sincerely meant it. I knew Michael's core argued at the obscene idea of sacrificing humans to gain what he thought was a just reward, but his need for revenge was equally strong.

Looking at Michael, I shook my head and stood from my chair. If the war was knocking at our doorstep, and Gavin was to signal the attack, his death was imminent. He'd already sealed his fate.

"As much as I feel that Gavin deserves nothing more than a slow and agonizing demise, those people will not be a part of it." I looked at Michael as a slow and devious smile curved across his lips. Michael had a plan, something that must have satisfied his inner desires.

Michael stepped aside, and Gavin slipped past Michael with a mocking smile and pompous pose. Just before he opened the door to the dining hall, Gavin turned back. "Don't be too long. I don't want to keep Nicholas waiting." As Gavin reached for the smooth glass doors, Michael placed a heavy hand on his shoulder.

"Where are you going so quickly? There is still much to discuss."

"So, she is accepting surrender?" Gavin's voice was hopeful as he turned to me, but when he got a look at Michael's smile, he realized that wasn't what Michael was referring to.

"No, no, no. You misunderstand. I was talking about your life. Now, as I see it, Arri is right." Michael looked at Gavin with vengeance written in his eyes. "The people will not be held hostage." Gavin bumped back against the painted stone wall, and with Ash and Steven flanking Michael, his eyes froze in fear. "So, after the restaurant is empty, and the wolves have verified that they have all made it out safely, then," Michael's devilish grin widened, "and only then, will we face your men. Now, I know you are a man of many things, but I doubt that valor is in your makeup. So, I know that you will not sacrifice your life for theirs." Michael ran the tip of the steak knife along Gavin's neck once again, etching his skin, and Gavin swallowed hard. "Now, you and I will calmly walk out of here, and you will tell your men that the humans will leave without harm. When we have established that the humans are gone, this trivial and diminutive fight will commence. Do I make myself clear?" Michael gave Gavin a look that made his legs tremble, and the knife set against his neck had all but carved into his skin. With a simple nod and a gulping breath, Gavin accepted Michael's terms.

As Michael and Gavin made their way out, looking as normal as possible, Ash stood nearby. Although he had remained quiet throughout the encounter, he was still and unwavering, waiting for Gavin to make the wrong move. He reminded me of the silent but dangerous type.

When Michael and Gavin were out of the glass doors, and halfway to the restaurant's entrance, Ash, Phoenix, and my parents jumped into action. With little to almost no words, the four of them looked to each other. Catherine pulled out her cell phone and called for Alex.

"Yes, Alex? This is Catherine. There has been a development. We need backup to the Sage Grill in Richfield—and fast. Escorts for the humans, too." With that, and no closing sentiment, she snapped her cell phone shut and joined the rest.

I stood in shock as fear replaced my anger toward Gavin and watched the events around me unfold. Did I just hear Michael say that we were fighting, and now? Catherine had called reinforcements. We were preparing for battle. My breaths came out in small, short spurts as panic and hysteria threatened to overtake me.

Boom!

There was a large noise and the lights went out as the emergency lighting flickered on. A chirping noise came from the ceiling alarms and commotion sounded from the other side of the dividing doors.

The manager's voice was strong over the crowd's growing panicked chatter and cries. "Now, please remain calm. The front doors are jammed so we will need to leave through the kitchen. If you can remain calm and follow the exit sign in the back of the room, everything will be fine." From the way his voice wavered, I could tell he was just as scared. I could feel it coming off him in waves.

Just then, Ash's phone buzzed.

"Nine-one-one emergency," he answered. I looked at him, puzzled. Then, through the doors I heard the faint echo of the manager telling Ash of the events and the situation and I linked it all together. The humans wouldn't leave without a reason, and with all the vampires out front, we needed to create a scene and direct them to the back exit.

"We're on our way. Please have the building evacuated and get as far away as you can. It appears to be a gas leak, and the building could blow any minute." Ash ended the call.

Through the glass doors, the manager shouted, still on the line. "Hello? Hello?" There was a second of hesitation and he must've turned to address the crowed, "Okay, now please stay calm, but hurry as fast as you can through the kitchen exit." Within minutes, the restaurant was cleared, and the pack secured the building and surrounding area.

"Huh, that went rather well, as far as humans go," Ash said, breaking the silence.

"All right. Are we ready?" my dad asked. As everyone nodded, I was the only one standing frozen.

"Are you ready, little girl?" My dad came to stand in front of me. With concern, confidence, and love shining in his eyes, he pulled me into a bear hug. "I know that you are afraid. I can hear it in the pounding of your heart. But we've got this. We will all be there to protect you. We will surround you and keep you safe. Nothing will get by us. Okay?" Dad's soothing and neutral voice calmed my inner demons, and a bit of bravery started to emerge in my heart.

Taking a firm step forward, I turned to face the war outside. With Ash and my dad in front of me, Mom and Catherine flanking me, and Phoenix behind me, I walked through the empty and deserted restaurant with the rest.

As if knowingly facing a war wasn't bad enough, we finally cleared the entrance doors and saw the scene unfold: Michael holding Gavin hostage with a knife against his neck as forty bloodthirsty, mouth-foaming, power-hungry vampires looked on with anticipation and impatience.

As Michael felt our presence, he thrust Gavin at the enemy, and stepped right into formation with the rest of us.

Gavin scampered away, smoothing out his suit, and dusting himself off, he sneered with narrowed eyes in our direction.

"It is obvious that you have chosen war," he said, popping his neck and squaring his shoulders, "but are you sure that that thing, that inconsequential and disgraceful little cur, is worth losing your lives over?" Gavin was obviously feeling a little braver with his troops behind him. Although he sounded and looked confident, I knew his inferiority to Michael, Ash, and my dad weakened his certainty of the fight's outcome.

"Now, now, Gavin. Let's not be so hasty." A man to his right stepped forward. I froze. This was the man that my dad had been talking to in town. His blond hair and well-tailored brown suit contrasted with the mistrust stamped across his features. "Nicholas's instructions were to negotiate for her surrender."

Gavin shot the man a look. "It's no use. They won't listen. Look," he said, gesturing toward our little group, "even now they surround her."

"But let us see what we are fighting for. Maybe a bargain could be struck."

"Terrish," Gavin spat as the man approached us.

"That's far enough." My dad's voice was stern.

Terrish lifted his hands. "I'm just looking," he offered. With a critical eye, and with thin, tight-pursed lips, Terrish scanned me, his eyes roaming from head to foot and back again. "I can see the appeal. She is definitely a nice specimen." Terrish looked to Michael. "Is she more human or vampire?"

I looked at Michael, expecting him to scold the man, but Michael said nothing, just shook his head slightly.

Really? I thought. I reached out and felt the emotions churning around me. From my little group, there was nothing but certainty. We were as sound as we could be. Mom was a bit angry, and Dad may have been a little annoyed, but that wasn't the odd part; I would have expected such emotions. I would have expected anger, frustration, maybe even a bit of fear and anxiety as we neared the fight, but no: my group excelled in the confidence department. Michael was determined, resolute, and calm. The impending fight, their numbers being greater than ours, the savage looks on their hostile faces made me sick to my stomach. Personally, I wanted to run for the hills, but Michael knew something. I could feel it. I could feel him waiting, and there was no worry in him. Then, I reached out and felt Gavin's group. They were mostly angry, hotheaded, and impatient, but then there were a few that surprised me: keyed up, yes, but their hostility was directed at the men surrounding them.

"Her slim and tight physique is definitely appealing and made for speed. Her trim face matches. She's timeless." He looked at Mom and nodded. "But I feel that, although her panic-stricken eyes and tight stance shows her fear, she probably packs quite a wallop."

An Australian accent tainted Terrish's words. "What are you asking for the little treasure?" he asked like he was just buying a gallon of milk.

My dad just about jumped out of his skin, but Michael raised a steady hand.

"What are you offering?" Michael countered.

"Are you seriously going to bid on me like a calf at the county auction?" I asked through clenched teeth. I trusted he had a plan but didn't know it was this!

"I'm offering you ten," Terrish said with certainty. Michael reached back and took my hand in his.

"Ten is the best you could do?" Michael asked as he squeezed my hand.

"Michael," my dad warned.

"Yes, well, Nicholas set the price and the men," Terrish added as he paced back and forth, as if deciding on his next move.

"Fine then," Michael said as he backed up and our group surrounded us.

"So, what's the big plan?" my dad asked, his voice lower than a whisper.

"I would have to admit, I was expecting more, but unfortunately Nicholas is being stingy yet again."

At this, my dad wasted no time and grabbed Michael by the throat. "I should wring your little neck. I trusted you to protect my daughter, not sell her to the highest bidder." My dad's temper was rising, and his anger clouded his better judgment.

"I didn't sell her," Michael mouthed.

My dad loosened his grip as Michael's eyes landed on me. "No, you misunderstand; Terrish is on our side." Michael's eyes pleaded with mine.

"Let him go, Dad," I said as I placed a secure hand on my dad's arm. "Let him talk." I had to admit that I was a little concerned by what just happened: Michael seemed to have sold me to this Terrish guy, but he also claimed that he was on our side.

Turning to Gavin, Michael held up a finger, indicating for

them to wait a moment. Gavin ground his teeth as he growled.

"No!" Gavin yelled. "You are wasting my time. I have had to put up with the pretense of following your orders as you play patty-cake with this worthless child, but not anymore. What's your answer?"

Michael squared his shoulders, clenched his jaw, and stared Gavin dead on.

"I accept your ten, but Arri is not for sale."

Gavin shook his head. "You are as dumb as Steven, thinking that you could take on Nicholas. He is rightfully your leader, and that mongrel is nothing but a child. The only thing she deserves is to die a slow and agonizing death." Gavin's lips turned into a slow grin. "So, what have we?"

As the grueling bartering commenced, I was fully aware of Phoenix's presence behind me. Although her movements were slow and deliberate, they were planned to the millisecond. With stealth and grace came the unmistakable sound of her drawing her swords. Beside me, my mom and Catherine moved in closer to us as the three men were preoccupied with Gavin.

"Michael said you should have this," Phoenix whispered. The familiar smooth hilt of a sword pressed firmly against my sweating palm. I gripped it and took a few shaky breaths.

This was really going to happen. For a moment, I was hoping that the dealings with Gavin, the auction and appraisal, was all an elaborate dream. I was waiting to wake up in my bed dripping with sweat and chills, but as the first man plunged toward us, it was clear that this was reality; the battle was beginning. The circle that encased me slowly broke apart. As my friends, family, and lover patiently waited for the fight to come to them, the world froze, and our wolfish comrades encircled us from behind.

TWO

At first, everything lurched in slow motion. The silent air swept past the cruel faces of our enemy. Time stopped and so did my heartbeat. The wind picked up speed as the whirl of my storming emotions grew. My ears rang with the sound of faint footsteps as the enemy rushed our lines. Pebbles and dirt scraped the pavement as we braced for the hit. This was it—the battle of good versus evil had started. With my life teetering in the balance, I cringed as fear squeezed my heart. Then, the telltale clang of metal hitting metal filled the void.

Phoenix was the first to approach her target. She disappeared from behind me, only to show up somewhere in the middle of Gavin's men. As the men saw her, recognition of who and what she was reflected in their eyes. She took the fight head-on. She fought as she lived life: without restraint and with total abandon.

Several men turned and homed in on Phoenix. Their mouths watered and their anger swelled as each one headed right for her. As she fought them off and engaged wholeheartedly, I could hear her sword sing through the air, and the distinctive sound of her weapons hitting flesh and bone filled the silence. They kept storming in from all sides until eventually they overtook her.

My breath came out in a gasp as I watched and waited for her to resurface, but she showed no movement. Then, as my heart sank, a shifting and stirring motion churned from underneath the men. Breathing a little heavily, I could see the bodies starting to fall one by one, and at last, Phoenix reappeared through the pile of Gavin's men. With a roar and a crazed look, Phoenix pushed up with swords drawn. Still and lifeless bodies fell before her as she panted and winced in pain, kicking and swearing. Her footing stabilized, but a good-sized gash split the flesh of her left shoulder. Switching the sword to her other hand, she rounded her eyes in shock as she focused in on Mom and yelled something inaudible. The sound blended into the background noise of war cries and yells.

At that point, I looked at Mom, who was just a few feet from me, and I gasped anew. Mom had one of Gavin's men pinned under her foot. With determination gleaming in her eyes, she drew her sword back and, with a quick downward motion, laid forth his demise. Then, as I glimpsed movement, I realized what Phoenix was saying. Right behind Mom was a vampire with his sword drawn and poised to take my mother's life.

The situation dawned on Mom as she heard Phoenix's cries. With frightening speed, Mom changed the direction of her thin silver sword and lunged it upward, stabbing the man through the chest. Pain and surprise crossed the vampire's face, but only until she tore the sword from his torso, and in one swift, clean motion, she took his life as well.

I turned to see Ash and my dad standing side by side as a dozen or so men surrounded them. They were obviously the two most feared of our group, and even the brute force facing them was no match for their power. My dad waited calmly for the enemies to make their move, and Ash stood still with his head down and eyes closed. One by one the men tried and failed to derail them. My dad, with brutal speed and flawless technique, pinned and disposed of them before they even raised their swords.

Then, Mom cried my name and shouted for me to look out. Her eyes filled with terror as she focused behind me. I turned to see one of Gavin's minions; his malicious expression and his sword were both aimed right at me. Wormwood, the redhaired coward that followed Gavin around like a yellow-bellied shadow, had found his courage and was ready for the kill. I paused, but only briefly. In the moments it took him to bring the sword down, the demon within me reared its beautiful head. With instinct, impulse, and a bit of fear, I lifted my sword from my side, and blocked his hit with my sword. Before he raised his blade again, I swung, and this time, I hit flesh. As my sword sliced onward, catching him in the mouth, my own blade slowed and stopped halfway through his head. His shattered teeth bit down in pain. As his head bobbed back his sword hit the ground. With revulsion, I tried to jerk my sword from his face, but it was stuck. Placing my foot on his knee, I yanked again, and with the sound of bone scraping against the blade, I managed to pull it free.

He fell to his hands and knees, gurgling and gasping. Before I could raise my blade again to finish the job, his head parted from his body in a flash and a whistle and fell to the ground. Immediately, my attention turned to the small, mousy woman behind him.

With a small smile, Catherine bowed.

"I got ya," she said, then turned away and joined the rest of the battle.

Stunned and terrified by what I'd just done, I felt goosebumps rise on the back of my neck. A tingling sensation covered my body as my heart froze. Something was coming at me, and fast. I quickly searched the space around me and ducked just as a dagger flew through the air. It whizzed past me and pegged itself into the stucco wall of the restaurant sixty feet behind me.

Gavin! The coward. He couldn't even fight me face-to-face. Feeling a sting on my cheek, I raised a hand and dabbed the tender skin. A small trickle of blood dripped from my face and landed on my shirt. With one look in Gavin's direction, I felt darkness envelop my heart. Absolute rage surged through my veins as my vision narrowed in on Gavin. Silence filled my ears. I heard almost nothing, just the pounding of my own heart and the air as I breathed in and out. As we made eye contact, his cowardly gaze and his panicked heart fed my rage. The untamed demon within me stirred and stormed. My eyes burned in full madness as the cut on my cheek seared. Then, as if Gavin sensed his own impending death, he darted into the shadows. With Gavin out of sight but not out of mind, I started to tap into the power inside. The demon pushed for freedom. With one last lurch, it crawled its way to the surface. As power and rage pulsed through my veins, maddening fury took over.

Approaching me was a tall, well-built vampire, his face contorted into an expression of bold and fearless certainty. But when his sword came about and aimed right at my head, I ducked and turned the tables on him. He faced me, stunned, and barely registered the failed aftermath of his cockiness before his eyes dulled along with his life force. Behind him, my mom's eyes focused on mine just before her blade sliced right through his neck with a swift and accurate swing.

As I searched the crowd for Gavin, I could feel his presence. He was close. A man from the surrounding fight fell at my feet. With one fleeting look, he jumped up and fled into the crowd with terror-filled eyes. The distraction was short-lived, but it provided Gavin with the gap he needed. The sound of gravel crunching beneath his shoes caught my attention.

I turned just in time to duck and lost sight of him for a second. Then, I felt his body press against mine from behind: one arm reached out and held me close, and the other whirled his sword to my neck. I blocked it, and from then on it was a battle of strength. With two hands on the hilt, I used my sword to force his sword away. He let go and backed off, then came at me again. This time I was prepared. With a steel-like grip on my weapon, I took a few steady steps forward, pushing him back and further into the fight. All around us, the action slowed, then stopped and stilled as all eyes turned to us. A growl rumbled through me as I watched their collective expressions turn to one of fear.

As Gavin saw the undying fury that burned behind my eyes and through my heart, his breathing froze. He raised his sword and aimed it at me. With a swift stroke, he came at me. I had to defend myself, so I picked up my sword and knocked his hilt from his hand. As his sword fell to the ground, I raised my hand again, and this time I hit him with the hilt of my own weapon. His head flung back, and I heard the sound of crunching bones as he fell to his knees. I pushed his body back with a foot to the chest as he gasped for air. Silence filled the battlefield, but I never took my eyes off Gavin. In blind fear, he stood up on shaky legs. His breathing was fast and erratic as he lifted his sword again. Looking for help, he found none; his men were either dead or in battle.

"Cowards," he yelled, then looked back at me, panicked. "Now look, Arri," he started with a shaky breath, "if you kill me, he will only send another. If you let me go, I can try to renegotiate. He listens to me." Before I could register his movements, Gavin scooped up a handful of dirt from the ground and threw the debris in my direction. I closed my eyes and tilted my head away from the onslaught as tiny pricks of glass and rock scratched my face.

Opening my eyes, I found Gavin trying to slither by me like the snake he was. He brought his sword up, going for the kill, but I didn't even flinch. With a mind of its own, my weapon swiftly blocked his blow just inches from my own throat. This only infuriated me more. I pivoted and came down on him with hit after hit as he scrambled and scurried to block. I was relentless. After I knocked Gavin on his back and he pulled his way across the pavement, still struggling to block my nonstop hits, he eventually faltered.

His sword fell and his breathing stopped as I aimed one last strike in his direction. Then, just as my sword hit his flesh and the first signs of his death flashed before him, I stopped. I stooped to pick up the sword he had dropped and held the jewel-encrusted metal. Breathing hard, I could feel the fury—the vampire inside of me—withering; I still couldn't bring myself to kill him. His eyes were creased with fear, and tears slowly streaked down his cheeks as he faced his death. But his expression turned to a smug smile as he picked up on my weakness, and he laughed nervously. He pushed to his feet and took a few steps back, dusting himself off.

"I knew you couldn't do it," he said, looking down at me through resentful eyes. "You are a coward. You're trying to be something you will never be—one of us." He flashed a toothy grin.

He was right. I would never be like that, but his words bit into me like steal then, I realized something about myself. "You're right. I'm not like you. I'm not a coward." Then, with quick and precise aim, I crossed the two swords at his neck and pulled them apart, slicing into flesh. A shocked look barely skittered over his face before his eyes dulled and his head fell to the ground. My anger died down, and my tunnel vision cleared just enough for me to watch his body go limp and fall at my feet.

As his head rolled to a stop, I felt a heavy hand on my shoulder. I had forgotten about the rest of Gavin's men that still surrounded me, about the fight. Reaching up, I heaved and threw the man over my head to land a good fifty feet away. Raising my swords and poised for more, I heard the faint sound of my dad's groan.

"Arri?" Michael's voice was low. He had dropped his sword and raised his hands. "It's just me." He signaled the rest to drop their weapons and metal clamored against the pavement as they obeyed.

One by one Gavin's men were disposed of. Bereft of life, the bodies slumped and hit the ground.

As the fight ended, the remaining men stood with swords at their sides and a look of defeat across their faces. Michael, my dad, and Ash lowered their swords and looked around at the war scene. Many men had died here today, and this was just the beginning. My mom, Catherine, and Phoenix approached me, each wearing new and fresh battle wounds that they seemed to give little thought to.

"Are you okay, honey?" Michael's sweet voice cut through the fog in my head as he whispered in my ear. He pulled me into a hug, and my swords fell to the ground with the weight of the fight baring down on me.

I took a life. The thought was loud and clear, like a banner waving in my mind. I knew that if I hadn't killed Gavin, he would have come for me day after day, forever. Even though I felt his death was deserved, his death was on my conscience. The power that helped me fight—the demon within—had already calmed. From the moment he fell to his knees, the rest was all me. No excuses. No justification or pretext. I killed Gavin.

After allowing myself that brief moment, I slumped further into Michael's arms.

THREE

When I was calmer, I pulled away from Michael and took in the scene, and my heart filled with fear, anger, and regret. Looking down at the man who had been bent on taking my life, regardless of the consequences, my heart stilled. Silent gasps escaped my throat as I realized what had just happened.

Nearby, I heard my dad mention something about the cleaners being on their way, but I didn't care.

The lifeless body lying on the ground at my feet haunted me like it was already a ghost. The regret I felt for what I had just done had me falling to my knees, dizzy and nauseated as I hit the ground. Michael was next to me in an instant, soothing me with sweet and calming words. He brushed his fingertips down my back, then back up again. The motion consoled me like the steady rhythm of waves upon the sand. Then, as I remembered the look of hope and rage in Gavin's eyes, and the words he spoke in a plea to spare his life, fear rocked through me anew.

If you kill me, he will only send another.

Several green and white utility trucks with Natural Gas logos showed up only a few minutes after the battle ended and parked at the entrance of the parking lot. Several men in white collared shirts and jeans spilled out of the trucks and started the process of eliminating the evidence.

Getting to my feet, I tried to calm myself. The bodies that were scattered across the parking lot were already being cleaned up and were practically all gone. The few of Gavin's men that still remained were surrendering to my dad and Ash. Together, the two of them looked more than intimidating, unnerving the men with the threat of impending death, but it was nothing compared to the look of anger that contorted Michael's face. Although he showed me concern and love as I remained in his arms, he looked dangerous and menacing toward the men Ash and my dad were talking to. Something told me that there had been a development and Michael was definitely less than happy about it.

"I'm sorry, sir, but the locals will be here within minutes," the man Michael had called Terrish said as he approached us.

As I turned my attention to him, Michael was careful to place his body between the two of us. I didn't know if it was for my protection or for Terrish's, but I was sure Michael picked up on the way every muscle in my body tensed when this man got near me.

"We need to get her out of here. She can't be linked to this. She has been exposed as a local. This would raise suspicion." Terrish offered me a slight, apologetic smile.

Two men in suits approached Gavin's body. One took his arms and the other his legs.

"No," I said in a voice I barely recognized, anger and fear raging through me.

"My lady?" one asked as he looked at me then, expectantly, at Michael.

"He was right," I plainly stated to no one in particular.

"I beg your pardon, but we really do need to go." Terrish sounded panicked. I could hear the tires of law enforcement wheels on the pavement just outside the parking lot. It was only a matter of seconds before the police rounded the corner and found us all.

"Evidence?" Michael asked.

"A broken pipe in the kitchen. Let's hope no one lights a match," Ash said as he, my dad, and a dozen or so men surrounded Michael and me.

"Let's go," Michael commanded. He tugged me away from the scene and we took off at a full run. Just as we cleared a warehouse about one hundred yards away, a police car turned and parked in front of the restaurant, followed by an ambulance.

When we reached the manor, Michael punched his way

through the old timber doors. The hinges broke, and the wood cracked and splintered against the floors. His vile temper hummed around him and even the familiar faces I knew in the house scattered and fled from his path.

"What happened?" he yelled, shooting each and every person in the room a glare that would chill bones. "Where were my point men?"

"Sir?" someone asked. He looked vaguely familiar, but I couldn't be sure. His broad shoulders and tall, toned body made him look like a bouncer.

"Speak" Michael demanded. While still holding me close, he scanned the group. Catherine and Phoenix were front and center. Phoenix looked a little rough around the edges. Her clothing was torn in a few places, though the cut on her shoulder looked better. Catherine had lost her bounce. Her shoulders were hunched, her gaze focused on the ground. Meanwhile, Mom's usually flawless clothes were less than stellar. Her hair was mussed, and fleeting anger glinted in her eyes. Then, there were the several dozen men who bowed at Michael expectantly.

"Well?" he asked, his impatience and anger rising.

"I'm not sure, sir. I was unaware of the development. When Nicholas sent us down here, it was strictly for observation, and there were only the ten of us. Gavin must have sent for reinforcements," Terrish said with his head down. No one wanted to look at Michael. The torrent of anger running through him had them cowering.

"That's not entirely true, my lord." The vaguely familiar man took a step forward and fell to his knees.

"Explain," Michael demanded.

"It was Gavin, sir." His voice shook. "He kept talking about redeeming his name. He spoke of killing the girl regardless of what Nicholas ordered."

Terrish took a step toward the man, grumbling and seething at the betrayal. "This information would have been helpful before the fight."

"I know." He struggled for breath as Terrish grabbed him by

the neck and lifted him from the ground. "It was right before you and your men showed up." His voice pleaded for understanding.

"How do you know of this plan?" Terrish's anger roared.

The fight replayed in my mind. I heard the valiant war cries as Nicholas's men charged the front lines. I cringed at the memory. Remembering the men one by one, I recalled each of them ready for the fight. The men in front ran headfirst, anticipating victory. The men in the middle charged, but they were backup, the ones who waited for the first to fall so they could fill their void. Then there were the ones in the back. They didn't move when the fight started. They were different. While Nicholas's men were fighting for their lives, the last ten in the back were moving themselves along the inner circle of the wolves to keep them from leaving. They never engaged. They were merely acting as a buffer, padding for the wolves to make sure there were no survivors.

That's where I knew him from. The familiar man had been the one closest to me. When Gavin had come up from behind me, this man was the one who let him come. He didn't stop Gavin or warn me; he allowed the injustice. Pulling myself from Michael's grip, I reached to his side and yanked his sword from its sheath. Whirling the blade about me, I turned the hilt around in my palms, weighing the weapon.

Michael stayed close, and Terrish didn't budge, but the remainder of the coven, including my parents, backed up as anger burned within me.

As the room around me faded, and my memories pushed to the surface, I replayed the fight. I outlined everyone's position and recounted their skirmishes with frightening accuracy, all while wielding the sword like an extension of my own arm and marking the steps.

The man in Terrish's grip started to tremble as I recalled his position in the fight. The way he purposefully scooted his way forward until he ended up nearest me. The entire fight, he had been a silent participant in Nicholas's plan. He was a man who knew the outcome and was only waiting for his opportunity.

"Nicholas knew Terrish and his men were traitors, so to even the odds, he planted a few surprises of his own. Gavin was right. If Gavin were to die, or if we were to win, Nicholas would only send another. Or perhaps he already had." Pointing the sword in the man's direction, I stepped forward. "The fight's not over, is it?" I said, placing the blade at his neck. "I have already killed one man tonight. Give me one good reason I shouldn't kill you as well," I continued, cringing at the thought that I might have to actually follow through with my threat.

"It was Gavin's idea," the man started to spill. "He was convinced that one of us had betrayed Nicholas. He was determined that, were he to fail, one of us should kill you before the fight was over. And I would have succeeded, too." His eyes darted back and forth between Michael and Terrish. Even as Terrish held him by the neck, the man seemed more concerned with the look of promised retaliation and vengeance on Michael's face.

Although Michael was furious, Terrish was the one to act first. The man's features froze in solid fear as Terrish twisted his head off his body and disposed of his life.

I knew now that death would likely follow me wherever I went. Starting with the first night I had been attacked outside the bank and all the way up to the morning Alex killed his own wife on my behalf, I had been surrounded by trouble and chaos. Somehow, I felt as if I myself was courting death—my own death. The realization dawned on me that, regardless of how safe and secure I thought I was, Nicholas would always find me, no matter how long it took. He would always be there.

Word of my existence had already spread like wildfire. It was only a matter of time before covens started to take sides. Factions would form, and if the vampire world were to be rid of Nicholas, who would bring us together and unite us? With that, I felt a twinge of fear tightening my heart.

"I can try to renegotiate." Even in death, Gavin's voice echoed behind my thoughts and fear. Negotiate? Negotiate for what? My life? There would be no negotiations. Nicholas has made it clear that there is only one leader, only one possible ruler: him. Any negotiations for my life will be no better than promises made on wisps of air and false pledges. I ran my hands through my hair, frustration and anger flowing through me.

After the night's activities, I was beyond worn out and tired. I headed to the stairs without a word, leaving the rest of the coven, and Michael, staring after me.

"Arri?" Terrish called from behind me as I reached the stairs.

Still in shock and feeling as if the world was falling out from under me, I turned to him, a lifeless look on my face and the icy tone in my voice as I answered him.

"Yes?"

Terrish faltered for a moment. Whatever he was going to say died on his lips and vanished into thin air as he gazed somewhere over my shoulder. I didn't need to turn around to know that Michael was there, right behind me, shaking his head at Terrish.

"Was there something you wanted?"

"No, ma'am. You have a good night."

When I turned around, Michael placed his arm behind me and escorted me upstairs.

"Do you think she'll be all right?" I heard my mom's concerned voice drift up the stairs.

"She's pretty tough, ma'am," Terrish said with admiration in his voice. By then, we had reached my room. Michael lead me in and closed the door behind us.

"Arri," Michael said, turning me around and pushing my unruly hair from my face. He placed his palm against my cheek, a loving smile on his lips. The touch calmed the storm within me. I didn't give Michael a chance to speak. I shook my head, kicked off my shoes, and got into bed fully dressed—I couldn't care less. I was done. I'd fought the fight tonight, but now, I needed to be left alone.

The fight replayed itself over and over again in my head. The cries of war, the swinging of swords, the sight of splitting flesh, and the horror of decapitation seared themselves into my memory. Watching each man try and fail against our small band of seven showed how powerful Michael was. My dad, a man with a past, was fighting for his daughter. My mom protected me like a mama bear protecting her young. Alex and the pack defended the world against anyone who would chance a coward's retreat. Even Phoenix, a new friend brought in especially for my training, had put herself in the line of fire—twice—to protect me.

My mind ran circles around the events. From the moment Gavin walked into the restaurant to the moment Michael held me close on the sacred and hallowed ground of the manor, it all played and rewound, each time bringing me to the same conclusion: The lengths that Gavin went to were beyond comprehension, and Nicholas was yet more complex than Gavin. Nicholas was driven—crazed—about power and control.

But once he gets me, once he has me in his grasp… then what?

I knew my life meant nothing to him, and that my death meant everything. The mere symbol of me had scared him enough to initiate the hunt.

As my mind started to sort out the puzzle pieces, a chilling presence surrounded me. I opened my eyes and Nicholas's dark and gloomy face was before me, taunting me from the darkness. His menacing smile gave me goosebumps. Nicholas had placed a reward on my head. He had sent his most prized men out to capture me, dead or alive, and yet for some miraculous reason, I had survived.

"You have not defeated me yet, my pet." Nicholas's voice rasped as if he was out of breath. "I will make an example of you as a warning to all of those who oppose me." His face drew back, and then he stepped forward from the darkness and circled me. He looked more like a mortician than a well-off, self-proclaimed vampire king. His skin was pale and taut with a bluish hue as he traced his long, icy-cold finger down my jawline. The scrape of his nail left a trail of burning pain behind. I tried to recoil but was frozen in place. As his touch reached the back of my jaw, I felt his clammy hand wrap around my neck, one bony finger at a time, until his hand encompassed me in a vice-like grip. He squeezed the breath from my lungs. I gasped. I felt so powerless, so weak and incapable.

"I'm going to make a nice, slow, tortuous example of you. I'm going to make you watch me kill everyone you have ever loved and cared for. Then, after I have broken your spirit, I will make you suffer slowly and painfully, making you cry out in agony, until you give up. Only then will I end your life. That is my promise."

His rancid breath, his cold fingers, and his deathly look chilled me, but the words he spoke, the words he hoped would instill fear in my heart, only fueled a fire of fury and wrath that I only barely held at bay.

"I'm not going to be the one who dies," I bit out as I raised my hands and broke his grip on my throat. "You will regret ever starting this war. I will see to it," I spat as I pushed him away. But just as I reached out to grab him, he disappeared and turned into smoke.

With a gasp and a wild whirlwind of fear and fury swirling inside me, I sat up. A light burning sensation lingered on my throat as I brushed my fingertip against the warm skin. I could still feel the contrast between the scorching trail left by his fingers and their curiously icy grip. I searched the room for any remaining signs of the dream but saw nothing. The curtains were closed. No outside light trickled in; only the dim illumination of the sconces filtered through the room. As I sat up, my head spun and pounded. One of the wonderful side effects of nightmares, I'm sure.

Looking around at the room once again, I saw nothing was different. In fact, I was alone. Michael must have left so I could sleep in peace and undisturbed—though not without making sure I was taken care of. He had placed a glass of water on the nightstand and draped new clothes over the foot of the bed. Everything was as it should be.

After showering, dressing, and assessing any damage from the fight, I stared at the person in the mirror. My eyes, storm gray, gleamed with light and swirling flecks of blue and red, a contrast to my green top. I felt fragile, confused, scared; turmoil churned and simmered under the surface of my skin. Nicholas was stepping it up. His bland and unadventurous life was spiced up when I walked in the picture and challenged his credibility as the leader. Now more than ever, he was hell-bent on getting rid of me.

Emotionless, I considered who I had become. I waited for the telltale pang of regret, the hollow and soulless burning that had accompanied the recent fight, but there wasn't any. Shaking my head, I took a deep breath and turned to the door. I would have to face the music eventually; it might as well be now.

As I rounded the corner of the staircase, I heard voices coming from the library.

"Last night, Gavin attacked us in town! Nicholas is getting aggressive with each attempt—each failed attempt—to retrieve Arri." Michael's voice was accusatory.

"Yes, but why her?" There was doubt in Terrish's voice. "From what I saw of her last night, she is scared, not at all the opponent that Nicholas expects." Terrish paused. "Are you sure she is the one in the prophecy? Is it possible there is another half-breed?"

I could feel frustration running off Michael in torrents, but he didn't have time to answer, because I had arrived at the library doors and pushed them open. Now that I had realized my fate, I felt rather bold and addressed the situation directly.

"It doesn't matter," I said, walking up to Michael and planting a simple, affectionate kiss on his cheek. My eyes started to burn with anger, but I tried to calm the blaze down to a light flame.

"Are you feeling better?" Michael asked, kissing me on the forehead and wrapping a protective arm around me. I could feel that he saw my rising anger almost as strongly as I felt it.

"Fact of the matter is, Nicholas believes it," I said. "As long as he believes I am the one in the prophecy, it doesn't matter whether I am or not. Even if there is another out there, he would never be sure which of us it is, so he would be after us both."

Terrish looked skeptical. I tried to pull in and harness my anger. After all, my fury wasn't directed at Terrish; it was directed at Nicholas.

"So, you believe you are this prodigy?"

"No. Yes. I don't know." I shook my head and let out a hollow laugh. "All I know is that it really doesn't matter what I think, what I want, or who I'd like to be. Nicholas pursued me before I knew who and what I was. He's determined that I am the one he needs to kill, and until my head is on his wall, or he falls at my feet, he will continue to chase me." I ended it with a small smile that said I was anything but okay with the situation.

"So, you'd fight him? Fight alongside us?" Terrish looked unconvinced that I could—or would.

"Yes, I will fight Nicholas. Yes, I will fight alongside you. Yes, I intend to win."

Terrish looked a little stunned that I was so assured.

With a shake of my head, I chuckled. "I may need a little training, but as for you thinking that I am weak, and not the opponent that Nicholas expects, well… I guess we'll just have to make me into the opponent he fears."

FOUR

It had been three days since I killed Gavin and the weight of his death still haunted me. Every time I closed my eyes, I could see the look of fear that shocked his face, the dullness that glazed over his features. From the moment Wormwood came up behind me to the moment I took Gavin's life, the demon inside me had churned and clawed to get out.

I could still feel its very essence raging inside me. Normally, it took a strong emotion like anger or fear to set in before it became present, but now, the demon lingered near the surface as if it knew what was coming, just waiting for the opportunity.

I left the self-imposed confines of my room and ventured through the house, avoiding everyone. A few turns here and a few turns there had me flipped around and in a part of the house I'd never been in before. There were two mahogany doors at the end of the dimly lit hallway leading to two different rooms. I opened the door on the left, and the room smelled like rubbing alcohol, reminding me of an uninviting, sterile hospital. I chose to stay clear of the room and turned my attention to the other door.

With great effort, and a good deal of muscle, I pushed it open. The ancient hinges creaked, and the smell of dust and stale air wafted past me. With no outside windows, the room was dark and foreboding. The lingering scent of leather and rubber hid beneath the taint of dirt and musty air. Reaching around the door, I found a light switch and flicked it on. One by one, the lights slowly flickered to life: rows of old, outdated fluorescent tubes that lined the ceiling.

Out of the darkness, a workout room came into focus. As each light blinked on, a new set of equipment became visible. I didn't know what I was expecting, but I wasn't expecting a gym. A laugh escaped my lips. It was comical. A vampire workout room? I tried to imagine Michael in here throwing a few punches, but I couldn't fathom him taking out his aggression on a punching bag. A vampire would annihilate this stuff in a matter of seconds. Which left me wondering… why is this here?

I walked in, tracing my finger over some of the equipment. Most of it was ancient. Old sparring gear, wooden fighting dummies, and large bowl-like objects that I could easily curl up in with room to spare. I settled on a bench that looked to be from sometime in the Renaissance period, then closed my eyes and took a deep breath.

What was this room used for? I wondered. Michael and his fellow vampires fought with swords, and bullets left no wounds on them. Besides, their strength alone would destroy anything in this room, but the equipment looked well used, once upon a time. I stood and approached one of the hanging bags, then balled up my fist and tapped it. It swayed back and forth rhythmically. Dust falling off the bag billowed and fell to my feet. I pulled my fist back a bit farther and punched it again, this time with a little more force.

"Follow through with your swing." Michael stood at the door with a slight grin curving his lips.

"Sorry." I stepped away from the hanging bag and clasped my hands behind my back.

"Here," Michael said, walking toward me. Placing his arms around me, he kissed my neck. He smelled of citrus and cologne and everything Michael. It was wonderful. I inhaled his scent as my mind fogged and my heart swooned. He intertwined his hands with mine, brought our joined fists forward, and kissed my knuckles. "Don't tuck your thumb," he said, positioning my fingers. "You could break a bone it if the hit is hard enough."

He stood behind me and placed his arms around me. Then, gripping my wrists, he pulled my right arm back, then pushed it forward and straight ahead until my arm was almost fully extended.

"Follow through." Michael's mouth was right next to my ear and my body hummed at his breath brushing against my skin. "Keep your eyes on the target," he said with a light chuckle. Realizing I'd shut my eyes to enjoy his touch, I snapped them open.

"What was this room used for?" I asked, trying to keep my mind off the way his body felt pressed against mine, the smell of him as he held me, and the way his breath and lips teased the nape of my neck. I was completely aware of his presence, both physical and emotional. Similarly, he tried and fought to keep his passion at bay, but it was a futile effort. His emotions were too strong. He clenched his jaw, and I could hear the hitch in his breathing.

"I built this room back when times were different." Michael offered no further explanation, and with that, my mind wandered. The possibilities were endless, but it was his feelings of regret and shame that caught my attention.

"Is this where you have been hiding the last several days?" Michael asked, pulling my left arm back then extending it again.

"No. I just came across it this morning."

"Then where have you been?" Michael asked as he planted several kisses on my neck and wrapped his arms around me once again.

"Avoiding the coven," I answered honestly.

"I've missed you. I came to your room the other night and you were gone." I knew what night he was talking about. Gavin's face had filled my dreams and Nicholas's threat had filled my heart. I'd woken up in a cold sweat only a few hours after I went to bed. My inner demon meandered through my every emotion and snaked its way to the surface. I'd splashed my face with cold water, looked in the mirror, and seen my eyes burning red. With my pupils a deep crimson, and the rim a deep scarlet, I looked possessed, evil. The sight of my own face frightened me to tears. I feared for the person I was becoming. My inner anger was a constant presence, and it was getting closer to the surface by the second. I shuddered. What would become of me if it ever did reach the surface and I wasn't able to calm it back into submission?

Michael felt the change in my disposition and held me closer still. "Do you want to tell me where you were just now?" He sounded concerned. Taking my hands again, he stepped us closer to the bag. We went through the motions again, this time hitting the bag.

"Ever since the altercation at the restaurant, that same inner demon that helps me fight has broken to the surface," I admitted. "I can feel it, clawing at me to let it loose. If it breaks free, I'm not sure I can push it down again. I don't know what it is, but I can't lose control."

Michael made no comment. He just continued to show me the moves over and over and then stood beside me as I kept punching.

"Just remember, keep your eyes on the target. Your opponent will take your distraction as a weakness and capitalize on it," Michael said. I hit harder.

I tried to keep my mind off Nicholas, but it wasn't easy. Every time I hit the bag, I saw Nicholas's face, taunting me, sneering at me, telling me I wasn't good enough. With a jolt of fear that he might be right, I swung and hit the bag. My knuckles scraped along the nylon, and the chain clinked and splintered. The seam ripped open as I followed through with my swing, and sand cascaded out onto the floor before the broken bag fell with a thud.

I cringed, breathing heavily as the remaining fear throttled through me. I felt out of my element, out of control. The power that surged through me quaked and threatened my inner restraint. Turning to Michael, I could see his doubt and uneasiness written across his face. My human side fought and screamed for dominance, but it was out of my hands.

"Arri, talk to me."

As I looked at Michael, my human side cried out for help, but the other side of me—the side that had been pushed down, dismissed, and ignored for years—broke free and now controlled me.

"Talk?" I heard myself say. It was like someone else was speaking and I was stuck on the inside. "About what? How scared I am, how insecure I feel about fulfilling the prophecy? Or did you want to hear how afraid and frail I really am?" My inner self was saying everything I was feeling, everything I thought, and everything I hid. Then, as if the roles changed, I felt my real self fighting to the surface. My two sides, battling for the same position, human and vampire both struggling to control me.

Something familiar grazed my palm, jolting me to awareness. Michael had pressed the hilt of a sword into my hand. I could feel the coolness of the metal caressing my skin. The blade, sharp and straight, was firm and unyielding, nicely weighted. It felt like the sword itself represented balance, power, and weight working together in harmony to create something capable of either destruction or leadership when wielded by the right person.

I looked up at Michael, who took a few steps back. When I finally finished admiring the blade in my hands, Michael had already cleaned the mats, and pushed the equipment to the sides of the room. Circling around me, Michael took the flat end of the sword he was now holding and swatted me gently on the rear.

"Now advance," he ordered, poised for battle. His playful banter caught the attention of my human and vampire side alike, both humming in anticipation. My vampire side was thrilled to come out and play, but my human side recoiled and tried to hold back.

After holding the sword up, Michael took a slow strike at me. I blocked it easily enough, but I didn't strike back. He came at me again, this time a little faster. I blocked it, but still didn't retaliate. Michael's playful look faltered and was replaced by one a little more serious and determined. I could feel his attitude change and his demeanor take on a more combative edge.

"Don't hold back, Arri. Hit me," he said, raising his voice. At that, my two sides stopped competing for dominance and became one cohesive instinct.

As Michael's sword came at me again, I blocked it and swung back. The two blades collided, and sparks flew. With each attempt to break through his defenses, I could feel my vampire side take hold and aggress further into the fight. My human side, waiting in the background, just held on for the ride.

"Fight me, Arri," Michael demanded as his hits became harder and more aggressive.

"I can't."

"Can't? Or won't?" Michael asked as he circled me and came at me again. This time, his swing was aimed right at my legs.

"Both!" I yelled as I jumped to avoid his swing.

"Both won't cut it. You need to decide. Are you human or vampire?" he asked as he came at me with a new set of swings.

I have to choose? Michael's words stunned me momentarily, and when he took a few thrusts at me, I didn't block. Only the feeling of falling brought me back to reality, but by then, it was too late. I was lying on my back with Michael's sword resting against my neck.

"Your opponent won't hesitate to kill you." Michael's eyes were still glazed over with the thrill of the fight, and in that small, revolutionary moment, I realized that I didn't have to choose. I was, and could be, both. My problem wasn't having to choose which side I wanted to be, it was learning how to be both.

I had been raised human. I'd been forced to be in control, to push down my vampire side in order to be the daughter I always had to be. In doing that, I never got a chance to know who I was.

As my breathing became steady and slow, Michael helped me to my feet and took my sword.

"Are you okay?" Michael asked as he pulled me into his arms. All my inhibitions fell away as he held me.

"I'm fine," I said, pulling back and looking into his eyes. My inner battle died, and a new sense of power and peace coursed through me. The war between vampire and human might have been far from over, but the fight for my inner control was at a truce.

"You seemed to be having an inner conflict that needed sorting. Is it sorted?" Michael asked as he interlaced his fingers with mine and we headed for the door.

"Yes, I think so. At least… it's a start."

Michael and I climbed the stairs until we reached the main floor. I hadn't realized I had wandered so far.

"How did you find me?"

Michael chuckled. "I'm not sure. I just felt like I should look there, and there you were." I felt Michael's heart leap with emotion when he thought back to wanting to find me. His want and need to be with me was strong.

The manor buzzed with conversation, and Michael and I were almost invisible as we ascended the stairs. When we came to a stop in front of his room, Michael paused.

"Would you like to come in?" he asked nervously.

"Sure."

Michael opened the door and ushered me inside. The drapes were pulled back. His desk was spotless. His bed was made. All in all, I couldn't see or even think of a single thing that would make him nervous.

"Would you like something to drink?" he asked, opening the door to a cabinet hidden in the paneling of the wall.

"A Coke?"

I doubted he would have a non-blood beverage, but since the fight, I was alarmingly hungry and thirsty.

"Here." Michael pulled out a Coke and handed it to me then closed the fridge.

Walking around his room, I opened the Coke and took a few gulps. The cool liquid felt good against the back of my throat, and the sugar and caffeine gave me a little boost.

"I didn't know sparring could take so much out of me." I reached the window and looked out over the yard. The pine trees swayed to the dance of the wind, bowing to nature's force. It was a beautiful scene. With all the movement outside, I was strangely aware of Michael's pacing behind me—the wind forgotten, the trees disappearing, as I honed in on Michael. Looking down at the mark that bonded me to him, I thought back to the night Michael asked me for permission to bind himself to me. Turning, I saw he was by his desk, sifting through some papers.

"Did you mean it?" I asked.

Michael stopped and looked at me in confusion. "Mean what? About the fight taking it out of you?"

I laughed. "No, about you proposing. Well, proposing in vampire terms." I stared at him, waiting for his eyes to betray how he felt, waiting for the pang of hurt. But his eyes sparkled with lust and longing. A seductive smile tugged at his lips and his gaze turned predatory.

"Yes. Every word." He came around the desk in two easy and smooth strides, closing the distance between us. "Are you backing out?" he asked, a playful tone in his voice.

"No. It's just that after the fight, it was never brought up. I was hoping that you could tell me a little more about what it entails."

He lifted the drink from my hand and placed it on the table by the window. Then, taking my hands in his, he led me to the bed and I sat.

"What would you like to know?" Michael sat down next to me.

"Well, I'm not really sure. Maybe you can walk me through it."

Michael went quiet. His heart jumped with excitement, but his expression gave nothing away.

He traced the lining of my wrist, stopping every so often, feeling for my pulse. He brought my hand up to his mouth and placed a kiss on my wrist. The slow, deliberate kiss lingered, forcing my pulse to quicken.

"There is no ceremony," he said in between kisses as he worked his way up my arm. "There will be an introduction at the ball as I announce you as my mate and we will be introduced as Arch Leaders with everyone as witness." He placed a few stray kisses on my collarbone. "But first," he kissed my neck, "you need to accept me as purely yours, and I will need to accept you wholeheartedly, like you trusted and loved me the night I saved you."

My heart raged and pounded as he lingered at my neck, leaning toward me, resting his hands on the bed caging me in his arms. His breath caressed my skin and my body swooned, begging for his touch.

"Then..." he paused, "I will need to take your blood." His body tensed as he waited for the cold splash of reality to hit me. Frankly, I was waiting for it too, but the cold never came. My mind registered what he was saying, and I knew I should be appalled at the thought, but I wasn't.

"Okay." My heart skipped a few beats when I heard myself whisper my acceptance. Michael pulled away and stared at me in amazement.

"You do realize what I have to do, right?" As he said it, I saw the fear of rejection in his eyes. The panic and worry that followed made my heart hurt. Michael was asking if I knew what he had to do, and he feared that I would balk and refuse his love.

"Yes," I said, offering him a reassuring smile as I leaned in to kiss him. At first, it was tentative and light, but as I poured my heart into the kiss, Michael reciprocated with fever and passion.

FIVE

Michael kissed and teased his way from my lips to the pulsing vein in my throat. His teeth grazed and nipped. He gave me time to back out as he patiently waited for me to get accustomed to the idea. Lust and passion surged through me as I accepted Michael. I knew what I was doing and what he would have to do. In that moment, I was willing, and I waited for us to be bound together. I loved Michael with all my heart. I needed and wanted him. His teeth made one more trek across my skin before he backed away.

"Are you ready?" he asked. His voice was deep, gruff, and laced with passion.

The catch of my breath and the way I gently pressed myself closer gave him the invitation he needed. As he kissed his way down my cheeks, over my chin, and across my throat, I waited for the pinch of pain as he sunk his teeth into my skin to drink. The moment was close. I could feel his breath as he opened his mouth. My heart hitched and yearned for this moment.

"My lord!" someone yelled through the door, followed by a several raps. "My lord!" the urgent voice repeated, sounding more panicked than the first time.

A groan escaped Michael's throat before he dropped his head in the crook of my neck in defeat. He hesitated, then licked his lips and let his tongue graze my neck, sending shivers skating through me. As he tried to control his temper, he growled and hissed. The commotion on the other side of the door continued as Michael's anger seethed below the surface.

"I give up," he said, springing from the bed and raking his

hands through his hair. Turning back to me, he searched my eyes for understanding. "I'm sorry, Arri," he said, leaning to give me a kiss on the forehead. "I'm so sorry."

Those three little words were all I needed to know that the moment wasn't going to happen. Letting out a regretful sigh, I nodded. Michael's expression was a pained mixture of frustration, anger, and sadness.

After helping me from the bed, Michael fixed his disheveled clothes, then smoothed his hands over my head and secured my hair back with a headband.

"I promise, this moment will happen, and when it does, we will not be interrupted." Regret filled his eyes as hurt churned inside me.

"I'll hold you to that," I said.

Michael pulled me in for one last kiss that made my knees weak.

Then, in a whirlwind of rage, Michael grabbed the handle of the door and threw it open. It broke clean off its hinges. The doorknob ripped out of the wood and fell to the floor in a mangled and contorted mess. I knew right then that whatever happened would be dealt with, and with the deadliest means, if possible.

As I followed him out of the door, Michael took my hand.

"My lord, my lady," Terrish greeted us.

"What is it?" Michael's voice was a blend of pure anger and concern.

"It's Phillip, my lord." Michael turned to me, then back to Terrish.

"Yes? What of him?"

Terrish's expression flashed with sadness and despair before he nodded and closed his eyes. Michael's inner turmoil was more than a cyclone of emotions. He must know what Terrish meant, even without hearing the words.

"Who found him?" Worry colored Michael's words.

"Catherine." Terrish's expression faltered before he hung his head. "She received confirmation by carrier."

Michael's head shot up, and his eyes seared with anger.

"From whom?" Rage dripped from his words.

At this point, Terrish started to cower. Fear-struck, Terrish couldn't answer. Michael grumbled and nodded. He must have known the answer to his own question, because without another word, he headed toward the stairs.

"My lord, my lady." My dad bowed as he greeted Michael and me. He was brimming with animosity, as was my mom and most of the coven as well.

"Where is Catherine?" Michael demanded as he glanced around the crowded room.

Mom looked over her shoulder. Sadness gleamed in her eyes. Grief flowed through her. The contrition that slowly moved across her features broke my heart. I placed my hand on her shoulder and squeezed lightly.

"Are you okay, Mom?"

"Yes, dear." She covered my hand with hers.

"I'm sorry," I whispered.

As my mom pulled her hand away, my dad swooped her up in his arms and held her tight.

Leaving the two of them alone, Michael grabbed my hand and led me to the library. The doors were closed, and from the feel of anguished grief coming from the other side, Catherine was beyond agony.

As Michael opened the door, Catherine's small form was curled up in the corner of the room. Her legs were drawn up to her chest, and her hands trembled as she held her knees. Catherine took one look at Michael and staggered to her feet.

"No, Catherine," Michael said, as he rushed to her side. "Please." He placed a hand on hers and looked in her eyes.

"I am truly sorry for your loss. Phillip was an amazing vampire, and his death will be avenged. I promise." Michael's voice was full of conviction and concern.

Phillip was—had been—Catherine's mate. She used to tell me stories about their travels and adventures before she became a manager. I didn't know Phillip personally; he was always spoken of, but I'd never met him. At times, I thought she'd made him up, but seeing the heartbreak on her face jolted a string of fear, anger, and sadness deep inside me. I'd never seen vampires show sorrow, heartache, or misery, but today, propriety had been thrown out the window.

Catherine blinked up at him and nodded her appreciation.

Michael sat alongside her for a few moments as he allowed the silence and familiar tinge of gloom to drape over us. Catherine was quiet.

Finally, Michael stood, offering Catherine a few more words of consolation before leaving me alone with her.

"Where is the carrier?" I heard Michael snap just before he gently closed the door behind him. When the handle clicked and he was gone, Catherine unhooked her arms and pulled me in beside her.

"I'm trying to be strong, but I'm not sure how long I can hold it."

"Then don't," I said, trying to console her. "It's okay to feel."

At that moment, I could sense the change, the shift in her demeanor. The weight on her heart grew. The sadness had transformed and something dark and sinful had joined it. The turmoil and turbulence within her were unnerving. It wasn't just sorrow that filled her heart. It was regret and frustration, too. The emotions tainted her, and she was on the verge of destruction.

As she pulled away, a threatening, almost evil look glistened in her eyes and something vengeful dominated her. With a nefarious grin, she pushed herself to her feet and walked to the door.

I was so confused. I knew I hadn't known Phillip enough to say anything more personal, but Catherine's behavior was still rather odd. There was normally a period of grief and mourning, but Catherine seemed to only feel those briefly before she turned the other cheek. Something was off.

As she walked toward the door, a small white piece of paper fell from her tailored coat pocket and fluttered under a large leather reading chair. I debated whether or not I was going to tell her, but when she reached the door, the wild swirl of emotional chaos whisked around her like a warning sign of death, and I opted to leave her alone and return the paper later.

She gripped the doorknob with her tiny, delicate hand, and the sound of metal grating beneath her strength made my heart cringe. Catherine had snapped, replacing her sweet and calm temperament with a raging and untamed vampire bent on retribution.

"Thank you, sweetheart. You're right." With that, her kind smile fell into a look of determination and resolve. "Goodbye, sweet girl." With those last words, she left the room in a full-on sprint.

"What happened?" Michael asked as he rushed back in. I was still in shock as I stared after her.

"I don't know what happened. She told me she didn't know how long she could hold it together, so I told her she didn't have to be strong. Then something snapped inside her, and she ran out."

I looked at Michael for answers, but all he showed me was confusion and worry. He held my hand as we left the library.

"What happened? Where did Catherine go?" My mom's panicked voice betrayed her calm exterior.

Michael didn't answer. He just shrugged.

"What now?" my dad asked, coming in from the hall.

"I'm not sure. When I talked to the carrier, it was clear he knew nothing, but it is obvious Nicholas sent it."

A wide range of gasps was heard around the room as the other coven members looked on.

"Why Catherine?" I was confused.

"I'm not sure. Maybe he's upping the ante or it was a message." I knew Michael didn't feel as certain as his voice sounded.

Message? I thought. Message, message, message. There was something that caught my attention. Leaving the room as everyone talked and discussed what our next move should be, I headed back into the library. I knelt by the dark brown leather reading chair and fished out the crumpled piece of paper.

Carefully, I unwrapped the scrunched and folded mess. Seeing the slant of the writing, the familiar script, fear seized my heart. My breathing came out in uneven gasps. I fell to my knees. This letter was from Nicholas himself. I closed my eyes, trying to still the tears that threatened to fall, then looked down at the letter and read on.

What do I get for a child—a demon—that should never exist? It would have been all too easy to give her something wicked, or at least something dreadful, but neither seemed an appropriate gift. After searching and pondering what to give the worthless wraith, I'm sure you will find my alternative gift satisfactory.

I'm lifting a glass to my shameless defeat, a small token of what will come to the futile and insignificant life of a child who dares to defy me. May this moment torment you for the rest of your endless life. Phillip's head will serve as proof that my fury hath no end.

With everlasting love,

–N

The edge of the paper was coated in blood, and a small clump of hair was stuck in the folds. Nicholas had sent Catherine her lover's head in a bag. As I got back to my feet, equally chilled with fear and boiling with rage, my heart raced. Nicholas had killed Phillip in an attempt to get to me. Killing and murdering helpless humans was no longer his goal. He was going for the gut. He was targeting my family, aiming for those closest to me.

I gritted my teeth in anger. His ridiculous claim of being the high ruler of the vampires was now hurting the ones I loved. Crumpling the paper in my hand, I stormed out of the library. The door crashing against the wall drew everyone's attention.

"Where is Catherine?" I demanded.

"Arri?" My mom's voice was just a whisper, but the concern in it was carrying the weight of the world. With burning rage inside me, and the weight of Phillip's death on my shoulders, I asked again.

"Where is Catherine?" I asked again, my voice now a growl.

"We don't know. As soon as she calms down, she'll return. She's just lost her mate. These things take time." My mom was trying to be as supportive and comforting as possible.

"No!" I yelled as I ran my hands through my hair. Frustration and a deep understanding of how Catherine felt washed through me. I could understand the sadness, but I could also understand the need to seek revenge. I was only surprised she wasn't blaming his death on me.

With everything I was feeling and thinking, I still felt Michael's arms when they wrapped around me.

"Honey, talk to me."

The sound of his soothing voice and the feel of his reassuring touch calmed me.

"Where is the carrier?"

Michael pulled away. Confusion and curiosity marred his brow. "He was human. He was paid to deliver the package. He knew not what it contained."

I shot Michael a glare.

"I don't know. I would guess he is in town having his dinner by now. Why do you ask?" His head tilted in question. "He knew nothing," Michael tried to reassure me.

"It's not him I'm after. Nicholas was kind enough to send Catherine a little letter in hopes it would reach me."

I shoved the letter into Michael's hand, the weight of Catherine's actions on my behalf ripping at my heart.

"She tried to hide it, but it fell to the floor on her way out. Michael, she's out for blood. She isn't going to stop until she gets her revenge."

My voice sounded broken and pained. I needed to find Catherine and stop her before she killed her way to her own death.

Michael opened the letter, growing still as he read it. Torrents and tides of rage rolled off Michael and he pounded his fist on an old wooden table, which crumbled beneath the force, shards and fragments exploding and littering the floor.

"Ava, Steven, you know her. Where would she have gone?" Michael's voice was barely controlled.

My mom's eyes met mine. A trace of fear glinted in them before she hid it away.

"She would have tracked the messenger," Mom said as she started for the door.

The sun had already set behind the mountains. After calling on every vampire in the surrounding area to keep an eye out for the renegade, Michael and I made our way to town. With only a handful of coven members to join us, we went in pairs. Because of my speed handicap, Michael and I took the traditional way in a car while the rest of them took byways, trails, and random courses until we could reconvene in town.

As Michael and I reached the freeway, his phone buzzed.

"Yeah?" His tone was short and clipped. As he listened to the caller, panic and fear pumped through his veins. "Where? Thank you, Lyle. Keep an eye on her, but do not engage unless necessary." He threw the phone against the dash, shattering it. Glass and plastic were strewn around the car as he picked up a new phone from the console.

"She's gone mad," Michael stated. He glanced at me. Registering my confusion, he continued, "When a vampire loses a mate, the despair and anguish that follows is unbearable, so three things can occur: one, the vampire will take their own life; two, the heartbreak can lead to rage and fills the heart with revenge, causing them to go mad; and three, the vampire may choose to live through their mate's death. Catherine went mad. Once pure, untamed, and full-on rage courses through a vampire, it is rare for them to recover. It usually consumes us until retribution is achieved. In Catherine's case, retribution can only come with the death of the one who killed Phillip. She'll never find them. Phillip was still in Egypt when he died. He's been there since before you came to live with me." Michael's voice was morose as he thought about Catherine's loss. Michael was sad and testy, and for good reason.

As we reached the edge of town, the obvious vibe of confrontation suffused the air. Mom and Dad were positioned outside the borders of town. Alex and Jonathan appeared out of nowhere, flanking my parents. Oddly enough, the wolves had a habit of appearing magically when we needed them, which was a lifesaver.

Lena, the cowgirl with a red cowboy hat and four-inch-high

designer boots, and Tack, her mate, were on the other side of the diner, keeping an eye out. Lyle and a few of the Ravens, Michael's personal bodyguards that protect him and his home, met us at the old flower shop.

"She's pacing the town, but she hasn't made a move." Lyle filled Michael in.

Tack signaled as Catherine paused in front of the diner. On the other side of the thin glass window, the clueless messenger quietly ate his dinner, not knowing death was just around the corner.

SIX

As the air stilled, Catherine's fingers twitched at her sides. With her attention drawn to the man happily eating his turkey and potatoes at the table less than ten feet away, she waited, biding her time until the moment was right.

"You know, Marcus, I would have paid to have seen the look on her pathetic little face," I heard a man's voice say as he and a friend rounded the corner.

I directed my attention back to Catherine, watching her slowly dart into the shadows, unseen by the approaching men. Her small form and her spiked, bleach-blonde hair blended in with the diner crowd. Yet even from the cover and distance of the flower shop across the street, I could feel her anger build and grow.

"Yeah, but it was genius using the carrier. Thus, untraceable," the second man said, chortling vilely.

"Sure, but now we need to get rid of the evidence. We wouldn't want him spilling to the child," the first man said.

Looking around, I searched for my parents, but Lena and Tack were the only ones I could find. Even the werewolves were well hidden in the shadows of night.

Stopping just in front of the clear glass doors, one of the men reached into his pocket and fished out a small vial, no bigger than my pinky finger. The smaller of the men entered the diner first. He made a show of looking around as if trying to spot his dining companion.

"Josh," the carrier called out, and eagerly waved as if the first man—Josh—couldn't see him in a mostly empty room, sitting near the window, and less than fifteen feet away. After a few moments of waiting, the second man entered and walked behind the carrier.

"Ah, Marcus," the carrier happily greeted the second man as they shook hands. "I hate to be the one to bring it up, but may I?" He extended his hand to the second guy—Marcus—expectantly.

"Ah, yes, of course. I apologize for the delay," Marcus said. His smile looked forced, but the carrier didn't seem to notice. Marcus reached into his coat pocket and withdrew a plain manila envelope. Then, while their human accomplice counted the large wad of cash that the envelope contained, Marcus held his attention as his comrade emptied the small vial into their human friend's drink.

As the three men exchanged pleasantries and idle conversation, Catherine gradually unfolded herself from the shadows. The slight quiver of the streetlights pulsed against her hair, which flashed and gleamed in erratic lighting. In the time it took for Catherine to make her final decision, I could feel her fear. Her heart turned and tightened.

Then, as the men recognized her presence, their expressions turned determined.

Within Catherine, however, hope turned into anger. Love turned into heartless rage, and sympathy turned into cruelty. As far as I could feel, my beloved Catherine was lost forever.

"Michael." My word came out in a warning.

The men's expressions turned smug.

Movement from the far corner of the building caught my attention. I had been so wrapped up in the scene in the diner, I had forgotten about my parents. I watched as my mom fought and wrestled against my dad to free herself and help her friend. Jonathan and Alex were close by, waiting for things to go wrong. Then, as movement inside the diner drew my attention back, I saw the two cowards do the unthinkable.

Within seconds, Josh and Marcus, the two vampires, jumped from their seats and placed a few humans between them. Catherine, scoffing at the idea of humans stopping her when she was already making her advance, walked right up to one of the vampires. Setting a hand on his human shield's shoulder, she threw him across the diner as if waving a wand in dismissal. The shattering glass and the broken body slumped against the floor, causing a few of the women to scream. The noise of the fearful humans didn't faze Catherine as she moved in on the retreating vampires.

I started to move so I could run to Catherine and stop her, but Michael and two of his Ravens held me tight. Their death grip forced me to stay as I watched Catherine from the cover of the flower shop. As she flung people around, I cringed. This was not the Catherine I knew.

Catherine discarded human after human as Josh and Marcus desperately used the mortals as makeshift shields. She didn't care for their lives as she disposed of each one, throwing, flinging and... killing. Josh was unwittingly being cornered.

"Now, listen," he tried to explain, "I didn't do it. I was only sent to deliver the package." He put his hands up in surrender.

"Did you know what was in that bag?" Catherine growled. The man had the nerve to shake his head. "Oh, I think you did. *I would have paid to see the look on her pathetic little face.*" She threw his previous words back at him. "Well, how does my pathetic little face look now?" she countered as he took a few steps back. "You think an apology will save you? You think that will stop me?" Catherine yelled. Her shrieks echoed off the diner walls. Every man and woman cried out in terror as she narrowed her eyes.

Marcus carefully and slowly moved his way around back, so that he and Josh could surround her. As Josh held her attention, it looked like the plan would work, but every move Catherine made was calculated and premeditated. As Josh talked and circled his way around her, a cocky grin swept over his face.

I froze in fear.

Josh's almighty smile faded as he realized that not only did Catherine know what they were doing, but they had also lost the battle. Catherine had moved and stalked until they were out of maneuvers.

In a moment of panic, Josh reached down and grabbed a large, well-fed lady. He tossed the human at Catherine, but with a wave of her hand, and a last-minute duck, Catherine easily dodged, and the flying woman landed in Marcus's lap. As the vampire stumbled back and fell to the floor in shock, Catherine took the opportunity to efficiently behead the smaller man.

Sickly whimpers muted the sound of Catherine's triumphant yell as she rode his headless body to the ground. At the hollow thud of a dead body, the humans cowered, and Catherine now narrowed her gaze on the remaining vampire. With a smooth and knowing smile, the vampire bowed to Catherine.

"It looks like you have yet again defied my attempts to circumvent you."

"Marcus," Catherine bit out.

"You thought that I would just give up after what you and Phillip did? It only felt right that I return the favor." His icy voice sent chills through me.

"Yes, well, I think it was well deserved," Catherine said as her face contorted into a sneer. She pursed her lips and narrowed her eyes. The man retreated slowly until his back hit the wall. Catherine walked toward him like a panther stalking its prey, each step calculated and purposeful. As she approached him, he reached out in desperation, trying to fight against her, but Catherine's anger and need for revenge outweighed his advance.

Now that her victim had no way out, Catherine closed her hands around his neck. Leaning into him until her tiny but powerful form was pressed against his, and her mouth was only centimeters from his ear, she whispered to him.

I couldn't hear what she said, but his response was enough to know that with each and every word she spoke, she slowly tightened her grip. The horrified look on his face showed his pain before his demise. With a sinful smile that chilled my heart, Catherine let out a small grunt, twisted his head, and disposed of it on the floor behind her.

The uncontrolled sobbing of the remaining patrons huddled in the corner drew Catherine's attention. The last remaining humans fought each other as they pressed themselves further against the wall.

With a devilish grin and a menacing cackle, Catherine slowly stalked toward the helpless people.

Before I could see what was going on, Michael quickly picked me up and nodded to his Ravens. With stealth and speed, they made it to her just in time. As she reached for the closest victim, one of the Ravens—followed by Lena and Tack—grabbed her hands and pinned them to her sides. Her full-out furious laugh gave me goosebumps.

"Michael, what are they doing?" I asked in horror as I saw them bring her to her knees. Her struggle intensified as two more of the Ravens joined in to help hold her down.

"They are stopping her from killing the humans. The fight with the vampires is over, but she is still fighting. She must be stopped." Michael's voice was sorrowful.

"No!" Catherine cried as Lyle walked up from behind her with a sword in his hands. "No!"

Without a second thought, Lyle let the sword swing in one elegant motion. I sat in shock as the sword slid through her neck. In this small fraction of a second, everything was suspended.

My heart raced as I felt for Catherine. I waited and watched. My heart stuttered and I felt my limitations falter. As my breathing came out in sputters, I tried to grasp onto the last of my control, but my fear and anger were too strong. As I sat there, helpless, the last thread holding me together snapped. Shaking all over and clenching my jaw, I let my boundaries dissolve and allowed my emotions to soar.

"Michael!" I yelled as I released the power that surged through my veins. I felt the ground beneath me tremble. The streetlights quivered, then popped and exploded. Michael struggled to hold me back but lost his grip. Startled, he blocked the glass from the bursting bulbs in the streetlights. The ground beneath me rumbled and roared with each step I took. I barely heard the car alarms and dogs over the sound of my own blood rushing through my veins.

"No!" I shrieked as I ran to the diner. Michael and the Ravens scurried and rushed to catch me, but I was already at the door before the last of the eight lights broke.

As I approached Catherine, I reached for her hands, but her body fell back, and her head landed in my palms.

"No!" I yelled. Looking up at Lyle, my sorrow faded as anger took over. "You could have waited—you didn't have to kill her." I stood and stalked toward him with a vengeance. The fear that gleamed in his eyes grew, as did my rage. My own eyes burned, the telltale sign of them turning red. With a thin, tight-lipped smile, I walked toward the man responsible for killing Catherine. His retreat suggested that he feared me, but I knew better than that. He was a Raven. He was one of the strongest and most feared of Michael's men, only used in extreme circumstances.

"She had gone mad," the Raven said.

"She was hurt. She—"

A swift and powerful blow landed in the small of my back.

My lungs deflated as I face-planted onto the hard wood floor. I gasped for air and tried to push myself up.

"Don't get up," a rather large unfamiliar man in a white suit and black polished shoes said as he pointed a sword at me. "I'm not in the habit of losing." His tone was low and rumbling.

His gruff voice dampened my anger, and an unease seeped through me. As I turned away from his penetrating glare, I saw Catherine's head lying on the floor just a few feet from my face. Her angelic features were frozen in fear.

"Catherine?" I whimpered. This was not how it was supposed to be. Silent sobs shook through me as reality hit. Then, covering my face with my hands, I wept.

It didn't take long for my tears to subside and courage and fortitude to take root in my broken heart. My banked anger fired right back up, and I growled.

With renewed strength, I carefully pushed myself up onto my knees. Two additional vampires, dressed in the same white suits, stalked up beside the man, their swords loosely held at their sides. I glared up at the man who held his sword against my neck. Ever so slowly, I turned my head to meet him eye to eye. A slight, almost imperceptible smirk creased my face.

In a move faster than I knew I was capable of, I swung my leg around in an arc, aiming for the man in the middle. I caught him by the ankles and swept him to the ground. He flailed his arms in a vain attempt to regain his balance, but only succeeded in taking the man to his left down with him. As their bodies thudded, I heard the sound of metal clanging and scattering across the diner's wooden floor. The last remaining vampire swung his sword in an attempt to end the quarrel. I pushed myself up, stepped in close to him, and grabbed the hilt, stopping his swing. Standing fully, I broke his grip and heard his fingers snap one by one. I turned around and swung the sword right at his neck. Then, at the last possible moment, I stopped. The gentle, residual sound of the ringing steel was all I heard as the man's eyes widened in pain and fear. He fell to his knees. When the two other men managed to find their feet with not a weapon between them, the quarrel was indeed over.

"It's funny you're not in the habit of losing," I said, looking at them in disgust. "Neither am I." I dropped the sword and ran to Catherine's side, where my mom was now weeping. I knelt down beside her and placed my hand on her shaking shoulder. Her quiet sobs shook through her as she gazed down at Catherine's head, her eyes welling up with tears.

With a faint quiver to her lips, she whispered, almost inaudibly, "Did you know she saved my life five times? My best friend in the whole world, my one blood sister." Her words trembled. "She sacrificed herself for me countless times and I was powerless to stop this. I at least could have done… something, anything." She hung her head as her breath came out in uneven gasps. Then, with no sound whatsoever, her lips formed words. "I'm sorry," she told her friend. "I'm so sorry."

My mom closed her eyes. A single tear fell from her face and landed on Catherine's cheek. The loss of her best and closest friend had killed a part of her. I could feel her heart shatter and break as she held her friend's head.

Michael quietly came up from behind and held me. The moment was surreal. My mom felt broken as she watched her best friend die. My dad was filled with anger, and Michael felt torn between wanting to seek revenge and being here for me. But as the four of us sat there, the feeling of several unfamiliar vampires started to seep through the chaotic emotions.

"I know," Michael said, sensing my worry as I moved uncomfortably.

"Who are they?" I asked, standing and watching the vampires that surrounded us.

"Shadows," he said with an exaggerated sigh.

"Shadows? Who are the Shadows?"

"They are like… cleaners. They come in and sweep away the mess left by vampires, but they only come when—" Michael was cut off when Mr. Not-In-The-Habit-Of-Losing walked up beside us, his white suit oddly formal in this setting. With pains not to offend Michael, he bowed his head to me, then to Michael.

"Is she yours?" he asked, gesturing toward Catherine's remains.

"Yes," was Michael's simple and direct answer.

"We'll need to talk about the ramifications of today's little display, but first we need to dispose of the witnesses and clean up this mess. How many will you donate?" The man's comment was heartless in a way that infuriated me. He spoke as if Catherine meant nothing and the issue had been her fault. He didn't take Nicholas's actions into account.

With fury boiling just below my surface, I let a surge of power fly free in an attempt to calm myself. The lights in the diner suddenly shattered, littering the room with exploded glass.

Michael moved to cover me from the onslaught of debris, and the Shadow took Michael's sudden movement as a threat.

"No!" was the last thing I heard as Michael's form blurred and blackness enveloped me.

SEVEN

I woke up with sun beating through the window. A light breeze drifted through the air, rustling the trees as the branches scratched against the glass.

Sitting up, I heard voices talking from behind the door.

"When she wakes, bring her to me. I see no reason for the District and the Coven Masters to be delayed any longer."

The cold, hard voice sounded familiar, but only vaguely. Then yesterday's events started to come back to me. The fight in the diner, the Shadows, and the—

I paused. Carefully touching my hand to the back of my head, I felt a raised knot. The Shadow knocked me out when… when…

My mind stuttered. Michael! My heart pounded as fear over what happened to him consumed me. Looking around the room, I tried to gauge where I was and who had me, but nothing had changed. The room I had occupied since moving into the manor over three years ago was the same.

I concentrated on breathing in a slow and steady rhythm, waiting for the piercing ringing in my ears to subside. My head pounded in protest, hammering with an entire warlike drumline.

I tried to recall exactly what happened. After Catherine went rogue and practically leveled an entire diner as she killed Nicholas's deliverymen, she turned on the humans, then Lyle killed her. My heart ached as I recalled her death, but just as quickly after, my sorrow faded into anger.

I pulled my knees in to myself, wrapped my arms around them, and held tight. My chest tightened. Taking slow, quivering breaths, I tried to calm myself, but the lamp on the nightstand flickered, and the handles on the dresser jiggled as I rocked back and forth. The bed creaked with every move I made.

Creak… creak… creak.

I don't know how I was making the lampshade flicker or the dresser handles jiggle, but I knew it was me, and I needed to control it. I willed my emotional tidal wave to calm, but all I could think about was everything that led up to this moment. The vibrations got stronger.

Eventually, the constant squeaking from the sway of my body and the jingling of the dresser handles drew the guard's attention.

"Ma'am?" I barely heard the deep, hesitant, voice as he cracked the door open, almost as though using it as a shield. "Are you awake?"

I sat there, staring at the door as I narrowed my eyes at him.

I knew him. He wasn't a member of Michael's coven. He was a Shadow. One of the men who'd attempted to bully me in the diner.

"Who are you?" I asked, eyeing him with suspicion. The man cringed.

"I'm Jakob, first commander of the western clan."

Yep, judging by his wide eyes and the intense grip on his hilt, I could tell he was afraid of me.

"If you'll kindly accompany me, the others are expecting your attendance." He swallowed hard.

"What do you mean, the others?" I said, seething.

"The District leaders, the Coven Masters, and the Shadows, of course. Due to the horrendous show you put on at the diner, the Shadows are naturally…" he trailed off as he adjusted his stance. "Well, I'm pretty sure you know." There was a slight pause as he assessed me from head to toe. Fear crept into my heart. "Hey, uh… are you okay, ma'am? You look a little pale."

"Yeah." Then it hit me. He specifically said the show I put on at the diner, not Catherine, and judging by the way Jakob described the situation, I didn't think the others wanted to have tea. Something was going on, and it wasn't pretty. I could feel it.

Annoyance rose up and took its place in the forefront of my mind. In the last twenty minutes since I'd woken up, it had been an emotional tug of war inside me.

On the other side of the door, torrents of confusion and tension came rolling in like a fog, and it wasn't just from Jakob. I needed to get out of here. I needed to calm down and find a place to think, and that wasn't here.

My heart rate tripled as my emotional tide swelled. Seeing that Jakob had widened his pose and withdrew the blade of his sword just enough to show silver, I assumed he heard it too.

I bit my lip, hesitating.

"I'm fine," I repeated, trying to smile past my anger. They were basically treating me as the threat. "Could you please get Michael for me?" I knew the answer would be no, but I had to try.

"I'm sorry, ma'am."

"Please, call me Arri." Maybe if he thought we were on a first name basis, he'd loosen up a bit.

"I'm sorry, Arri, but Michael is currently..." He glanced around the hallway, as if looking to see if someone was listening. "He is currently in his office with Nizari." His face showed reverence as he spoke the name Nizari in a hushed, polite, and fearful tone.

"Fine." I folded my arms in front of me. I knew the name should mean something, but fortunately for me, it didn't. There were only a few names I cared to know, and Nizari was not one of them.

"Well." I looked down at his shoes, trying to act compliant and submissive. I needed to get him away from the room so I could get out of here. Once I calmed down, I'd need to see Michael. He'll know what's going on. "Okay, well, since I just woke up and need to get dressed and ready, would you please tell them I'll be down in a minute?" I asked, lowering my head with an exaggerated sigh.

As I walked toward the bathroom, I heard the soft click of the door as it shut. I quietly listened for his retreating footsteps, but there were none. I bit the side of my cheek as I thought. He must have figured out my little ploy and was waiting just outside the door to trap me. I tiptoed to the door, carefully gripped the handle, and turned the knob, praying the hinges didn't creak.

As I cracked the door, the general rustling of the coven as they walked and talked downstairs filled the empty hallway. Jakob had, in fact, left, presumably to tell everyone that I would be down shortly. I took a few calming breaths, and my pulse began to slow. I didn't want them to hear the pounding of my erratic heart. That would give me away. At last, I closed my eyes and took the first step outside my room.

After I made it downstairs without being caught, I took a deep breath and hid behind a chair in the foyer. I didn't expect it to be so busy. I debated the actual possibility of me making it out of the foyer without being seen, but the odds were against me.

"I heard she was responsible for Catherine's death," Tayla said as I skirted around her, ducking and hiding.

"The poor dear. Her mother must be absolutely furious with her. She had no business being there. Catherine might even still be alive today if the child had just stayed out of the way and let Michael and her mother do their job," Rosa, an older vampire, said. Although her appearance indicated she couldn't have been older than twenty, I knew for a fact that she was over four hundred years old.

When I heard those words, I froze.

I fought myself, trying to control my inner demon and not kill Tayla and Rosa for blaming me for Catherine's death. I shook my head in disgust.

I could see now that the Shadows' presence had started to turn a few of the coven members against me. New and reclaimed fury swept through me like a roaring tide. Eyeing the doors less than twenty feet away, I knew I needed to make a break for it without being seen. If I had to stay in here any longer, everyone in the foyer would be dead.

A single vampire in dull, flat, white material entered the mansion, and I paused only a moment to analyze his dress. All the Shadows dressed in variations of the same thing: white material, loose-legged pants, and a form-fitting shirt of thin fabric. Basically, they were white ninjas. Knowing that there were more than one or two Shadows walking around the manor, I shook off the sinking feeling that I might have bitten off more than I could chew. Before I had a chance to overthink it, I quietly slipped out from behind the chair and took a few steps toward the front doors.

"And where are you going?" a deep male voice said from behind me.

I slowly turned and came face-to-face with Jakob. I tried to ignore the murmuring voices and the various coven members who stopped and stared at the two of us.

"I see you decided not to change." His tone was light and mocking.

"No."

"Where are you going, Arri?" he asked again.

I looked over my shoulder at the front door. Twenty feet away, my freedom awaited, and I was stuck in here.

"Out."

"I thought I told you the others were expecting you." He cocked his head at a set of old wood and wrought-iron doors and smirked.

I looked at the doors, which were situated between the two grand staircases. They had never been open, or at least not that I'd seen. That doorway led to what once would have been the king's throne room. It was the one part of the castle that Michael left in its original form. The noise on the other side of their polished cherrywood grew a bit before subsiding into a whisper. My heart stilled. They were undoubtedly talking about me—as many conversations often did.

"Tell me, Jakob. What awaits me beyond that door?" I asked in a soft voice, gesturing to the throne room.

"It's not for me to say. I am merely following orders."

Orders. The word sounded so impersonal, so cold. "Orders?" I asked, closing my eyes, trying to rein in my feelings. "Whose orders?"

Rosa snickered. "Obviously she's not one of us if she doesn't know who Nizari is." She chuckled again.

I clenched my jaw and took a deep breath. As some of my anger released into the air, the pictures on the wall started to vibrate.

I turned to Rosa, my gaze fierce. "Until now, I've had no reason to know Nizari, but obviously you have."

I slowly stalked toward her. Rosa was one of the lowest ranking vampires in Michael's coven. She was ill-mannered, a sneak, and one of the biggest rumor-starters I've ever known.

"His name means nothing to me because I have no need to know who he is or why I should fear him. You, on the other hand," I said, taking a few more steps in her direction, seeing terror evident on her face, "have more than him to fear. I had nothing to do with Catherine's beheading. She went rogue after Phillip's head was delivered to her in a bag. The men in the diner died by her hands, not mine. The only reason she is dead now is because she went after the humans. I didn't kill her; Lyle did. So if you have anything to say about Catherine, you'll have me to answer to."

By the time I had finished yelling, I was towering over her, and the chair she and Tayla had been sitting on shook violently.

"Arri." Jakob said my name as if he, too, feared me. He laid a strong, sturdy hand on my shoulder, and Rosa looked relieved. "Come on," he said, pulling me away from the revolting woman. "She's not worth it, and it's time to go. The leaders are waiting." As I turned away from her, I took one last look over my shoulder at her cowering form.

"There's more to me than you think," I said, glowering at her. Just then, the picture of the night sky above her head fell to the floor. The sound of shattering glass echoed throughout the room.

With his hand still on my shoulder, Jakob steered me to the wooden doors. My anger melted just a smidgen.

If I were to be honest with myself, I was intimidated. All the heads of the vampire world—besides Nicholas—were supposed to be waiting for me beyond those doors.

"She doesn't belong. She's a threat. She is obviously risking the discovery of vampires," came one man's voice.

"She is not a threat," Michael's voice boomed. "She is just

young and new to our world. She has never shown or flaunted who she is. If anything, she has hidden her true potential."

"She made a mess of a small diner within minutes!" A woman's unfriendly voice drifted through the silence.

"No!" Michael's voice raised a few decibels. "She did nothing. Catherine was the sole perpetrator. Arri had nothing to do with Catherine's behavior or actions."

Michael was defending me.

"Yes, but we need to make sure she is not a threat. We—the council and I—are not intimately involved with her. We are not so easily swayed." The suggestive tone of this man's voice infuriated me. Like I was manipulating Michael.

Just then, Jakob pulled me to a halt and reached around me to knock on the door. He must have realized I'd heard the last few bits of the conversation, because I felt his disposition change. He made three quick, resounding raps on the door, and voices echoed from the opposite side.

"Enter."

Angry thoughts flooded my mind as I heard the last person's comments echo through my whole being: *We need to make sure she is not a threat. We—the council and I—are not intimately involved with her. We are not so easily swayed.*

I tried to put an emotionless and impassive expression on as Jakob opened the door.

"Ah, Arri," a man said, standing as I entered. "I'm glad you chose to join us."

A small, tentative smile curved my lips.

As if I had a choice.

EIGHT

"We were just talking about you. Please, come in and have a seat."

I looked to where the odious-looking man gestured.

My footsteps echoed throughout the enormous space as I walked toward the chair that sat in the middle of the hallowed room. The high, stained-glass ceiling ran the entire length of the space as the light beamed in and painted the room in rainbows. Yet what should have been a bright and cheerful space felt only threatening as the coven heads and Shadows stared at me with intense glares and curiosity.

I looked around. Chairs lined the room in rows and rows. Each was filled with a coven head or bodyguard.

"Arri," a deceptively calm voice called out to me. Michael, in his formal attire, stepped up behind me and intertwined his hands with mine as he pulled me in close. "I did not call for this meeting. I'm sorry." His pleading voice both soothed my heart and enraged my inner demon. I knew he didn't call for the meeting—the Shadows did, and that is what infuriated me.

"They have determined that you are to blame for the recent acts of exposure," Michael said. I opened my mouth to protest the allegation, but he placed a quick, chaste kiss to my lips. "Our relationship is also under question." His words were forlorn, like he hated to speak them aloud, even if they were necessary.

"Arri, please sit," a bellowing voice boomed.

I turned my attention to the man sitting in what was presumably a judge's chair. Even the setup of the room was arranged to intimidate me—like a courtroom, except the rows of chairs were on either side of me to face the center of the room, the door was behind me, and the judge before me.

I willed myself to feel respect for this man who was glaring at me like I was an enemy, but I felt nothing. The low, churning tide of whatever emotion I did feel was quiet.

"Arri? Would you care to take a seat so we may begin the meeting?" The man in the judge's chair motioned for me to sit.

Meeting? Is that what he thinks this is? I tried to rein in my anger, but all I could manage was a wry and mocking smirk.

"Come on. Let's not give him any reason to hold something against you." Michael's voice was laced with concern.

The small white chair in the center of the room might as well have been ten feet tall and covered in spikes for how welcoming it felt. With each step I took, I could sense the anticipation coming off the members of Michael's coven. Michael kissed my forehead, then turned to leave.

"Where are you going?" I asked as my heart filled with dread.

"I will be next to Nizari." It sounded like he would almost rather be anywhere but there.

I looked to the man sitting before us, as if he ruled all. His black cloak flowed behind him like a train on a gothic bridal gown; his white tailored suit contrasted against the fabric nicely, and his long, coarse, jet-black hair was pulled back into a stiff, wiry braid.

So this is Nizari, I thought, looking at the man before me. He looked mean and rude from his ridged back with his permanent frown and his stoic expression. And yet, I could feel the unease coming from the other members in the room. Something was off.

As Michael took his seat, Nizari glared at him, and the coven quieted. The room became stagnant, and the air seemed to chill.

"State your name," Nizari commanded.

I took a calming breath and bit my lip. Staring right at Nizari, I shook my head. "I'm sorry, but who are you?"

The room broke out into amazed and shocked conversation.

Nizari sputtered. "Me?" he asked, his tone sounding as though I had slapped him.

"Yes." Then, my inner demon, which I was beginning to love, came to the surface—and so did my confidence.

"I am Nizari, King of the Shadows," he said, rising up to his full height.

"Hello, Nizari. I am Arri. It is a pleasure to meet you." I offered him a placating smile.

"Indeed. Now state your full name," he commanded again.

"No," was my simple response. He was being demanding and rude. There was no telling why I was here. No explanation of what this was all about. As far as I knew, anything I said could hang me out to dry without anyone finding a single drop of blood on my hands.

"Pardon me?" His voice was grave and harsh.

"I said no." I gave a defiant tilt of my head. "I want to know what this is all about first. If I am being tried for something or accused of something, I have the right to know."

This only seemed to upset Nizari even more. I could see the muscle in his cheek twitch as he clenched his jaw.

"The allegations and claims against you will be revealed in time. Right now, I want your name."

"You know my name." From the corner of my eye, I could see my mom and dad withholding smiles that threatened to escape. I, too, had to suppress a smile when I remembered how Mom and I used to get into it. Neither of us ever had a chance of winning. We never raised our voices, but the arguments could go on for days, each of us taking turns to point out facts to support our side. It was part of the additional classes and life-training sessions my parents demanded I take when I was growing up. I could almost out-debate my own parents.

"Miss Stone, are you trying to be difficult? Because if you are, it will only result in a harsher punishment," Nizari practically barked.

There it was. I was already convicted. He said "a harsher punishment," not that my attitude would help my case.

"So, I am already convicted? Please, at least tell me what I am being charged with so I can defend myself."

"All right, I will assume we all know your name as Arri Stone, seeing as you're not willing to cooperate." Nizari sounded exasperated. I gave myself an internal high-five. "Okay, now to get back to business." Nizari continued and eyed me warily, waiting for me to interject. "Arri, I have come here to put an end to the exposure you have caused and the number of cleanups we have had to assist in over the last two and a half years. According to my understanding, you have left many a human privy to our existence. As such, I convict you, Arri Stone, with the crimes of exposure, neglect, and the blatant disregard for our secrecy."

Nizari nodded toward three men at the rear of the room. Automatically, my hands were bound behind my back. Something forced me to my knees.

"*What?*" Michael yelled as he jumped to his feet. He shot an expression of downright fury at Nizari before reaching for his collar.

I stared at the two of them for a moment in shock. Did he just say that I was convicted before I even had a chance to defend myself? What kind of court is this?

The room went into an uproar. Michael's coven was on its feet and yelling at Nizari. My parents were being held back by several nervous Shadows, and many other Shadows approached Michael, looking equally fearful and wary.

"Let her go!" Michael yelled over the crowd as he shook Nizari.

"I can't," Nizari responded calmly, although his heart, which I could feel pounding, was as fearful as a kitten cornered by a pack of hungry wild dogs. "You have no jurisdiction over my ruling."

Michael growled in a thunderous rumble.

"And you have no authority over my coven," he snapped. "You let her go now, or I will take your life before your Shadows have a chance to stop me." Michael's seething voice came from the heart. I knew he meant every word. As I searched the room, I saw Nizari's Shadows closing in on Michael, but I also saw my parents and Michael's Ravens making it difficult for the Shadows to reach him.

My heart sank and hit my toes as the sound of metal scraping against its sheath brought me back to my own physical predicament.

One of the Shadows holding me on my knees placed an open palm against the back of my head and forced it down. With this, my shock and fear turned into pure and uninhibited rage. The old wood floors bit painfully into my knees as the pressure on my shoulders crammed me down harder onto the polished surface. From the corner of my eye, I saw the feet of my assailants as they stood their ground next to me.

"No," I said in a low, angry tone.

"What?" one asked, bending to hear my response.

"I said *no!*" I yelled. With the slight shift in his weight, I threw my shoulder forward, and that small but consequential movement sent the Shadow stumbling.

One down.

The motion caught Nizari's attention. "Now!" he screeched.

The man with the sword stepped up behind me as the remaining Shadow attempted to hold me down again.

Panic surged through me, along with rage and fury at Nizari's attempt to execute me. The demon within was so close to my surface. It thrust its way through the invisible shield I'd put up in an attempt to rein it in. With one powerful surge of strength, I rose to my feet, shrugged the Shadow off my shoulder, and faced the vampire with a sword. Part of me wanted to laugh. It was the same moron who had held a sword to my neck in the diner. The same one I'd tripped.

"Well, hello again," he said with a smile in his voice. "I must say, you surprised me before, but it won't happen again." His expression was the same as when we met, but I wasn't buying his bravado. I could feel the way his heart jumped in fear, the way his inner self shook, unsure of what I was going to do.

Waiting for his move, I watched him closely. The steady rasp of his breath, the twitch in his lips, even his tightening grip on the hilt of the sword.

I knew I was at a major disadvantage with my hands tied behind my back. All I could do was wait for his move.

As my mind scrambled to find a solution that didn't end in my death or a horrific, crippling wound, I froze. The knot on my hands was loosening. Just as realization hit me, I felt the light, too-close brush of a knife blade at my feet. Looking back toward the crowd, I saw Phoenix among them, playing the part of defender against a few of the Shadows who tried to take on Michael.

A smile was spreading across my face when I was blessed again when the familiar feel of smooth, finely worn leather graced the palm of my hand. Phoenix. I smiled. With a swift and easy glide of the metal through the air, the Shadow blocked my hit effortlessly.

"So, do you play to fight or to win?" he asked mockingly.

I couldn't help but chuckle. Then, with one quick move that even surprised me, I turned about and landed the thin metal against his neck.

"This is the second time I have spared your life. The next time my sword swings at you, you won't be as lucky," I said as I eased the blade from his neck. He nodded, placing two fingers against the scratch and dabbing at the single drop of blood that beaded on his skin.

As I looked through the roaring crowd, and the many vampires that had swarmed into the middle of the room, I saw Michael and Nizari.

Michael still had Nizari by the collar, but the Shadows were close on his heels. With my pent-up emotion at the point of explosion as I reached the head of the fight, I finally let it all out. Every second of anger, each moment of rage, everything that brought me to this point blew out in a powerful but disciplined force.

"*Enough!*" I yelled, my voice booming throughout the room. The silver and gold chandeliers shook, the lights flickered, and the floor rumbled.

The room quieted and everyone stilled. They all stared at me in wonderment.

"What is going on here?" I asked as Nizari smoothed out his collar and tie, as if recovering from nothing more than a minor argument. And, of course, it was Nizari who was the first to make a move.

"All right, now. Everyone back to your seats," he said in a commanding voice. Then, with a pointed glare at me, he added, "I will humor your request and hear your defense." With an exaggerated sigh, he nodded to his Shadows, and they quickly backed off, though they stayed tense and alert.

With a surge of fury, I gave him something between a smile and a scowl. I took a gander around the room. Everyone had taken a seat. My parents and Michael remained standing, but they had moved from the jury and were now right next to me: Michael in front of me, Mom to my left, and Dad to my right. Then there was Phoenix and Ash, who stood at the rear. Each family member watched and waited.

"Now, if it pleases you," Nizari's voice reeked of arrogance and disdain, "you may attempt to vindicate yourself." His arrogant tone and his condescending smile infuriated me. It irritated me to think he thought he was above me. Not to say that I was above anyone in any way, but still. That didn't excuse his behavior.

"I want to know on what grounds you claim I am responsible for the exposure of the vampire world to humans," I said evenly, although I was as scared as scared could be.

"I need no evidence. Your actions during this meeting alone are proof enough that you are guilty," Nizari stated as if that was an answer.

"You don't need real proof?" I asked with a tilt of my chin.

"No." He sat back in his chair.

"So, by that logic, I could also convict you of the same crime. I could sentence you to a beheading for conspiracy, no?"

"What conspiracy?" Nizari's face was grim with disbelief.

"For committing treason and conspiracy against Michael and members of his coven. For working and planning with Nicholas." At last, I had everyone's attention.

"I do not take sides, nor am I working with Nicholas." He looked unaffected as he sat back and dismissed me with a noticeable yawn.

"Well, I believe you are," I spat.

"Do you have any proof to justify or validate such a ridiculous allegation?" He eyed me with suspicion.

"No. But if you don't need any proof, then neither do I." I cocked my head to the side. My lips twitched as I held back a smile.

"Your accusations hold no merit!" he yelled as he sprang to his feet. He planted his hands and leaned over the top of the wooden stand. It creaked, but only from his weight, not his power.

"Neither do yours, but you were willing to kill me with no more evidence than I have against you for committing treason," I said, never breaking eye contact with him. "If you ask me, you did nothing but come here willy-nilly and slap a conviction on me without knowing what happened or who is really to blame. You simply showed up at the diner, saw me, and assumed I was responsible for the exposure. I had nothing to do with the diner incident, and I won't let you drag Michael's coven and my name through the mud and put me on trial for something I didn't do. If you actually did your homework, as you should have—you are the King of Shadows, after all—you would have found out that I was in the flower shop the entire time. I only emerged when Catherine, the real culprit, was put to death. When I finally made it to her side, her head fell into the palm of my hands." I stopped for a much-needed moment to calm myself.

I didn't realize that as I was speaking, I'd been pacing, and as I paced, the stained-glass ceiling around me had been cracking and splintering. Small pieces of glass fell from the fragile canopy, covering the room in shards. The bodyguards were shielding the coven heads, and the polished wooden floors were now a carpet of shiny, knife-sharp glass.

I raised my hands chest-high, then pushed them back down again in an attempt to control my rage. A rush of air mimicked my movements, then blew around my feet and out toward the crowd. The burst of energy that flowed freely through my veins calmed, but only slightly.

"If this is how you are ruling as 'King of the Shadows,'" I said, drawing air quotes around his title, "then I see no reason why you should rule. Keeping our world a secret is of utmost importance, but if you are sentencing innocent people to death just because they are present at the time of an exposure, then you have most likely killed the wrong person—which does nothing but increase the chances of another exposure." The room around me was still and quiet as everyone looked back and forth between the king and me. The anger in me rolled off in waves as I allowed my emotional chaos to run free. The air around me seemed to swirl and flurry as I moved about the room.

I waited for him to rebut, but he didn't. I could feel his eyes following me as I paced. With each step I took, his eyes narrowed in on my feet. I kept my same stride, still walking back and forth. My internal rage and confusion were much too strong for me to remain still. I could feel my control slipping as I thought of Nizari's ability to dispose of and convict whomever he saw fit, and not have to answer to such things as facts, evidence, and proof. He was a walking, talking vampire dictator. No different than Nicholas.

"You say you don't take sides, but if you are blindly convicting and punishing those who are innocent, then you are no better than Nicholas." As I spat Nicholas's name, the reined-in anger I reserved specifically for Nicholas came out in a burst. A series of gasps filled the room as heads nodded.

It was only then did I realize I was still pacing, and with every move I made, the glass that fell from the ceiling kept landing all around me… but nothing fell on me. The same stunned look flickered on the faces of the Shadows as they watched the floor at my feet. When I stepped forward, the fallen glass moved away from me, allowing me to walk on clean, shard-free, polished wood. I had been clenching and unclenching my fists, which allowed me to control my fury, but I couldn't rein it back in, and as my inner turmoil still flowed free, it cut a path of untouched and clean space as I paced.

"I resent your lack of respect for me and my men. You have only lived among us for a short while. You have no say in the matters of our world," Nizari said, walking around the table and toward me. I stopped mid-stride and allowed his approach.

The air around me seemed to cool a few degrees as a chill filled the empty space between us. Tingles and sharp prickles skated across his skin as I felt his inner self fight against the stinging pain.

"I may not have lived within this world of fairytales and fiction for long, but it is obvious you have been taking advantage of your role as secret keeper." My eyes burned with the sudden want to bestow as much pain on him as he had bestowed upon others. With one last deep and controlled breath, I let out a surge of energy that knocked Nizari back a few steps.

"I see you as just as much of a threat to the vampire world as Nicholas," I cried. "No one has the right to commit someone to death without the proper proof and chance at self-defense. Not even you."

I watched as Nizari fought against the stinging pain I created around him. His face contorted into an expression of anger and torturous pain.

"You wonder why I think I have the right?" His voice boomed with outrage. "I have the right because if vampires like you are allowed to roam free, we are all doomed to die. Not to mention that no one should possess your power. So, in either case, you should die." He bit out the threat with passion and fury.

I thought about it for a moment. Where have I heard that phrase before? The thought churned inside my head until the dots finally connected.

"Who sent you?" I asked in a cold, controlled voice that didn't hide the accusation behind my words.

"No one. Your own mess drew me to you," he said. Beneath his well-articulated words, I could feel his deceit and lies as if they were burning fire.

I let out another burst of power, and Nizari struggled to compose himself against my anger. I reached out and took his arm. Then, just as with Nana, the pictures started to form in my head. Like a black and white vision of truth, I saw his memories as though they were happening before me.

"Nizari, my old friend," Nicholas's voice cut through the space between them. "It has been a while. What are you up to in today's world?"

"The usual. Although the cleanups are getting a little slow." Nizari's words were sad and thoughtful.

"Yes, well, your reputation as a cold-blooded killer could have something to do with it." Nicholas chuckled, a cold and eerie sound.

"So, why have you summoned me?" Nizari asked, his tone very "cut the crap," like he wanted to focus on the kill.

"I have a proposition for you." Nicholas turned his cold eyes onto Nizari. "I want Steven's daughter dead."

"I don't like to take sides, Nicholas. You know that. Besides, Steven is a vampire. We cannot father children."

"And yet, he has still managed to father one."

"The rumors of the prodigy are just that: rumors."

As the words left Nizari's mouth, Nicholas reached out and pinned him to the clean, painted wall behind him. Nizari's expression remained emotionless.

"I am in a dreadful mood, my old friend. I need not play any games. I want the little cur dead. Her mere existence has started rumblings. I will have none from you. You will kill the wretched child. Here, use this." Nicholas slid a piece of paper into Nizari's hand. "Be creative," he suggested. "For I'd hate for your position to be vacated and filled by someone selected by my own hand."

The threat was enough to wipe the placidity from Nizari's face. The realization that Nicholas could and would do it shone through his eyes. Satisfied, Nicholas lowered Nizari to his feet and bid him good day.

As I came back to reality, I felt my face falter for a moment as fatigue hit me, but I quickly hid the expression and let anger rumble through me instead. I realized Nizari was being manipulated, but the fact that he didn't fight for justice disturbed me even more. Nizari, the all-mighty Shadow King, had let his services be bought and paid for.

Releasing the death-like grip on his arm, I sneered at the man.

"I asked who sent you!" I yelled.

"No one," he snapped. "I told you before, we don't take sides. We have no opinion or position on the guilty." Beneath his façade, a faint glimmer of fear and contempt flickered in his eyes before he pulled the veil back into place.

"I'm calling your bluff," I said. My sense of fear jumped up a notch or two, as I noticed his Shadows had circled in behind me. I knew I had the power to hold off Nizari, but I didn't know how long I could defend myself against them.

Just as I had noticed the cracks in his composure, so did his fellow Shadows. His slipup had them questioning the nature of his conviction.

"My liege, what defense do you have?" Jakob asked as he stood next to me, but at a distance.

"My will and actions need no defense."

"No, my liege. We have no will. We take no sides."

Jakob had pointed out the king's mistake. Nizari was cornered, and anger pulsed through him with a vengeance. As Nizari fought against my invisible hold on him, his added force and strength started to break through my shield. I clenched my jaw and tightened my fists at my sides as I tried with all my might to hold him back, but the power within me had grown tired. Although my vampire side was waiting and willing to fight the fight, my human side was growing shakier by the moment.

As Nizari caught on to my weakness, he made a lunge at me that my unseen hold couldn't stop. He pulled out the sword from the sheath at his waist. In a last-minute decision to defend myself as Nizari came at me with his sword, I conjured all the strength I had left and forced my inner power to enact my will. Thanks to a bit of hope and a dash of luck, the glass shards skidded across the floor and surrounded him in a circle of wind. The whirl of air moved its way up until it enveloped Nizari from head to foot. Then, with my remaining strength, I forced the tiny shards of glass toward the sputtering, confused king. But my strength wasn't enough. All I had managed to do was scratch his immaculate clothing and upset him more.

The Shadows nearest to me did nothing to help their leader; however, the ones by my parents still obeyed Nizari's commands, holding my mother, Ash, and Michael back. My mom seemed helpless as she struggled against the Shadows for freedom, but right behind them was my dad—fighting. With the speed of his sword, he took life after life, Shadow after Shadow, but it wasn't enough to free my mom and Ash. Just as one life was lost, another Shadow swept into the empty place it left. Michael and Phoenix fought as hard as they could as well, but they, too, were overwhelmed.

The coven stood in shock after seeing Nizari's and my display, the Shadows torn between their leader—their king—and me. The room was chaos.

I fell to the floor and scooted away from the approaching vampire. Even in my vulnerable state, the glass and debris littering the floor fled from my path, leaving me untouched. Then, when my back hit the wall, and I had nowhere else to run, Nizari lifted his sword.

"You will die by my hands." A crazed smirk creased his lips as his sword bore down on me.

I watched and waited for the end. My strength was barely enough to keep me breathing, my powers were nil. I had nowhere to run.

Suddenly, the air hummed with a sense of reverence. Everyone was looking at us in astonishment and awe. Then, I heard the ting of metal.

Time and space stood still as all eyes, including mine, watched Jakob stop Nizari's blade. With a flip of the wrist, and a grunt of force, Jakob disarmed his master and king.

"You were wrong, my liege. Arri isn't the threat you claimed her to be. You are." Jakob's last words left his lips as his sword swung a mighty blow and Nizari's body fell to my side.

As I closed my eyes in relief, I heard Michael's approach. Tears fell from my cheeks as I felt his presence.

"Arri?" His voice calmed my heart. "Arri? Are you okay? Honey? Please talk to me."

I heard the panic in his voice, and it brought me back to reality. I opened my eyes.

I took a few deep, revitalizing breaths and nodded. Although I was still weak and tired, I pushed past all that and sat up. The room was stock-still as all eyes watched me. I turned to Michael and gave him a relieved smile, but it didn't make my aches and pains dissipate. I pushed myself to stand, but my balance was off, and I stumbled. Michael reached out to stabilize me, as did Jakob.

"Whoa there, toots. Where are you going?" Jakob's voice rang with authority. I held my breath as I looked into his eyes, waiting for him to tell me the meeting wasn't over, but he just smiled.

"Do you feel well enough to walk?" he asked, gesturing to the unwelcoming white chair sitting in the middle of the large, devastated space. Glass littered the room, the ceiling was crumbled and shattered, and the once-polished wooden floors were now scarred.

Michael growled, and I grimaced as I held my arm. The warm, sticky fabric of my shirt clung to my skin as I felt blood soak through my clothes. I closed my eyes, shook my head, and let out a hollow laugh. Even after all of this, I'm still on trial. There had to be humor in this. After all, from what I have heard, the Shadows aren't known for their forgiving nature.

"No!" Michael bellowed as he placed himself between Jakob and me. "This meeting is over. Arri has done nothing wrong. She is under my protection, and I say this is over." Michael's murderous glare and threatening mood registered loud and clear as Jakob took a gracious step back.

"I agree. Arri has been through enough. I was merely trying to be a gentleman and offer her a seat, as she seems too weak to stay upright for long." Jakob's voice was soft and understanding. "Please—she is injured. Do you have someone who could tend to her wounds?"

Michael looked back at me, and then nodded.

"No," I said. Jakob's words hit me deep. "I may have been wounded, and I am tired and drained, but I am not weak." I fought back tears as I shook my head.

I turned on my heel and headed for the doors, leaving the room silent and stunned. As I reached the outer hall, Michael's grip on me tightened as I lost my balance again. My teetering stance and my unsteady composure caught the remaining coven members' attention.

Silence filled the castle and a sense of reverence drifted

throughout the muted halls. Michael bent down to lift me into an embrace. As he saw the blood from my arm staining the tips of my fingers, saw the tiny droplets of blood that fell to the floor, his heart broke.

Yet when I felt his strong arms envelop me in a blanket of warmth and security, I relaxed, leaning my head against his shoulder. In mere seconds, Michael had climbed the stairs and opened the door to my room.

"Here," he said as he gently deposited me on the chair near the window. He went to turn on the shower.

The curtains were open, but I wasn't interested in anything outside. I was still focused on the events from downstairs. My head spun. It wasn't the fact that Nizari had betrayed the Shadows or the fight between them and us. No, what I couldn't figure out was how I had managed to displace so much energy. The ceiling shattered and the broken glass moved out of my way. Even the way I held Nizari at bay with sheer force stunned me. I closed my eyes as I thought of how dangerous I could be, not just to the coven, but to Michael. I didn't know how to control this power, and until I did, I was a danger to everyone. Had Nizari been right?

I nearly jumped out of my skin as Michael placed a reassuring hand on my shoulder.

"Arri, hon, the shower is ready."

His soft voice caressed my heart and sent tingles throughout my body. Looking into his angelic, emerald-green eyes, I saw a maelstrom of emotion—concern, pain, love, fear—all wrapped around him like a heavy blanket. It was everything he felt for me.

I took Michael's outstretched hand and let him help me to my feet. In all my life, I had never felt so depleted. Even when I died in Michael's arms, I was still fighting. Now all I could feel was the gaping, hollow space where my strength used to be.

As the hot water drenched me, the large gash on my arm screamed out in pain. My knees buckled, and I hit the shower floor. Then it dawned on me: this is exactly what Nicholas wants. He wanted me vulnerable and weak. He wanted me to feel tired and spent. But he thought wrong. Every attack, every attempt, made me that much stronger. Maybe not physically, not always, but emotionally. It took me a moment to recover from the stinging wound, but in my core, a renewed sense of power and confidence rose up from the ashes. First, though, I needed to rest.

Dawn came faster than I wanted. From the other side of the door, low rumbles caressed the silence. Finally, the castle was back to normal, as it should be.

"Morning." Michael's voice eased through my half-awake state and brought me fully aware. His body was pressed against mine, and he pulled me toward him.

Last night, even though I'd been so wiped out I couldn't have gotten out of bed if I had tried, Michael insisted on staying with me, which was okay. His warm body and his captivating embrace called to me. After that little visit from the Shadows, I needed the comfort and sense of security.

Feeling the brush of his lips against my cheek, I warmed from the inside out. His fingers drew lazy circles on my arms.

Even as my sore muscles screamed in protest, my body automatically drifted toward him. In all this madness and chaos, Michael was my one true anchor. His faith and confidence in me were unyielding and his love for me absolute.

He pulled me on top of him and brought my mouth to his for a searching and soulful kiss.

"How do you feel?" he asked against my lips.

I pulled away and braced myself upon his chest.

"I'm sore and bruised, but other than that, I'm fine." I smiled down at him as he looked into my eyes.

"I've been watching you sleep." His words were more than an admission; they were a probing question. "Nightmares?" he asked, brushing a few strands of hair behind my ear.

"Yeah. Nicholas again," I admitted. "It's not enough that he hunts me by day, he has to haunt me by night, too." I gave Michael a half-hearted smile. "He's going to kill me, you know. I've seen it, and in a way, I've felt it. I just wish I knew why." Saying it was harder than I expected it would be. I looked away to hide my fear.

Michael sat up with no effort at all and brought me up with him. He moved me to his side, then turned to face me. The concern in his eyes broke me.

"I have the same recurring nightmares all the time," I told him. "Nicholas shackles me, and then tortures me. He uses hot branding irons, thin-wired whips, and scalding water, but I never break. He wants me to submit to him, admit that I am below him, but I never do. He hobbles me and parades me before his followers."

The catch in my voice was an obvious sign that I was about to cry, but I held the tears back, and Michael calmly and willingly listened without interruption. I continued, twisting my hands in my lap.

"Then there are others, about some sort of past memory or something. I haven't quite figured these dreams out yet, but they are about my dad. He is walking aimlessly, fear-stricken and hungry, and then, as if in a blaze of fire, the vision changes and he sees a man drinking from another man's heart—his lips stained with blood, his teeth sharp. And the barbarian seems to recognize my dad. The scenes blur, then, I see my dad kneeling over Nicholas, pity filling his heart as he watches him gasp and fight for air. My dad takes pity on him and bites his neck, leaving a scar on his collarbone, an X marking him like a brand. My dad leaves him and lets nature take its course."

I shivered as a chill ran down my spine. There was something poetic about the nightmare, but it was frightening, nonetheless.

"I know what Nicholas has planned for me, but what I can't figure out is why. In my dreams, Nicholas stabs me through the heart. His satisfied cackle echoes off the white marble room. His coven laughs and jeers as they cheer in victory. But then the pain stops. My life ends, and I wake up. Each nightmare I have reveals something different: a new pain, a different torture, even different deaths, but the endings are always the same. I die. My heart stops, the lights dim until darkness takes over, and the sound of blood rushing through my veins ceases."

I swallowed past a knot in my throat. I looked into Michael's rich green eyes, a sob breaking through my defenses.

"Michael," I whimper, "I'm afraid that I'm going to die."

Michael pulled me into his arms. I cried on his shoulder as he rubbed my back in comfort.

"Shh, my love," he whispered. "They are only dreams. The endings can still change." His soothing words stoked the love in my heart. But deep down, I knew he was wrong. Whatever Nicholas had against me, whatever reason he wanted me dead, he was never going to stop until either he or I was no longer living.

I pulled back from Michael's embrace just in time to catch a smile skate across his face.

"What?" I asked before he pulled me into a kiss. He started out slow, exploratory and beseeching, his lips parting slightly as if asking for permission. His hands stroked my ribs, and my mind lost all thought or logic. Only Michael could make me forget about my impending death, why I was marked to die, even why I was destined to end my life fighting for my own freedom. Michael was the one person that could take me from scared and panic-stricken to passionate and willing in a heartbeat.

TEN

A few weeks had passed since the Shadows left. Their unsubtle promise that they would be back soon left everyone on edge—everyone except me. All I needed to know was that they were going to be back. For a human, the word "soon" meant anytime within the next few months, but for a vampire, it meant anytime within the next hundred years or so. They didn't exactly see time the same way I did. They measured it by major or world-changing events like wars, man walking on the moon… the kinds of things that make a big impact.

I stood under the wilted willow tree, pondering the reality of my situation and looking over Michael's vast yard. In the past, the grounds would have been pristine. The well-groomed, bucolic setting wouldn't have normally had so much as a blade of grass out of place, but what I saw now made my insides cringe. The bushes were overgrown and untrimmed. The grass was tall and uneven. In short, it looked more like a pasture than a manicured and well-maintained lawn.

Thump… thump… thump… thump…

The pounding of my heart drowned out all the noise. The wind, though subtle and quiet, seemed to match the rhythm of my heartbeat. As the trees swayed back and forth, a calm feeling settled over my heart. My mind cleared and my thoughts drifted to the past several weeks. Catherine's death, the Shadow King Nizari trying to execute me, even the show of my strong, if untamed, abilities all haunted my memory. Catherine's death was a hit to the gut. It was then that this fantastical life became a reality. I lived in a castle. My life was posh. I was even able to function with the fact that Nicholas was after me because it had only been me that he targeted for so long. No one close to me had suffered. Not until Catherine.

With that, my serenity crumbled. As I wiped the tears from my face, a familiar presence came close. Looking over my shoulder, I offered my dad a polite smile.

"Hey, Dad," I said, turning away to hide my tears.

"You know, there once was a time when you called me Daddy."

His light tone and easy stride calmed me as he closed the distance between us. My dad and I had never been especially close. He and I were always at arm's length. Always hovering near each other, but never quite within reach.

"Yeah, there was, wasn't there?"

I nudged my dad with my shoulder as he came to stand next to me. Since he and my mom had come to the castle, I had made an unconscious decision to keep a bit of distance. They'd hidden who and what I was from me, but more than that, they'd suffocated me. I was never allowed to be myself. Then, when I moved away from home, they disappeared, leaving me to find out who and what I was alone. I resented them. They'd lived a life of secrecy and adventure, but I hadn't really lived a life at all.

"So when did Daddy become just plain old Dad?" he asked. We didn't look at each other. We just stared off into the distance at nothing and everything.

I didn't answer. I just looked over the empty scenery before me. My emotions clouded, and I closed my eyes in an attempt to calm them. I understood why my parents hid me and did everything in their power to protect me, but understanding didn't make it hurt less. I swallowed the lump in my throat and opened my eyes only to see my dad looking at me.

His features were cast in iron: his mouth set in a grim line, and his eyes forged with anger and pain. His thoughts, however, were almost visible. I could practically see them. Light flickers of images and hints of voices and sounds drifted through my head. I saw pain and agony. The heart-wrenching guilt that twisted within him, the pleading in his eyes—they broke me.

The distance between us had hurt him as much as it hurt me. Keeping me at a distance was related to his past. He was protecting me from what he had done, who he was, and what was to come.

"Oh, honey." His voice was tired and exhausted. "I didn't plan on us having a child, let alone you." His words fell from his mouth in a painful mess. Letting go of my hand, he took a few steps back until he sat on the bench surrounding the willow tree. After burying his face, he lifted his head and slowly shook it. "It wasn't supposed to be you," he admitted in a pained whisper. With those words, he caught my attention.

My dad stopped shaking his head and looked up at me. He patted the seat next to him on the bench, and I reluctantly moved closer. The air between us crackled with nervous energy. I could feel the tidal waves of emotion coming off my dad in crashing billows.

My parents weren't bad people. Actually, they were the exact opposite. They were caring, loving, and, despite the distance that had grown between us over the years, they had sacrificed themselves for me, day in and day out. Even now, as Nicholas closed the gap between him and me, my parents were still ready to fight my fight.

I grabbed his hand. The simple gesture, the small movement, meant more than just words.

"I'm sorry, dear." My dad's voice touched my heart. A tear or two fell from my cheek as we sat on the bench in absolute silence.

His swirling emotions calmed, and a quiet ambiance surrounded us. My dad scooted closer and placed a finger under my chin to bring my gaze to his.

"Do you want to tell me why you are out here all alone?" His penetrating gaze broke past my usual façade.

"Just thinking."

This was not the usual type of conversation my dad and I had. We were formal, polite, never the comforting and consoling type. This was new.

"Trying to figure out my next move." I smiled but kept looking off into the distance.

"I know what you mean. Nicholas has made some gutsy moves."

"No. He has made more than gutsy moves. He's made hefty promises and tireless threats. This goes beyond minor disagreements, Daddy. This is war."

War. The word felt heavy and appalling. Unfortunately, it was also unavoidable.

"Yes, it is, but are you ready for it?" My dad's voice was calm, but I could feel the undercurrent of concern just below the surface as his insides screamed for him to protect me. "I'd love to tell you that this conflict doesn't involve you, but I don't think you'll listen."

"How could it not, Daddy?" I was incredulous. "Nicholas has all but sent me a formal invitation. This goes well beyond diplomacy. He has done everything in his power to ensure that I take the bait. The attacks, Sarah, Nizari, and Catherine... these were all to ensure that this war occurs. This fight will happen, Daddy. It is only a matter of time."

I felt like I was signing my own death certificate. I've seen the outcome. I've seen the torture, the berating and humiliation before his coven. I've seen it all. Fear crept through me as I again relived the nightmares. The flashing images of Nicholas, the pain as he tore me down until I was weak and almost powerless, everything that my premonitions had shown me teased and manipulated their way back into my thoughts.

"It sounds like you already know where things are headed."

"Yeah, but this is about more than me."

This was about Michael's coven, the human lives, and the other covens I hadn't even met yet. This was about everyone in the vampire world. It may have started out with Nicholas's idea of me being the heir to the prophecy, but it wouldn't stop with me. It wouldn't stop until Nicholas had undisputed control over the entire vampire world. And who knows—the human world could be next.

"So, if you know what needs to be done, what's stopping you?"

His honest question made me think.

"Because I know how it ends," I said. "I don't know if I can go through with it."

My mind wandered to the many painful ways I'd died in my

dreams. Even the actual death as he stabbed me through the heart. It was all part of defeating Nicholas. All the things leading up to the moment before I died scared me.

My dad watched me. His eyes bore into me as if searching my very thoughts.

"Are you okay, honey?" My dad's tone matched the concern in his eyes.

"Yeah," I lied, pasting on a plastic smile, as was my usual MO. Between the two of us, we never shared emotions or feelings. It was always superficial and empty.

"I lied," I said, closing my eyes. "I'm not okay." I turned to look at my dad and decided to tell him how I really felt.

"I'm scared." My voice cracked, but I kept going. "The Shadows were only the beginning. Nicholas probably has his hands in every coven from here to Hades." I paused and attempted to be okay with what I was saying.

Placing his hands on my shoulders, my dad looked me straight in the eyes. "A boatload of responsibility has been dumped on your shoulders." His eyes calmed until they were almost sad. "But you are not in this alone. You have your mother, Michael, and me. Even the coven and wolf pack are behind you." In the depths of his heart, I could sense a hidden secret, a masked Picasso. Whatever it was he was hiding sent shivers down my spine. For a moment, his eyes shone with intangible excitement. Then, with a deep and controlled breath, he hid the feeling behind a mask of indifference.

A sympathetic smile curved his lips. "Okay, what can I do to help?" His offer was genuine, and my heart smiled knowing that in these last few minutes, we'd made leaps and bounds to becoming closer than we had ever been.

"I don't know yet. I just know that in the end, I hope that my nightmares are wrong and that I don't die before I have a chance to kill Nicholas." I bowed my head as my chest tightened and fear and hope broke through my barriers. As the fight got closer, I could almost feel it. There was a sort of finality preceding the war to come that sparked the air and ignited the demon inside me.

Then, as I tried to stifle my cries, my dad did something that he had never done before: He whisked away the strands of hair in my face, and then pulled me in for a hug, wrapping his arms tightly around me.

The tension in my shoulders loosened, and the mental pressure that I held deep inside slowly eased.

"You know, I don't know how to do this father-daughter thing," he said, shaking his head, "but, out of everything, I am most proud of you." Gently pushing me back he smiled.

"So, what's your next move?" He nudged me and smiled, trying to lighten the mood.

"Steven." A soft and sardonic voice broke the silence surrounding us.

My dad turned to see a tall, blond, curvy woman crossing the yard. He groaned. His temper rose only to be tamped back down as his self-control snapped into place.

"Michael is looking for you. He is in the library," she purred as she sidled up next to him.

With an exaggerated sigh, he leaned in and kissed me on the cheek.

"Shall we?" he asked, ignoring the daggered look the blonde sent him when he side-stepped her, and held out his arm for me.

The castle was as busy as always. The vampires walked the halls with unnerving grace as they spoke in hushed tones. The blond, who had followed us back to the castle, pouting and seething under the surface, joined a group by the door in idle conversation. The distasteful looks on their faces as she joined in uninvited made my insides smile. Apparently, she caused indigestion in everyone she met, not just my dad and me.

"I'll go see what Michael wants, then maybe we could have lunch?" my dad said. "I'd like to talk again about what happened in the throne room a few weeks ago and how you're feeling now. You have advanced beyond anything I've ever imagined."

I thought it was odd that my dad was the only one unfazed by my abilities. It was almost as if he had expected them.

Shaking the thought from my mind, I shucked off my small sweater and started upstairs. As I ascended the steps, I felt the odd sensation of being watched. When I reached the top of the stairs and rounded the banister, I took a sidelong glance down into the room below. The coven members, completely oblivious to my presence downstairs, continued their conversations, but the cold stare that followed me sent chills down my spine. The blond, however, stood with a murderous glare and was tracking my every move.

I ignored the woman and reminded myself to deal with her later. I wasn't sure what it was, but I had a feeling that her issues were not Nicholas-related. She held a grudge—apparently against me.

When I opened the door to my room, I stopped short. Something was amiss. The room was almost as I had left it. The bed was made. The window coverings were open, letting in the late morning sun. But what caught my attention was the suitcase, packed and waiting on my bed. The smaller cosmetic bag, stuffed almost to overflowing, looked right at home next to its matching counterpart.

Had I forgotten about taking a trip somewhere? Or had my room been mistakenly occupied by a new arrival? I stood stock-still as I stared at the luggage.

The light scent of springtime blooms and lavender teased my senses as it wafted in from behind me. It was Mom. I smiled as I turned around. She had a sorrowful expression on her face as she peered over my shoulder and looked at the packed suitcase.

"Are you going somewhere?"

Although she kept her voice level, I could feel traces of uncertainty and fear building up within her.

"Honey," she went on, "you were just going to… leave? Were you going to at least say goodbye?"

She sounded hurt and confused. I shook my head, but before I could respond, she continued. "If this is because of—"

"No, they're not mine. I didn't pack them." I interrupted, and then laughed as she visibly relaxed, her shoulders falling and a small smile touching her lips.

"Did Michael move your room?" Her voice was incredulous as she tried to put two and two together.

"No." I looked around the room. "I'm not sure what that is, really. Did you want to come in?" I asked, heading for the bathroom.

When I came out, my mom was perched on the bed, her back straight, her hands twisted in her lap, and a small frown marring her brow.

"What's up?" I asked, plopping down into the fluffy white chair by the window.

Since I'd first come here, I'd felt oddly at home. Especially lately, I wasn't afraid to be who I was. I only had to please Michael, and he seemed to be pleased regardless of what I did. Even from the confines of my room, I could feel him. He was close, and as always, he was thinking of me. Under his calm and collected surface, his emotions—emotions hidden beneath years of discipline— churned and roared within him.

"I just came up to see how you've been. It's been a while since you and I have talked." She offered a tentative smile as she awaited my response.

That's because you haven't been here for the last couple of years, I thought as I bit my lip. The two of us had had our bouts over the years. At some point, I would have to let go of the past when I had lived in Vegas. It's obvious she's trying.

"Yeah, I know. Things have been a little hectic." I offered her a half-truth. Things had been crazy, and as I unintentionally tried to avoid my parents as much as possible, it went from busy to chaotic in a heartbeat.

"Yes, they have. You seem to fit into this lifestyle fairly well."

Her words were hollow as she reciprocated my empty reply. I could feel her withdraw. I wasn't being fair. She was here, trying to put things right, and I was being difficult.

She stood to leave but paused at the door.

"This isn't easy for me, you know. I know you are mad, and are probably resentful, but I'm trying." Her voice sounded defeated. She still faced the door, but instead of turning around to me, she bowed her head.

"I didn't know what to do with a child as coveted as you. I can see now that it was a mistake, and I'm sorry for that."

Her words hit me like a brick.

"Mom, wait."

She stopped. Her hand was still on the doorknob and her stance still rigid.

"I'm sorry," I blurted out. "It's just…" I paused, looking for the words. "With everything I've learned in the last couple of years, I was afraid that now that you and Dad were here, you were going to try and put me back in the box. Somewhere safe and confined, where I'd never get to live. I'd be hidden and suffocated like before until I forgot what it felt like to be alive." My voice was strained. It hurt to tell her how I felt. "Until I forgot what it felt like to love and be loved. I'm afraid that you and Dad will try to take everything away from me—my new home, Michael, even the friends I have made in the coven. Being a vampire may not have been on the top of my adventure list. Neither was being on top of Nicholas's hit list. I wouldn't have normally chosen this path, but now that I'm here, and living a life outside of your guidelines, I've never been happier."

I let everything out in one burst—as though if I didn't tell her everything now, I'd never have the courage to do it again.

Many seconds passed before she finally turned around. I could see the pain and understanding in her eyes.

With inhuman grace, my mom crossed the room and hugged me. Her normally distant affection was tossed to the wind as she held me close.

"I'm sorry, dear. I wish I could go back and try again. But I can see now that you are strong—and, as always, a force to be reckoned with."

Just like that, all was well. Although the relationship between my parents and me was still rocky, there was a base to work on. It was a start.

"I'm sorry to interrupt," a male voice carried through the room.

The speaker was tall, well-built, and showed no emotion. His tight features were utterly stony. "If you could please come with me, ma'am. Michael is waiting for you downstairs," he boomed with a stern voice into the silence.

As my mom and I exchanged looks of confusion and bewilderment, two more men appeared in the doorway. They looked at Mr. Tall-Built-and-Expressionless for instructions. With a wave of his hand and a few mumbled orders, he signaled the men to enter the room. One grabbed the suitcase and exited without a single word. The second man stood behind us and gestured for us to leave first.

"Arri?" my mom asked. She and I both hesitated, readying ourselves for a fight if need be.

"I think it's okay," I said. "They look like Michael's Ravens," but I felt far from certain.

ELEVEN

As we entered the hallway, a light bristle of pent-up energy caught me off guard. I knew there was something brewing, and I also knew it had Michael and my dad upset. I could feel it. The worry and stress I felt from the two of them made me nauseous. I could almost feel their actual thoughts. The mixture had my head hurting as I tried to piece together their emotions, but it was their gradual onset of panic that really scared me.

Although it was clear something major going on, I was nervous that I wasn't privy to it. The small prickle may have caught my attention, but the buzz in the air said there was something else going on as well. Something a little closer to home.

When we got to the bottom of the stairs, the man with the suitcase walked right out of the front door without looking back. By now, I had figured that the luggage was for me. Apparently, I was going somewhere.

"Please wait here while I attend to my duties. Michael will be out here shortly," the man leading the way said, his lips turned up in a smile that didn't fit him. A permanent scowl seemed more suited to the surly man.

"Thank you," I said, as the man bowed his head and departed from our company.

As the two of us stood in the foyer, my mom snickered.

"What do you think this is all about?" she asked, curiosity spiking her attention. Then, as my mom looked behind me, her smile faded. Following Mom's glowering gaze, I noticed the tall blonde walking toward us with a bit of a sashay in her step.

"So, you are the woman who caught Michael's eye," she

drawled. The arrogance in her voice was accentuated by her English accent. "The one and only Arri Stone." Her sarcasm was a bit much, and it added to the bite in her voice. "I'm sure you are aware of the fact that Michael is the most sought-after vampire." She circled around me, assessing me from head to toe and from front to back. Her eyes seemed black with envy, and her voice reeked of jealousy.

It was all I could do to keep my temper in check. The woman circling me like a vulture rounding its prey now started to brush up against me. The scent of her perfume choked me. I could barely breathe the toxic air.

"Yet you have managed to accomplish what no other vampire has. You have manipulated him into falling for you—a nobody, a mongrel. You are nothing more than a mutt and deserve to be treated as such." It was obvious now that the bristled energy I felt earlier was hers.

I tilted my head and narrowed my eyes but said nothing. She didn't need prompting. Her emotions said all I needed to know.

"We could have been happy," she said through her teeth as she pointed a bony finger at me.

Looking over the woman, I could see her appeal. Her platinum-blonde hair, although I wasn't sure if it was natural, framed her face, accentuating her high cheekbones. Her long legs and too-short dress outlined her perfect physique, leaving nothing to the imagination. Everything about this woman was designed to draw male attention, yet she stood in front of me seemingly unattached. It was understandable that her narrowed eyes and stiff posture would be an unattractive quality to a prospective mate, but I think that look was reserved specifically for me.

"You two were together?" I asked, trying not to choke on the words. My heart tightened as I waited for her response. Given all the time Michael and I had spent together, the thought of him being with someone else before me hurt. I knew it was silly; he was well over several hundred years old, and I doubted he'd remained companionless that whole time, but still, my heart ached at the thought.

Looking over the bold woman as she scowled at me, I saw something flash within her hazel-green eyes. Hurt, maybe? I didn't know. But whatever it was, she quickly hid it.

"No," she scoffed.

"Then why are you angry with me?"

The woman's mouth fell open in disbelief. Then she chuckled, an evil and vile sound. "Ha! You don't know, do you?" That sarcastic tone of hers wasn't comforting.

"No, I don't. If you were a scorned lover, I could understand your animosity, but you two were never together. So how could you have been happy?" I was trying to keep my voice even and calm, but I still heard the anger in my tone. I could already see where this conversation was going, and I was going to end up defending myself again—just not in a court this time.

"Look at you. You are human," she said, as if it left a bad taste in her mouth. "You are everything we are not. You are fragile, weak, emotional, and at best, a royal pain." She folded her arms and cocked her hip. "You have managed to manipulate Michael into seeing you as a gift instead of the good-for-nothing little tart that you really are." Her smile said she knew everything, but when I closed the distance between us, that snippy little grin fell from her tight, thin lips. The arrogant posture and know-it-all demeanor sagged as she backed up and hit the wall behind her.

"I am sick and tired of this coven's half-witted thoughts and ideas about me," I snarled. "Let me tell you something," I stepped forward again and poked this hotheaded blonde in the chest, "I can't control Michael any more than I can control the weather." That wasn't entirely true; I had some control over some of the more basic elements, but still. "Nor would I want to." I chuckled and shook my head. "You think I wanted all of this?" I spread my arms wide at the entire manor. "The constant attacks, the distrust I hold, the fear that anyone could turn on me in a heartbeat? No. All I wanted was a normal life. All the stuff you think you know about me, everything you despise about me, has come at a great cost. So, the next time you decide to open your pretty little mouth, think before you speak."

"Great cost?" Her courage made a temporary comeback. "All I see is you living off Michael, using his resources as your own. You have no idea what great cost is."

I slammed my hand against the wall next to the woman's head.

"I know all too well about cost," I bit out. "I have lost everything I have ever known. I lost a childhood— friends, no life outside of studying. I lost what would and could have been a great relationship with my parents. In the last three years, I have faced death twice and lost the best friend a person could ever have." I slammed my hand again as the pain of Catherine's death stabbed through my heart.

My eyes narrowed, and the woman seemed to have the good sense to fear me. Strangely, I felt like crying. As I tried to tamp down the insecurity, fear, and pain that had me feeling tearful, I stepped back.

Her hazel-green eyes shimmered with triumph as a smile spread across her lips. "You can't fool me," she said through clenched teeth. "I don't care how powerful you think you are. You will never be one of us. You're too fragile and weak to accept the life he has. You will only be holding him back. You don't think we all know? Michael's feelings for you are out of pity and obligation." She took a breath. Her features were painted with pride.

I tried to ignore her hateful remarks, but a part of me still wondered how much truth was in her words.

"You were thrust upon him. Thrown into his care without even the option of having an out. Imagine how bound and forced he must have felt to have a creature of your making tossed at him like that. He had no choice but to protect you, the coveted and almighty prodigy you claim to be. You are no more than a pity project that he is tied to. Do you want to be responsible for keeping him from his destiny? To make him mate you because of the responsibility he feels for you? Yes, that's right. You are a responsibility. He doesn't love you. After all, who could love a half-breed like you?"

She widened her smile and planted her hands on her hips as if she had won.

The sad thing was, I could almost understand what she was saying. I was thrown at him, a burden cast upon his shoulders. He even told Alex when I arrived that he wanted nothing to do with me. But if he didn't, then why save me by willingly giving me his blood?

My thoughts kept circling as I stood stock-still, staring at the unholy woman who had torn me apart emotionally in seconds. My insecurities surged to the surface thanks to a half-witted blonde with no more sense than an anvil. But her vile, jealous words cut me to the quick. She was right. Michael deserved more than a half-breed. He deserved someone who didn't have trouble following in his wake.

Standing there stunned, I sensed a new, maternal fury growing beside me. In the moments it had taken me to realize this woman was right, my mom had pinned the blonde to the ground. Flailing beneath my mom, she looked terrified. As tiny as my mom was, she had managed to take down the towering woman in seconds.

"Enough! What is going on here?" Michael's voice boomed through the foyer. The sound reverberating through me made my heart stutter. I didn't have to look to feel Michael's fierce presence—his angry expression, his stiff posture—as he followed the fight between the blonde and my mom.

As the two of them scrambled to their feet, the blonde's expression changed. Her tight-lipped anger and hard look morphed into one of victimized pain.

"She attacked me," the blonde offered as she bowed low enough to sniff the wood flooring. A few fake and muffled whimpers fell from her cowering form.

My mom stood unmoving, but her anger rose at the sound of the woman's mewling.

"Ava?" My dad approached my mom and laid a hand on her shoulder. "Are her words true?" He himself had no doubt that Mom was innocent, but by now, the rest of the coven had surrounded us.

"No." My voice was low, but even then, the entire room quieted. The blonde looked up from her phony mewling. A glare twinkled in her eye as she quickly glanced at me before trading her daggered look for one of sadness.

"Arri?" Michael stepped in front of me as if to shield me from the rest of the coven. "May I ask you what happened?" His worried eyes looked into mine for truth.

"If I may, my lord?" Sebastian, a quiet and withdrawn vampire, interjected in a deep and husky voice. Although his eyes were glazed over and cloudy, there was calculation and sharpness in his wits. "I would have to agree with Arri." This was the first time I'd seen or heard Sebastian talking at all, let alone taking sides. "Faylene approached the youngblood first. She was spitting lies, but even within her dishonesty, there was some truth. Unfortunately, she was still in the wrong." With that, he stepped back and disappeared within the crowd, blending into the horde.

"Is this true?" Michael directed his question to the bowing woman. Anger and frustration suffused his words.

"Yes, my lord." Faylene stood and glared at my mom. "But she still attacked me. Arri and I were merely talking when she became overprotective of the..." her words faded for a moment as she decided on a less noticeable insult, "youngblood." She sneered. "If you ask me, Ava is too attached to the—" She stopped again and cleared her throat. "To Arri."

Faylene was careless to show such distaste toward me, and Michael immediately picked up on it. His hands fisted at his sides and his jaw clenched.

"You would take care how you address *amica mea* or those words will be your last. I have warned you before. This will be your last warning, understood?" As Michael spoke, he stepped closer and closer to her until he was practically hovering over the woman.

"I will not be addressing her again," Faylene scoffed. "I cannot be a part of a coven that allows misguided and manipulated vampires such as yourself to preside as Coven Master. She has manipulated you into believing that she is your one and only, when any one of us true, pure-blooded vampires could stay at your side and provide better companionship than she." With those final words, Faylene turned and started for the front doors. The tapping of her heels was the only sound as Michael stared after her. He waited, biding his time until she pushed the double doors open, before he made his move.

"Rogan," Michael whispered.

Rogan weaved through the crowd without touching a single vampire. Within half a heartbeat, he stood before Michael, eyes lowered and head bowed.

A stern look marred Michael's brow as his eyes narrowed on the retreating woman.

Michael gave a single nod to Rogan, and Rogan disappeared again. I thought I saw him exit the large front doors just as Michael's voice caught my attention.

"Are you okay?" Michael looked me up and down for any marks or bruises. "Did she hurt you?" Concern shone in his eyes.

"Just my pride." I gave him a half-smile, but even he saw that it was forced.

As my dad took my mom into his arms and whispered sweet nothings in her ear, Michael pulled away from me and approached Mom.

"I apologize for Faylene. I regret that you felt the need to protect your daughter, but if I may have a word or two with you and Sir Steven, it would be greatly appreciated."

My dad followed Michael, but Mom offered him a smile before she made her way to me. "Her words were lies, and nothing more." She placed her open palm on my cheek as she stared into my eyes. "You shouldn't take them to heart. You are a wonderful blessing; one I am proud to call my daughter. It'll be okay. Don't let her jealous words mess with what you know in here." She placed her other hand on my heart.

I gave her a placating nod as my dad and Michael returned from whatever they'd been discussing. The two of them took one quick glance at me, noticed the way I avoided their gaze, and shared a mutual look of worry.

Leaning over the several inches between us, Michael kissed my forehead. The moment was over far too quickly. A light brush of the lips, a fast peck, was all that was offered. My skin barely had a chance to feel his touch before it was gone. I missed his lingering kisses, the heat of his breath. I missed the unmistakable endearment, the feeling of being wanted and adored. What used to be love and affection was now simply commonplace, something that was done automatically, as if it were trivial. This almost cemented what Faylene had said.

"I'll be right back. Why don't you go into the kitchen? I'll be there in a minute." His voice was soft and sweet, but there was also a tinge of fear and nervousness behind it. He was hiding something. Something was veiled within him.

"Mmhmm." I smiled as he turned to follow my parents out of the room, leaving me alone in the middle of the foyer.

My heart sank as I replayed Faylene's words over and over again in my head. Nicholas's threats and random attacks I could handle. Being stabbed, wounded, and berated, I could handle. But Faylene had attacked me emotionally. She'd attacked my insecurities and brought them to the surface, where I had no choice but to face them.

I trusted Michael and loved him beyond words, but there was still a part of me, a part that I didn't know if I would ever truly lose, that wondered if he was with me out of obligation or because he loved me as much as I loved him.

As I blindly entered the kitchen, I breathed in the sterile smell of ammonia and vinegar permeating the room. It left me gasping for air.

"Sorry about that…"

Although Michael's voice was low and gentle, he still scared the tar out of me. My heart pounded, and my body went stiff until he wrapped his arms around me. That one simple show of affection made my heart skip, and for a moment, I could almost see the untruths in my doubts.

"There was a small accident a bit ago and the kitchen needed to be disinfected and decontaminated." Michael laughed and placed a lingering kiss on my cheek. The smell of soap, fresh linen, and everything Michael brought a smile to my face and made my knees weak. "Are you ready?" His words purred in my ear as he pulled me back against his chest.

"Ready? For what?" I gasped as he traced kisses along my jawline.

"Come on. I'll show you."

In one swift move, he lifted me into his arms. The fabric of his shirt was smooth and soft beneath my touch. His body warmed me as we slid into the pantry and through the tunnels under the mansion. The chilly air tingled against my cheek as he sprinted off into the darkness. Moments later, he gently set me down at the base of the tall and winding staircase.

"We're going to the lair?" I asked, confused. "I thought the brute-force man took the suitcase out the front doors."

"He might have. I merely told him to bring it here. How he got it here was up to him." Michael looked amused. "Do you object to going to the lair?"

"No." I closed my eyes and shook my head. A small smile touched my lips.

"Then why the sullen look?" He placed a finger under my chin, bringing my head up so he could look into my eyes, and waited. "Have I done something wrong? Have I not done it right for your day's traditions?" Michael looked worried.

"Huh? What are you talking about? What traditions?"

The feeling of insecurity was quickly replaced by one of curiosity.

"I thought your mom…" Michael stopped and smiled. "My apologies. I am doing this all wrong."

"Doing what wrong? Michael, what's going on?"

Instead of answering me in words, he placed a chaste kiss to my lips that melted all my mind's chatter as I succumbed to his pull, his lure.

"You will know soon enough, *mihi perpetuum amorem.*"

TWELVE

His kiss lingered on my neck, my jaw, and finally my lips, as he pulled me into his arms. As he teased and nibbled, I barely noticed we were moving. When he at last set me down, it was at the threshold of his lair. The smell of fresh floral arrangements and the scent of men's cologne mingled in the air. It was everything I could do to keep my knees from melting.

"Ahem." Lyle, Michael's most trusted Raven, cleared his throat.

Startled, I jumped back.

"Yes," Michael forced out as he kept his eyes glued on me.

"Everything is prepped and ready. The Ravens and I will leave you and Lady Arri." The lilting way he said my name sounded straight out of Ireland. "If you need our assistance, two of us will be placed just outside the entrances." That simple but loaded bit of information had me staring at Lyle in confusion. They were leaving?

No matter how private the situation, Lyle was always close by. Michael was never without his Ravens. They were his bodyguards—as if he needed any.

Michael smirked at my look of confusion and cocked his head before his smirk grew into a full-fledged smile.

"Thank you, Lyle. If I need you, I'll whistle." Although Michael was talking to Lyle, his eyes never left mine.

Lyle nodded as he backed out of the room.

As I heard Michael's steel doors shutting on the outside of the lair, my heartbeat picked up.

The two of us stared at each other in silence. Our combined emotions swirled inside me. I felt Michael's anticipation and fear, and I was also just plain nervous. Why was he locking us inside the lair?

Instantly, I thought something had happened at the manor, but then why wasn't he there handling the situation? I don't think Michael would dare to lock me up if there was any danger… would he?

"I can hear you thinking from here." There was a smile in Michael's voice.

I nodded, and a shy, embarrassed smile crossed my face.

"Where are they going?" I asked, pointing to where Lyle disappeared. My voice came out in a forced whisper even though I was trying to keep it calm and unassuming.

"They'll be close by. With all the interruptions, I thought it would be nice if we could have some uninterrupted, undisturbed time alone." Michael smiled his winning, knee-weakening smile before he enveloped me in his arms.

The warmth from his body erased any doubts or concerns I had as I relished the comfort of his embrace. Then he pulled away, gripping me by the shoulders.

"Are you hungry?" he asked, placing little pecks along my cheek bones, temple, and just below my ear.

I sighed as my heartbeat thundered and my breathing came out in gasps. He chuckled, realizing the effect he had on me.

"A little," I lied, knowing that I was actually starving. This morning, when I'd awoken to another cold sweat with Nicholas whispering his promise to a slow and torturous death in my ear, I'd left the confines of my room as fast as possible to the open spaciousness of the courtyard. In my haste, I had completely forgotten about breakfast. Then, after my little run-in with Faylene, lunch had been a total loss as well.

On cue, my stomach gave out a very unladylike grumble.

Michael chuckled.

"Okay, maybe I am a bit hungrier than a little," I clarified. I averted my eyes, hoping the warming in my cheeks was from the heat of the lair instead of the embarrassment that I felt.

"I'll make you a little something while you go and get changed. There is something for you under your bed."

Before I could ask what, he kissed me soundly on the lips then made his way to the kitchenette.

I looked down at the clothes I was wearing. It looked like I was ready to go all Mission Impossible. My hair was pulled back into a ponytail. My tight black shirt, black construction jeans, and boots were not suited to sit back and lounge around a place that made a five-star hotel look like a Motel 6.

As I wandered through the obscenely large, mountainous, castle-like cave, it felt oddly eerie. The last time I was here, I had heard the Ravens moving about and talking in hushed tones, even if they'd stayed unseen. Right now, the silence was deafening. The halls seemed to be tall and narrow instead of open and welcoming.

I shivered as I slipped into the room Michael deemed mine. At a glance, the room looked the same. The bed was as perfect as before. The fire in the fireplace heated up the open space giving the room a warm and comfortable feel.

After a shower, I paused at the old set of dark and rustic doors next to the bathroom. I could have sworn that these doors weren't there during my last visit. As I opened the double doors, I gasped. Behind them was a walk-in closet. The walls were lined with clothes, shoes, and any accessory a woman could want.

Fingering through the items, I decided on comfy-looking, lightweight flowing pants in a tan color and a beige metallic tank top. Barefoot, I walked to the bedroom.

I knelt and looked under the bed for the little something Michael mentioned. A satin box in pale pink caressed my fingertips as I pulled it out from under the bed. I placed it on the duvet and carefully untied the silk bow to open it.

My heart stilled and my hands froze as I pulled back the tissue paper. Three things rested in the box: a satin nightgown, a matching robe, and a thin silver bracelet. Instead of a hanging trinket, the charm was integrated into the bracelet band. It was an exact duplicate of my own tattoo in a thin crimson wire, made to copy the mark on my wrist. I couldn't help but smile.

Leaving the nightgown for later, I adorned my wrist with the bracelet and went to leave the bedroom in search of the wonderful man who pampered me and some much-needed food.

As I started to leave, I passed a tall oval mirror perched atop a sturdy wooden frame and I stopped. The contours and curves of the fabric lightly hugged my body and gave me a shape that would normally be hidden beneath my regular clothes. My hair fell over my shoulders in untamed waves and my makeup had been washed off, leaving my face a blank canvas.

As I stared at myself, Faylene's words came back to haunt me. *So, you are the woman who caught Michael's eye.*

The disbelief in her voice made sense now. Thinking back to her well-manicured looks, I couldn't help but feel a little out of place among vampires. I tried to block out her condescending tone, but her hateful words seeped through my defenses and into my worries and doubts. *You have manipulated him into falling for you.* Had I? *A nobody, a mongrel. You are nothing more than a mutt.*

I closed my eyes in hopes of erasing her look of disdain and arrogance, but I was unsuccessful. My heart twinged as I thought of how right she was.

Look at you. You are human.

I surveyed the woman staring back at me in the mirror. I was, in fact, human. I had all the imperfections to prove it. Granted, I didn't have trouble with my complexion like most, but that one little attribute didn't take away from the many ways I wasn't perfect.

You are fragile, weak, and emotional. Her words took my breath away and stabbed my heart.

What if Michael thought the same thing? What if she was right?

Michael's feelings for you are out of pity and obligation.

At this point, a few small tears glistened in the corner of my eyes, but they didn't fall. They were just proof that Faylene was right. I was emotional. My thoughts were drowning me in self-pity.

She said it herself: after all, who could love a half-breed like me?

The term half-breed had come up a lot over the past few years, and every time it did, I felt more and more like a polka dot among stripes.

“Feel any better?” Michael asked from the doorway as he peeked his head in. “Dinner is rea—”

His words fell short as he saw the crestfallen look on my face. My eyes were red and blotchy. My cheeks were pink, and my slouching shoulders showed my resignation.

“Yeah,” I said over the lump in my throat as I tried my best to stand up straight. Although my eyes were downcast and my hands trembled at my sides, I took a fortifying breath and tried to steel my heart.

“What’s wrong?” Walking up behind me, he looked over my outfit and his eyes darkened. He placed his hands on my waist, his touch soft and caressing.

“Nothing. Everything’s fine.” I pasted a placid smile on my face.

“Then why the tears?” he asked, as he slowly turned me to face him.

I shook my head and looked over his shoulder. I couldn’t look at him. I didn’t want to see the look of pity or obligation on his face. Faylene’s words would be all too real then.

“Arri?” Michael placed an open hand on my cheek and forced me to look him in the eyes, then dropped his hands back to my waist. “Why the tears, Arri?” he asked again, touching his forehead to mine.

“It’s nothing. Just something that Faylene said this afternoon.” I shrugged like it was nothing, when her words really weighed on me heavier than lead.

“And what could she have said to you to make you feel this way?” he asked, pulling back and pushing my hair back.

“I…” I closed my eyes and decided the truth was best. I knew a small part of me hoped he would laugh it off, but an even larger part was afraid he agreed with Faylene and the joke was on me. “Faylene may have suggested that someone of your stature would never love a mutt like me.” I opened my eyes, stared down at my bare feet, and continued. “She also let on that I was more of an obligation to you. That you took me in because you pity what I am.” I swallowed what felt like a boulder.

Michael's fingers pressed into my skin as he processed what I said. At that moment, I felt emotionally stripped and vulnerable. I had no room left to search for his emotions. My heart stuttered as I waited with bated breath to hear what I dreaded was true: that I really wasn't good enough, and that I was a charity case, just as Faylene had claimed I was.

"Arri," Michael's eyes were sad, "is that how you think I see you?" Loosening his hold on my waist, he stroked my cheek. The small act caressed my very soul. The gentle touch showed his tenderness.

"No. I mean, maybe. I mean… I don't know." I closed my eyes and tried to look away, but Michael's hand stopped me.

"Arri, look at me."

I took a slow deep breath and looked into his eyes.

"You are anything but a burden. Look into my heart, sweetheart. Feel what I feel."

He pulled me into his arms, tightening his hold, and all my fears disappeared. Faylene's words vanished from my mind as I looked into Michael's heart, a heart that belonged to me. The tenderness with which he held me, the way his lips moved along my jawline, even how his heart tightened at the sight of me said it all. He loved me.

"Can you feel it?" he asked. His light and loving tone reverberated through his chest.

I tried to answer, but my voice caught in my throat. I opened and closed my mouth several times until I finally gave up and nodded.

Michael stroked my back with his fingertips, calming me. He shifted away from me a bit. The light smile that adorned his features told me that this conversation was far from over.

"Michael…" I started, but Michael placed a finger to my lips, silencing me.

"I know." His troubled eyes searched mine. "I can see it in your face every time a coven member addresses your human nature."

His hand stilled on my neck and searched for my pulse. Taking in a deep breath, he smiled when the thumping of my heart grew stronger with every beat. Blood was pumping through my veins like a raging river toward a waterfall. "Your humanity. It does not define who and what you are. What you are destined for is not what I love about you. I love who you are," he placed his hand over my heart, "in here."

I smiled at him.

"I love the cunning, fun-loving, courageous woman you were, are, and always will be."

He didn't say beautiful, pretty, or stunning, I couldn't help but notice. He loved me, but I still didn't measure up. A vampire's beauty was perennial, immortal, everlasting. My own fine lines and puffy eyes showed my lack of sleep and betrayed my mortal status.

"My love for you is about more than appearance," he said as if reading my mind. His hand dipped to the small of my back. Pulling me close, he dragged his lips down the curve of my neck. A few light pecks below my ear had my eyes rolling into the back of my head as I sagged against him.

"As lovely as you may think they are," he said, nipping at my ear, "they are nothing compared to you." Then, his lips found mine. The way he held me, running his hand through my hair until he reached the nape of my neck and the rhythm of his mouth moving against mine, made my head spin.

As the moments passed, our wild embracing slowed.

The two of us stared at each other in silence. The rhythmic pulse of my pounding heart was the only sound until my stomach gave out a roar.

"Still hungry?" Michael asked, reaching for my hand.

The dinner Michael had prepared was fabulous—as if it would be any less than perfect. The fettuccine Alfredo made from scratch had me humming in pleasure as the creamy sauce melted on my tongue.

The awareness of Michael watching me eat made me a little uncomfortable. Every time I brought the fork to my mouth, his eyes darkened, and I could feel his restraint pounding at the surface.

"Did you enjoy your meal?" he asked as I set my fork down on my empty plate.

"Yes, it was delicious. Thank you." I blushed as he wiped a bit of sauce from the corner of my mouth.

"Feel better?" Michael said as he took my hand in his. "The color has returned to your cheeks." He brushed my face with his thumb. "It looks good on you." A smile spread across his face.

"So, the mysterious luggage on my bed, the trip to the lair, and the meal that made my knees weak… what's going on?" I asked as Michael showed me to the living room.

The two of us sat on the overstuffed couch. The lights were dim. The smell of damp earth permeated the room, a hint that the rainstorm that threatened earlier had finally reached us. The heavens must have opened up, judging by the moist, earthy air swirling around us.

"Is it so bad that I wanted you all to myself?" Michael's suggestive tone brought a laugh to his eyes.

The tension in his shoulders relaxed a little, but there was still something wreaking havoc inside him. I could feel it. The strain on his heart and the fear that electrified his every nerve, revealed his calmness to be false.

"Of course not." I laughed as he nuzzled my neck. As he leaned over me, his lips landed on mine while his hand searched for something. After a moment or two, the television on the far wall turned on, its sound slowly building. We broke apart briefly to settle on the couch to watch. As I cuddled into Michael's arms, I lost track of the characters, their lines, even the music as the movie faded and sleep caught up to me.

When the ending credits rolled, I felt Michael's lips brush my forehead.

"Let's get you to bed, sleeping beauty." His soft voice woke me.

"So, how was the movie? Did everyone get out in the end?" I asked him, leaning my head against his chest.

"Yes, well at least most of them did." Michael laughed.

My room was pitch black as Michael laid me down on the bed.

The silky sheets brushed against my bare shoulders as he pulled the covers over me.

"No," I protested, holding onto his arm. "The nightgown." I sat up and reached for the beautiful fabric, but a strong hand halted my attempt. The space between us was charged and ready, like the tingling in the air that precedes a lightning storm.

The room stilled for a moment. Neither of us breathed. Neither of us moved.

"Michael?" My whispered voice sounded like a plea. My throat tightened as my grogginess faded and awareness rushed through me.

"I'm here." It felt like he was practically whispering in my ear. His gentle and warming hand pressed slightly as he seated himself beside me.

"Stay with me?" I asked.

Without a sound, the bed dipped even further as Michael's body slid in close to mine. His warmth seeped through my clothes and into my body. I faced him and propped myself up on my elbow. A hint of faded and filtered light spilled into the open space. His features were barely lit by the light glow touching his face.

Michael tucked a lock of hair behind my ear before running his finger along my jaw, to the base of my throat, then to rest on my collarbone. My breath gradually quickened until I was practically panting. His slow and tantalizing trail left me quaking.

With a small shift, Michael had pulled me to him, his lips taking the same beautiful trail as his fingers.

"Did you mean it?" he asked in a husky voice.

"Mean what?" I asked.

My breath hitched as he nipped and nibbled at my earlobe.

Michael laughed. The bed quaked as a rumble bubbled in his chest.

"Mating me," he finished, his hope that I wouldn't balk at the suggestion invading my emotions. Hesitancy rippled off him as his features tightened and his heart tensed, waiting for my answer.

I'd known that the thought and want had been ripping through him over the last few weeks. The idea of branding me his had been at the forefront of his mind. But after the fight with Gavin, then Catherine's assassination by association, Michael had been careful not to push or broach the subject. He had almost kept me at an emotional distance.

Pulling away, he watched my features carefully. The vulnerability in the glassy green of his eyes softened my heart.

I leaned forward and kissed him. No holding back, no wavering. This is what I want. My heartbeat tripled as his hands found my cheeks and he kissed me back. His tongue traced my lips, asking for permission. The soft contours of his hands moved slowly and persuasively along the base of my throat, down my arms, then to my ribs, where he lifted me until I was laying atop his chest. Clothing was the only barrier between us. His hand found the back of my neck as his kisses grew deeper and more demanding.

Placing his hands on my waist, he quickly flipped us around until he was lying on top of me. Supporting his weight with his arms, he looked down at me.

"Are you sure?" His nervousness was almost arresting.

"Mmhmm," I managed as his thumb slid across my lips.

"It will only work if you and I both give and accept willingly. No doubts, no fear, just trust and absoluteness." His words were not a warning, but a simple plea. "Do you accept?"

I smiled up at him.

"I already have."

With just a hint of tender hunger, he kissed me. The slow and deliberate movements of his hands as they raked along my sides made me lose all sense of time and place.

He fiddled with the hem of my shirt, his fingertips tracing designs on my waist. I shuddered. My mind and body teetered as he caressed my skin. His lips nipped, tugged, and pulled at my neck.

At first, the bites were light and teasing. Then they grew stronger, balancing on the razor's edge between pain and pleasure.

"Are you ready?" he asked as his teeth skimmed along the tender skin of my throat. My heartbeat thundered in my ears as Michael let out a guttural growl of need and longing. The vibration through his chest sent shivers down my spine and made the hairs on the back of my neck stand up.

With one last small, tantalizing flourish, Michael lost control. A quick and cursory bite caught me off guard. The piercing pain came at me like a rock, then, as fast as it came, it dissipated, until there was nothing but a paralyzing numbness.

Although Michael stiffened, waiting until I was accustomed to the sensation and the act itself, his hands still wandered, drew, and teased the skin at my waist, ribs, and arms. As soon as my body relaxed, his light and effortless draw from my neck grew tighter, hungrier.

Silently, I closed my eyes, and gave myself to him, wholeheartedly, unconditionally, and willingly.

That was when the first flash came.

Black and white images raced before me like a flip book under a strobe light. Pictures of his mom and dad came first, the loving pairs of parental eyes beaming back at me with warm and tender affection. My heart ached with his loss as the next string of photos blurred past. I saw his parents as he left them, lifeless and alone, in their bed. The next few strands of his past came at me with a vengeance, the days after becoming a vampire. The eternal hunger, the internal struggle within him. It was what had made him and defined who he was today.

Then, as the flashing of his past slowed to a halt, the next images were of me. Just me. The background of every memory was blurred and out of focus.

When I looked in the mirror, I saw countless imperfections. Michael saw me as more. Not one photo or memory showed what I saw and felt. He saw beauty, grace, and strength—things I doubted I possessed. Each photo displayed me with smiles, worry, sadness, elation, and stubbornness. With every memory that flashed before me, Michael's heart opened more to me. His sorrows and doubts were washed away every time he saw me. I'd often wondered what he saw in me, a half-breed and a mutt who stumbled into his life, unwanted and unfit for either world. Now I knew. He saw the same thing in me that I saw and felt in him. My true mate, my one and only, my eternal love. The lines between perfection and fault faded and framed what we saw in each other—affection, respect, and tenderness.

As the pictures scrolled past, I felt the love, adoration, ardent passion, and fierce desire that burned inside him. First was me on the old broken-down brick wall in Elsinore. A look of strength, fear, and bravery flashed in my eyes as he teased me. Then me standing my ground when he first brought me home and I sparked his unbeating heart to life. The courage I showed, even in the face of such disadvantage, made his insides warm. The first time he made me smile, the first time he saw fear and retribution in my eyes, even our first kiss—all were among the miniseries of memories he had of me. I was the star of his life as he was of mine.

With each draw Michael took from me, with every pull, my head grew fuzzier. With a great deal of effort, I managed to push at his chest. I was beginning to feel weak, my body tingling as if I was going to pass out, and the world started to spin even behind my closed eyelids.

As Michael pulled back, I managed to open my eyes long enough to see the look of pure, untamed hunger and passion that beamed from him.

I tried to smile back but started to see black.

"Arri." Michael's voice broke into my darkness. "Here, drink." His voice, still laced with desire, held concern, too.

Even in my delirious haze, I felt the warmth of something metallic and copper touching my lips, and I readily drank. With each drop, my inner demon craved and frenzied for more, but it wasn't enough. I needed more and faster. Without thought or foresight, I gingerly grabbed the source and pulled it closer. Michael's neck was soft and warm. The small incision he offered was just above the collar. The calm and steady stream of blood cascaded from his neck. Closing my eyes, and taking a deep breath to fortify my strength, I sucked from the site.

The warm liquid burned my throat as I drank. With Michael's

intake of breath, I tried to pull away, but his hand shot to the back of my head and held me in place. His panting breaths quickened as he molded his body to mine. His weight above me was almost suffocating, but somehow, it just seemed right.

His blood was like a drug: exhilarating, sensual, and enticing. The euphoric feel of our bond took hold of my heart.

As the seconds turned into moments, I finally let go as my grogginess and tiredness gave way to uninhibited awareness, like for the first time, I was in tune. Michael's memories were added to my own. I saw the world through his eyes.

I slouched into the bed, my body relaxing and my head falling back onto the pillow. Michael bent down and traced the mark he had made, first with his finger, then with his mouth.

The tingling sensation of his breath, teeth, and tongue as he licked and stroked the soft, tender skin just above my collarbone soothed any discomfort I had. As he lay next to me, he studied me. A small smile touched his lips when he saw the grin that spread across my face.

The sweat and perspiration that clung to my skin was drying, and I felt sticky and tacky. Who knew that the blood exchange could be so wearing, exhilarating, and seductive all at once?

My weakness from blood loss was resolved as I replaced my own blood with his. The awareness of his every move, breath, and thought as he watched and studied me felt intoxicating. I could feel him as if I were him.

"Are you okay?" His hesitant and concerned voice purred through me as I lay there trying to calm my heart and steady my breathing.

"Yeah," I said breathlessly. My cheeks burned as I heard the need in my own voice.

Michael got up from the bed, retrieved the nightgown that had fallen to the floor, then walked to the adjoining room and turned on the shower. In only a few seconds, steam poured from the open door. When he walked back to me, I took his outstretched hand, and he led me to the bathroom.

Stopping in front of me, Michael tested the water, splashing me in the process.

Then, with a kiss on the cheek, Michael left the room. I was fired up, my skin ablaze with yearning.

I pulled my shirt over my head, my muscles tightening and pulling with every move. With each article of clothing I disposed of, my muscles grew more tense, but as I sank into the warmth and deliciousness of the shower, I relaxed. The delicate skin on my neck was just a start. My whole body ached and twinged with soreness. I washed the stickiness from my skin, light and rousing clouds of steam sending the scent of soap and cologne wafting through the air. The reminder of the bond Michael and I shared brought a permanent smile to my face.

After a shower that showed me that I was stiffer than I thought, I dried, moisturized, and dressed. Padding back into the room, I was a little hurt and disappointed to see that the bed was made and the room was empty, save for my frozen body in the doorway.

"Arri, did you enjoy your shower?" Michael's voice strummed my heartstrings. His silhouette shaded the frame of his doorway, outlined by the light that spilled in from behind him.

"Yes," I said, bowing my head and averting my gaze as a hint of embarrassment washed through me.

Michael crossed the space in a few easy strides, placed a finger under my chin, and lifted my head until my eyes met his.

"Will you come with me? I'd like to spend the night with you—my mate at my side." His caring voice, his loving eyes, his fulfilled heart—they all reached out to me, making me trust him and want him.

I bit my lip, smiled, and nodded. There are worse ways to spend the night than next to my mate. The last word made my heart giggle, and the smile on my face widened until my cheeks hurt.

THIRTEEN

As Michael ran tantalizing circles up and down my arms, my mind slowly woke up. I blinked away my sleep-induced fog and my lips twitched into a smile. It was like waking up after a storm. The night had been chaotic, intense, and turbulent, but as the sky cleared and the tempest blew over, a morning of peace and unity graced us. It was the same with Michael and me. Initially when he proposed that we finish the bond what seemed like ages ago, I wanted it but was also scared to death. The idea of Michael biting into my neck and sucking my blood had left me queasy. Just the thought made my stomach churn. But last night, the way that he teased and nibbled, awakening the skin and the inner demon inside, turned something fearful and intimidating into a sensual, rousing, and hedonic experience.

"Are you awake?" Michael's gruff and lustful voice whispered into my ear.

"Getting there," I said, smiling up at him.

I took in his roughly tousled hair, the lines in his shirt, and the way that even his eyes looked tired and hypnotized. I got the impression that, although vampires didn't sleep, Michael had somehow slept anyway.

"What time is it?" I asked, squinting around for a clock.

"About twelve in the afternoon." Michael smiled down at me, his eyes sparkling with mischief. "On Thursday."

I fingered the fabric of his shirt between my fingers, outlining one of the wrinkles. "Did you fall asleep?"

A confused expression etched over his brow.

"I did," was all he said.

I knew there was more to it. I could almost feel his thoughts, see what he was thinking.

"You took in my blood during the bond. For a moment, we were linked. I think my weariness transferred to you, made you tired."

I blinked, waiting for him to rebut my theory. Then it hit me. We left for the lair on Tuesday. He must have read my thoughts, because concern shaded his features, his fatigue forgotten as he focused on me.

"You were out for a while. I was nervous that perhaps I took too much." His features tightened. "I promise, it will never happen again." His voice was spiked with regret.

"Hey." I placed my hand on his cheek and turned his head until he was looking at me.

"I could have killed you," he said.

"But you didn't," I said sternly. "After everything I have been through, it's going to take a whole lot more than a little blood loss to stop me. Besides, if I remember right…" I dug through my hazy memories of what I remembered. "I took from you too."

Even though it nauseated me to think of it, let alone think of what possessed me to do it, I smiled.

Michael grumbled something inaudible, but in the end, he nodded and pulled me into his arms. "It was incredible, though." His voice rumbled through his chest.

"It was," I agreed.

As soon as his teeth pierced my skin, we'd shared something extraordinary. Time had stood still as his captivating pull lulled and entrapped me. That beautiful moment was more than just an exchange of blood; it was as though we were sharing our innermost desires and fears. I saw his memories, felt his pains, and relived his life through his eyes. Then, when I took from him, when I stirred and roused the demon within, his blood brought me closer to him in a way that was beyond explanation or words. It was a moment where we truly became one. It was the unity of the Statara. The blood bond bound us together for all time and eternity.

The one-time biting and sharing had turned into two or three by the time the night was over. It was as though we couldn't get close enough.

Now, even as I relished in the warmth of his embrace, I knew I had to get up. My body ached as I pulled myself up, stretching my neck. The way my muscles implored and pleaded for me to lie back down reminded me of how frail and human I was.

With a groan, I groped for the robe that rested at the end of the bed.

"Leaving me so soon?" Michael's playful voice tugged at my heart as he teasingly grabbed for me. I made a quick slip away, smiling down at the man on the bed beneath me. He always looked so perfect and flawless. Now he was almost human—almost. He tugged his shirt up over his head, revealing his perfectly toned, sculpted chest and abs for my perusal. In short, he was a god, my own personal Adonis. I bit my lip as I tried to rein in my desire to touch him. If I gave in, we would never leave each other's side.

"Not leaving, just a temporary leave of absence." I smiled back, using the same playfulness in my own voice.

A smile teased at his lips.

I attempted to stand up. The act should have been simple enough; I had done it millions of times. But now, lightheadedness struck me like a brick to the temples. The room spun, my limbs felt weak, and my knees buckled beneath me. The floor surged up toward me. As I grabbed for support, a pair of strong arms pulled me into them. I never hit the ground. Michael looked at me with pain written across his face.

"Arri." My name was a plea as he waited for the dizziness to subside.

"Yeah?" I paused as a second wave of vertigo graced me with its presence. Michael's form swayed and bent as I tried to focus on him. The blurry lines of his face and the shape of his perfectly contoured body sharpened and refined until, finally, the man I loved came back into focus.

"I must have gotten up too fast," I lied, knowing what I just experienced had nothing to do with the speed of my movement. There was only one explanation for what just happened. My mind sifted through my memories. Although I'd taken in Michael's blood, it hadn't been enough to replenish what he took.

As realization hit him, he dropped his head, ashamed.

"Arri, I am so sorry. I knew… I thought…" He shook his head with disgust in his eyes, berating himself for what he had done. "I never should have taken from you. I was blinded with lust, selfishness, and pride. I wanted us to be bound together, to finish the Statara, and in my haste, I ignored the fact that you were still…" He swallowed and turned away from me, as if he couldn't bear to see my disappointment or regret.

"Michael." I lifted his chin until I met his gaze. "I don't regret anything. Even if I knew it would have killed me, I still would have done it. To share such a rare and extraordinary gift would have been worth it." I touched his cheek and made a move to stand.

"Wha—" Before Michael could finish his protest, I leaned forward and placed a gentle and reassuring kiss to his lips.

With a wink and a smile, I slowly made my way to the bathroom. I stared at myself in the mirror. The reflection looked like me, smiled like me, but there was something different.

It wasn't my hair, or my new wardrobe. It was the way my eyes—my now green eyes—twinkled with lust and passion. It was the pink hue that touched my cheeks, the fact that I knew I was mated. It was the crimson marking on my wrist that had always lit up but now was practically glowing and pulsing. With each breath I took, I felt more confident, more assured, more poised. As Michael's blood ran through my veins, his memories were practically engraved into my mind. The way he saw me, felt about me, and loved only me, made my heart giggle.

As the warm water slipped over my skin, I was oddly aware of every place the downpour touched. The spray cascading over each and every square inch relaxed me. Closing my eyes, I felt the turbulence of Michael's thoughts battling each other. Guilt, remorse, and regret opposed pride, satisfaction, and an ancient calling to claim his eternal mate.

After a nice and calming shower, I stepped out onto the bathmat. I wiped the fog from the mirror, dressed, and combed my fingers through my hair to loosen knots or tangles. Silky strands of brown hair framed my face, my emerald-green eyes simmered with desire, and my smile warmed my whole appearance with satisfaction and passion.

"There you are." Michael watched me with intent and rapt attention as I entered the room. His eyes inspected me for any signs of wariness.

I smiled up at him as I wrapped my arms around his neck. I stood on my tippy-toes and kissed him.

"Yep, here I am," I said, unraveling my fingers from his hair.

"I was worried about you."

"Oh?" I playfully smirked at him and traced a single finger over his chest, down his arm, and came to rest on his mark, which was a match to my own. Our mating marks. I gently brought his mark to my lips and reverently kissed it.

"You are going to be the death of me, you know that?" Michael said, laughing as I pulled my hand away from the warmth of his body and seated myself at the kitchen table.

The last time I'd been here, the kitchen was just a notch dug out from the cave wall. It had nothing except a fridge. Now, it rivaled any modern kitchen: microwave, fridge, stove and oven, sink, cupboards, even an island with two barstools. The kitchen table was still small, with room for maybe four place settings at best, and two chairs beside it.

"So, with you practically spending the night with me every night, and most of the days, when did you have time to redecorate the lair?" I asked with playful skepticism.

"You may need to sleep every night." Michael eyed me with humor and mischief. "I, on the other hand, have had all night. Besides, it only took a half day," he said with a cocky assurance, obviously proud of his work.

"It looks great," I said as he bent over the table and kissed my nose.

Michael sat back into his chair. His calm outward façade may have been bricked into place, but his inner fight was wreaking havoc on his emotional state.

"I'm not broken, Michael. I had a little dizzy spell. It's not the end of the world."

I laughed as I finished the breakfast that he'd made me and brought my plate to the sink.

"It's not that," he stated as he made his way around the kitchen like he was on autopilot.

"Then, what is it?" I asked as I poured myself a glass of milk… just for him to pour it out into the sink and wash the glass.

"Michael!" I said, louder than I anticipated. Then, as if he was actually shaking the thoughts from his head, he turned to me, a pained expression distorting his features.

Michael opened his mouth but thought better of whatever he was going to say and closed it. The grief and fear that stained his heart stopped me in my tracks.

"Michael." I placed my hand on his broad shoulder. "What's wrong?" I asked, feeling his panic.

Michael flinched at my touch.

"Michael?" I asked again.

"Yeah, sorry," he said, raking his hands through his hair. The sadness that streamed from his every pore stilled my heart. As we made our way to the couch in the living room, he gingerly took my hand as if he were afraid it would break in his grip. He was careful to place a small distance between us when we sat.

"Michael, you're really starting to scare and annoy me. What's going on? Did something happen?" Uncertainty shook my every word as tears pricked the corners of my eyes.

"No! Yes…" Michael rubbed the back of his neck.

"Well, which one is it? Because I'm really freaking out now," I said. My heart rate went right from pounding to immeasurable speed.

"Yeah, well…" Michael hesitated, searching for the right words. "I don't know how to say it. I feel like I unwillingly violated your inner thoughts."

He might as well have said snorkel for all the sense it made. "Violated me? How so?"

"During the Statara."

Then it hit me. When I saw his memories, he must have seen mine.

"You saw my memories," I said, nodding.

"I'm sorry. I don't know what happened. When your mouth touched me, and you started to drink…" He couldn't finish. He just hung his head, waiting for the verdict.

"You saw my life, lived through my eyes. Just as I did through yours."

"Yeah, I saw it all. It was like watching a movie in fast-forward." His eyes narrowed. "I also saw your dreams, Nicholas… everything." He shook his head. "Are your dreams premonitions that become real? Do they come to life?" he asked, sounding scared that the answer was going to be yes.

"Usually. Well, mostly, in some form or fashion. You saw how I die." At that, Michael took my hands in his.

"It'll never happen, I won't allow it," he said, pulling me into his arms. "This is what you meant when you told me you saw how it ends?" His words hit me hard. Although I'd seen it over and over again, it had always been just me. I could never share it, or the way I saw it, felt it, and experienced it. To anyone else, they were just dreams. To me, they were real. A play-by-play of how I was going to die.

"You know, when two people bond, it is definitely an experience that brings them together. But memory exchange…" Michael didn't finish.

For the next few hours, we exchanged life stories, and explained anything that the other didn't understand. Michael was baffled that, with the life I'd led—bored, always feeling lost, even the suppression—I had managed to take vampires and werewolves in stride. Of course, he felt the fear and hesitation toward the others, but the fact that I didn't run around screaming for my life fascinated him.

"You mean your parents didn't tell you anything? They didn't encourage you to imagine or envision a life full of other beings besides humans?" Michael's mouth practically fell open when I told him how they reacted to me reading paranormal books. "And when you found out I was a vampire, you didn't feel fear. Not like I would expect."

We didn't know how long we would share each other's memories, but we exercised our knowledge, poking and prodding into every thought, every action, and every instant, until we were practically experts.

After hours on the couch, when I finally readjusted my seating, my legs ached and protested my every move.

"We better get you up and moving," Michael laughed. "I have just the thing."

The car ride into Richfield was pretty uneventful. It was the ending to the perfect respite. The winding road practically lulled me into a coma as I sifted back through the night that Michael and I bonded. The emotional connection and the physical awareness linked us together eternally. As the day went on, I noticed little, tiny things that made me smile. Like the way I felt his very presence. His distance, his emotional state, even his very thoughts, were unclouded.

FOURTEEN

The streets of Richfield buzzed with life, and I saw the town from a new, crystal clear point of view. An ordinary life used to appeal to me, but now, after the changes I had been through, such a fate seemed dull. My life had gone from colorless to bright and vibrant: living my days as a vampire, fighting evil like a superhero, saving the day in unseen silence even as I wore the mask of normality.

"You good?" Michael's voice was just a whisper in the deafening chaos that surrounded us.

The school year appeared to be in full swing, just another reminder that time had passed at the speed of light. Passersby ignored our presence as they hustled to and fro, frantically searching for the perfect outfit to go with the new backpack they just bought or the best shoes to impress the others—because everyone knows that the brand you wear is how you make your friends, right?

I shook my head in disbelief as the hoopla of humanity danced before me. These people were worried about how they looked or who they were seen with, while I was dealing with a life as a half-breed vampire.

As I stared off into the crowd, I was vaguely aware that Michael had asked me a question. My attention had been drawn to a man, so unlike the masses around us, as he leaned against a sleek white Lamborghini. He stood out like a sore thumb in his tailored suit and his porcelain features. He wasn't even trying to fit in.

"Do we know him?" I asked Michael, as he, too, saw the man I did.

"Yes, we do," Michael said with a cocky grin.

As the man pushed himself off the car and walked toward us, his expression showed nothing. His impassive look struck a nerve, and I waited for him to attack. Michael obviously knew him, but from what Michael was feeling, I couldn't tell if he was friend or foe.

"Brother." The man extended his hand to Michael, who visibly relaxed.

"Brother." Michael took his offered hand and pulled him into a light hug. The two patted each other's backs as if they had been friends forever. "Colton, how have you been, old friend?"

The man looked around. "Here?" he asked. "You could have had the tropics, anywhere you wanted, and you chose here?"

"Well..." Michael shrugged, a non-committal gesture of what he thought.

"And who might this be?" Colton turned his attention to me. The cool blue of his eyes perused me with interest.

Michael snaked his arm around my waist and pulled me closer. The sharp look in his eyes showed a possessiveness that told Colton to back off.

Colton put his hands up in mock surrender.

"Whoa, man, I was just asking." Colton let out a barking laugh. "You have it bad, man." Colton smirked in my direction as he stared at us with interest.

"So, what are you doing here?" Michael asked, his tone returning to normal.

"Is there a place we can talk?" The jovial look fell from Colton's face.

"Sure," Michael replied without missing a beat.

As the three of us walked into the small-town diner, I froze at the entrance. I had been here several times before. The vintage, eclectic look used to feel welcoming. Now, it terrified me. The last two times I'd been here were not good experiences. First, Gavin attacked me, then, Catherine was beheaded as a result of me being alive.

My breaths came out unsteady and shaky. Colton cocked his head, obviously not knowing my past, but Michael was by my side in a heartbeat. He stroked his hands up and down my arms as if rubbing away the chills snaking through my body, trying to reassure me.

"I'm sorry, I can't," I said, seeing the two events playing out in unison—ghosts of my past reenacting two different fights at the same time.

With a gasp, Michael pulled me into his arms.

"Oh, sweetheart, I'm sorry. I didn't think about what this place might mean to you." His words were genuine. "Here, we'll go somewhere else," Michael said with a wave of his hand.

"Is there something wrong?" Colton asked, eyeing me curiously.

"In my haste to hear why you are here, I had not thought about where we were going. Please, let us return to the manor. You are welcome to stay with us while you are visiting." Michael's voice was cordial and businesslike, but his attention was still on me.

"Is there a problem with the diner?" Colton's demeanor changed to defensive, as though readying himself for a fight.

"No," I said, finding my voice. "The last time I was here, my dear friend lost her head." I blurted it out, staring at where I'd kneeled next to Catherine, feeling my heart break into a thousand pieces.

Colton's large frame relaxed, but confusion floated behind his eyes.

"Please, let us leave," Michael said, leading me to the car.

As we drove back to the manor, silence grew between us. The diner would always be on my blacklist of places to avoid.

"So," Colton said, interrupting our silent drive, "the last time I saw you, you were in London. Do you know how hard it was to track you down? Everyone was so tight-lipped, I thought I'd never find you."

Nicholas's men sure don't have a problem finding him, I thought as Colton went on and on about how he finally ended up locating Michael.

As we reached the manor, Colton let out a whistle.

"Well, I'll be. You actually did it," he said in awe as we pulled into the circular driveway. Michael parked in front of the two massive castle doors and just shook his head.

"Do you approve?" Michael asked mockingly, as if he needed Colton's permission, but Colton didn't respond. He was stock-still as two people exited the manor.

Shock must have been plastered on Colton's face, because Michael laughed as he took off his jacket. He exited the car, opened my door, and helped me out. He and I approached my parents, leaving Colton frozen in his seat.

"My lord, my lady," my mom said as she and my dad both bowed to Michael and me.

"Lady Ava and Sir Steven," Michael greeted them. "Is everything okay?" he asked, reading the look on my dad's face.

Before my dad had a chance to answer, Colton spoke up from behind us.

"Michael?" Colton asked, his voice hesitant as he walked up next to Michael.

"Yes, my apologies," Michael said distractedly, his eyes not wavering from my dad. Then, finally, he pried his attention from my dad and regarded Colton. "Colton, I would like you to meet Sir Steven and Lady Ava. Ava, Steven, this is an old friend, Colton Le Mage."

"It's a pleasure," my mom said, as Colton bowed.

"Yes, it is," my dad said in a toneless greeting.

Colton was noticeably uncomfortable with my parents. It was as though he didn't know whether to run or fight. My dad was known as a tyrant, a murderer, and that was exactly how Colton saw him.

"Please—may I offer you a drink?" Michael asked, trying to break the uncomfortable silence.

"Yes, that would be great." Colton accepted Michael's offer but kept his attention half on my parents.

Once inside the castle, Michael, Colton, and I headed to the library, and Colton closed the double doors behind us.

"So, why are you here?" Michael asked as he poured Colton and himself each a glass of blood. I sat on the couch as he offered a glass to Colton, then downed his own glass before refilling it. Colton shot him a glare.

"Have you forgotten your manners, my lord?" Colton spat as he gestured to me.

"Manners? No, but I believe you have. In the future, please remember who you are speaking to," Michael warned, matching Colton's icy look with one of his own.

"I'm sorry, my lord, but I believe you have forgotten to offer Lady Arri a drink. It is generally customary that the lady be served before yourself." Colton's voice was apologetic, but his look was not.

"I don't think I need lessons in manners, though I see that living far from your Coven Master and District Leader has made you forget proper respect—something that will need to be rectified before you depart from my company," Michael said, with a calm that sent chills down my spine.

Although Colton was seething below the surface, he relaxed his shoulders, took a deep breath, and nodded.

"Yes, sir," Colton said, chin held high.

"Now, since Arri does not drink like you and I, she has already been taken care of. Her drink should be here momentarily."

Just then, a gentle knock at the door broke the tension in the room.

"Enter." Michael's voice carried over the expanse of the library.

As my mom entered with a Coke for me, she shot Michael a look.

"Steven has asked to speak with you as soon as you are done here." Her voice was tight.

"Yes, thank you," Michael said, as he took the Coke from her and handed it to me.

When the doors shut behind her, Colton looked between Michael and me.

"May I ask what Steven is doing here?"

"He is here as a personal guest of Arri's," Michael stated before returning the conversation back to Colton. "So, why are you here? You have gone through great difficulty to find me. Obviously, it is important," Michael said, sitting on the couch next to me.

I could tell that Colton was burning with questions, but from the curt tone in Michael's voice, questions would have to wait.

"Yes, as I was saying..." Colton's eyes flicked to me and he paused, a hesitant look crossing his face. "Maybe we should discuss this in private," he said with caution.

As Colton glanced between the two of us, it dawned on me what he was saying.

"Here—I'll just step outside and see what the coven's up to," I said, rising.

"No, that will not be necessary," Michael said, rising as well, before gesturing to me to sit back down. "I apologize for the delayed introductions. Colton, this is Arri, my mate. Arri, this is Colton, one of my oldest friends. He lives under Coven Master Amber."

Colton turned his head to the side in shock.

"Mate?" he repeated.

"Yes," Michael said, pinning him with a cold look.

Colton opened his mouth to speak, then snapped it shut when Michael took a warning step in his direction.

"Of course. Lady Arri, it is a pleasure to meet you... properly," Colton stammered out, obviously bewildered at Michael's choice in a mate.

"Now, as you were saying," Michael started, sitting back down next to me.

"Yes," Colton said. "I wanted to personally warn you about some rumblings that have reached me. Now, I know that Nicholas's men have been gradually infiltrating many of the covens, including my own. It is the nature of the rumblings that have me concerned."

At the mention of Nicholas's name, my breath hitched. Colton noticed but kept speaking as he eyed me for unheard answers.

"I know it is not my place, but Nicholas is saying that a young half-blood has declared war with him and is attempting to take his throne so she might reign as ruler of the vampires."

Colton glanced at the floor before meeting Michael's gaze once again. He squared his shoulders. "Are the rumors true?" he asked.

I sat there in shock at his words. I wasn't surprised that Nicholas spun this around, blaming me as if I were the one to declare war instead of him coming after me out of the blue, trying to kill me for having the audacity to be breathing—that was par for the course. It was the fact that other covens far from Michael's reach were being infested with Nicholas's parasites, and they might actually believe the lies Nicholas was selling by the truckload.

"Wait," I said, my own voice sounding foreign as my heartbeat rocketed.

Colton noticed this and his eyes narrowed on me, trying to find something he couldn't see on the surface.

"You said you have heard rumblings, and yet you have come to seek a personal audience with Michael to ask about the truth in these rumors. What other rumors have you been hearing?"

Colton looked to Michael and studied him carefully.

"Excuse me, my lord, for speaking out, but does she have permission to speak?"

Michael looked at him with arched brows.

"I'm sorry, but even though you have chosen to mate a…" Colton paused, searching for the right words, "human, well, to each his own. But with all due respect, she is not one of us and has no place in this conversation."

At this, my temper exploded. Michael put a hand on my shoulder as I tried to stand, wanting to make my way over to Colton and pound his face in for saying I had no place in this conversation. I was the only one who had a right to this conversation. Since I was bound to my seat, as Michael's hand anchored me to the chair, I looked to him, silently asking him if I could at least talk.

"Be wise, my brother. Her bark is nothing like her bite." With that, Michael nodded in my direction, allowing me to speak for myself, even though he was noticeably angry.

"I have no right?" I asked, keeping my voice eerily calm. "Interesting, because I have all the right. You may look at me and see me as human—and you'll get no argument there—but what you don't see is the other side of me. A side that is very much untamed. A side that has landed me in the smack-dab center of your feud. A side that has put my life in danger and drawn the attention of a very unhappy vampire who has been a thorn in my life for the last two years. In these two years, I have gone from a normal human who wanted nothing more than to live on her own to a girl who would give her life to save yours." With every point I made, I ticked them off on my fingers as my voice rose to yelling. "So, before you judge me by my human side, please be cautious of my vampire side," I spat as I narrowed my eyes at him.

Colton looked shocked. Then, as his eyes showed realization, fear and understanding seared through him. He now saw his error in judgment. Michael hadn't mated a human; he'd mated the half-blood Nicholas claimed to be the enemy. With true horror coursing through him, Colton leapt from his chair and dropped to his knees.

"Yes, I am the half-blood who Nicholas claimed declared war on his throne, but it was not me who declared war. He was the first to strike. He was the first to attack me. It was he who made me into the enemy he fears," I said, lifting my chin and squaring my shoulders.

"I'm sorry, my lady. I didn't realize… I didn't know who you were," Colton backpedaled as his eyes pleaded with me to spare him.

"You are correct in fearing her, but I have not forgotten your transgressions."

Michael's words were venomous as he stared Colton down until Colton was practically shaking. Then, when Michael looked at me and saw the hurt and unease that rippled through me, he almost lost it.

My eyes burned. I saw the look of awe that passed over Colton's features before I turned away.

"I think you should go," Michael said, his voice rumbling against my cheeks. "Please, retire to your quarters, and we will speak again before dinner tonight." There was no room in Michael's tone for argument.

The sound of the closing double doors was the only indication that Colton had left, but my heart still hurt. My last point was the actual truth. I would inevitably give my life to Nicholas to save the life of many.

The only question was where we went from here.

Do I surrender or do I fight?

FIFTEEN

Michael and I exited the library as Terrish stood just outside the door with his head slightly bowed. From what I could see and feel, his features were hard set, and anger brewed just below the surface. He was clenching and unclenching his fists at his sides. I could feel the disgust he harbored. It was as though he couldn't digest it. He'd lost all color at the mere thought.

As he meets Michael's gaze, Terrish set his lips in a grim line. His eyes were dark and burned with animosity.

"Yes?" Michael's voice sounded distant. I scanned Terrish's face. Something like regret and sadness flashed in his eyes before the flame of hatred returned.

"I'm sorry, but the matter has become urgent. We…" Terrish swallowed as if he were afraid to finish. "We found them." His voice was quiet.

At this, Michael stiffened, his heart constricted, and his grip on me tightened. As Michael pulled me in closer beside him, Terrish stared at me, and his features softened at the sight of my face and my tearstained cheeks. Grief and sorrow washed away all his steeliness.

The anger in Michael's heart mimicked the loathing that ricocheted through Terrish, and that is when I knew: whatever happened must be bad, really bad.

"I'm sorry, my liege, but… Alex and Jonathan… Nicholas…" Terrish knelt before us shaking his head back and forth.

The steel-cold dampness in the air chilled my heart as Terrish's words hit me like a stone. With ragged breaths, my vision blurred and I fell to my knees in horror.

As I gasped for air, I stared at Michael, unblinking. Shaking my head, I opened my mouth to speak, but what was there to say? My words stopped in my throat, refusing to leave, and my lungs pleaded for air as though my whole body was going to fail.

"Alex! Jonathan!" I cried out. My pleas were unheard in the commotion as Terrish told Michael of what he'd learned: Alex and Jonathan were gone.

Although the words registered, and I understood what Nicholas had done, my mind still stuttered.

"How? When?" was all I could manage to rasp out, my voice small and all but inaudible among the roaring crowd that had gathered.

How could this have happened and I not know? When? Alex and Jonathan were like my brothers, my best friends, and my bodyguards all wrapped into one. They were even welcomed among the coven as one of its own.

The last few weeks crashed through my mind, trying to remember the last time I saw them. I grasped for a single moment in which they appeared.

The fight with Gavin was all I could think of.

No, that can't be right; I could still feel them. My thoughts scrambled, hoping to feel them closer, hoping for… anything! My inner voice screamed at me to keep searching harder, but there was nothing. Days, weeks, maybe even months crashed into me as I sifted through each memory. But as panic set in, the crisp outline of each thought softened until they blended and fused together, making it all but impossible to distinguish one from another.

I sensed and glimpsed coven members gathering around as I struggled to accept what I'd just heard. Their forms swayed, their words were mumbled, and their combined emotions of confusion and anger raked against every fiber of my being. With unheard pleas, I lifted my eyes to my parents and Phoenix, who were pushing their way through the crowd.

With Michael and my dad at my side, the crowd grew quiet.

"Do you see the truth now?" Michael asked Colton, who had

joined the crowd and watched the scene unfold. "The lies you have been told, the misconception of the world around you, the war going on—all has been calculated by the one who created it. Do you see her?" Michael asked as he gestured to me, huddled in his arms. "Do you think that she alone has the ability to declare a war on Nicholas?" Michael shook his head.

Colton looked at Michael, the expression on his face clearly showing he needed more explanation.

"Don't you see it, Colton?" Michael continued, his voice raising a decibel or two. "When Nicholas heard of Arri, he saw the prophecy to be true."

At mention of the prophecy, Colton's eyes grew wide as acknowledgment registered.

"Can she defeat him?" Colton asked.

"She has the ability to defeat him, yes," Michael said with pride.

Colton looked confused. "But she is a child, no more than eighteen. What abilities could she possibly have that would defeat Nicholas? He has been an underlying current of power and strength, claiming it as his birthright to rule. What does she possess that would show her as the rightful leader of our people?" As Michael and I both looked at him in disbelief, Colton put his hands up in surrender. "I'm not supporting Nicholas, but to convince the coven leaders and their covens, we will need to have proof that she is the power that has been foretold."

Colton looked at my parents, Phoenix, then back at the two of us. His eyes grew wide, and his frame froze in disbelief as he saw the crimson marking on my forearm and my parents' protective nature over me. "I don't understand. How?" he asked as his large, awestruck gaze locked on me.

"You want proof?" I asked, my eyes burning with fury, my temper claiming me as anger and rage branded me as theirs. "The fact that Nicholas has kidnapped my friends, infiltrated your coven, and declared war on me—not to mention that I am stamped with the crimson mark—is not proof enough?" I asked. My voice was calm, but as wrath and fury consumed me, the emotionlessness of my tone made my words sound eerie.

Although the coven members surrounded me, I heard nothing. Each voice, each sound, blurred together until it resembled a wave of crashing chaos. Their individual voices became background noise.

I couldn't breathe, I couldn't see, and I couldn't hear, but I felt plenty. The combination of the coven's internal voices screamed and yelled at me. I couldn't control it. My head pounded and my mind spun as the massive noise overwhelmed me. My control splintered away, one sliver at a time, breaching my containment until there wasn't enough left to hold it back. I was close to losing it.

Then, as an outer calmness focused on me, my internal chatter ceased. That's when I felt Michael. His firm hands gripping my shoulders. His placid voice calmed my inner heart. As he spoke to me in low tones, his strength and energy retrieved me from the turmoil churning within and around me.

That was when I opened my eyes. My breathing became strained as I tried to control the raggedness of my inhales. Michael's green eyes focused on me, his gaze never wavering as the air around me pulsed with energy, his thoughts silently helping me calm down from a whirlwind of utter confusion and raging hatred as I secretly sought revenge.

The room shook and vibrated as my internal fight for control shared my torment with the world around me. My anger came off in waves as I processed Alex's and Jonathan's abduction. Although calmer now, my power still strained against my control, seeking any weakness as it pulsed through me. I felt the familiar tingles in the air coat Colton's skin along with the skin of everyone else in the room. I could sense the room, as though the air that crackled with my energy and fed me a map of each and every person surrounding me. I held everyone in place as my power explored its freedom. As Michael's grip on my shoulders tightened and brought my focus back to him, I physically relaxed.

I was vaguely aware of Colton as I struggled to pull myself together. As I released the invisible hold and energy from his body, Colton sagged against the wall with relief, and I pulled back the waves that rippled through the air. The question of whether or not

I would be able to beat Nicholas, and whether I possessed the power, was answered. He stared at me in fear and awe.

As my powers settled, the unseen current that tied me to everyone in the room and the energy that held them all captive as shivers and prickles crept along their skin, slowly released its hold.

After everything, after my raging sea of emotion and discord, my throat constricted and my heart broke. I took ragged breaths as sorrow and grief settled over me. Physically I couldn't handle anymore; I was exhausted. Sagging against Michael, I tried to pull myself together.

"That's not all, sire," Terrish said, clearing his throat and regarding me with caution. "There was a note."

"A note?" I asked. My head shot up, my heart clenched, and my emotional tide ceased.

As Michael held out his hand, Terrish shook his head. With noticeable hesitation, Terrish fell to his knees before me.

"The letter is addressed to Lady Arri." He cringed as Michael's features hardened and his eyes glassed over.

Michael snatched the letter from Terrish's outstretched hand and slowly handed it to me, but when I reached for it, he held on to it for a split second longer. Then, reluctantly, he released the letter and closed his eyes.

When I unfolded the thick parchment, my heart stopped, my mind went blank, and reborn fury raced through me.

Whose life will you choose?
Theirs—or yours?
Don't take too long. The clock is ticking.
Tick, tock, tick, tock.
How long do you think they'll last?
Yours truly,
–N

The familiar script and the scarlet writing made me ill. The maroon color of the pen, the burgundy tint made me cringe—but why?

Then bile rose in my throat.

The note was written in blood.

The loud crash of the door crackled through the air. For a moment, there was silence. The moment registered through my thoughts as the coven jumped at the forceful sound, then darted away at lightning speed. Michael was holding me in his arms as my mom and Phoenix stared at the doors of the castle, which were still reverberating from the force.

My dad was gone.

I stared at Michael in terrified silence—terrified for the kidnapping of my friends and the disappearance of my dad—before the world around me went black.

I don't remember much after I broke down. I was emotionally drained and weak as the demon within siphoned my strength, the downside of my human half. As I flexed and used my inner demon, it took tenfold from my human side.

The rest of the day went by in a blur. My mind constantly played and replayed Nicholas's words. Whose life will you choose?

Drained, numb, and devoid of all emotion, I felt my heart break. Alex's and Jonathan's suffering was at the hands of Nicholas, but I was the cause.

Before I knew it, the entire day had passed, and Michael was tucking me into bed. He crawled in next to me and held me as I slowly fell into a deep sleep.

The air in the room suffocated me as a single burning candle shone in the corner. The shiny, polished white marble flooring beneath my bare feet felt cold and icy.

"I was wondering when I'd see you again." Nicholas's frigid voice penetrated the room. The scene brightened to show Nicholas sitting in a high-backed chair in the center of a colorless room.

"Nicholas," I said through my teeth.

"Oh, good, you remember me," he said, rising out of the chair as if he were royalty instead of the bottom-feeder he was. "I was beginning to feel like you were avoiding me."

"As if I had a choice. But yes, I would avoid you like the plague if

you'd just leave me alone," I said, folding my arms over my chest and raising my chin.

"Oh, my dear, you are so young and unwise to provoke the likes of me," he said, walking over to me. He stepped in so close that I could smell the rank stench of his breath, like death and decay dripping and oozing from his every pore. He placed his finger under my chin, tilting my head until I met his eyes. I held my breath and tried to pull my head from his grip, to back away from him. His bony finger burned and seared my skin like hot iron.

"Let go of me," I seethed, anger and fury rippling off me in torrents. I slapped his hand and stepped away from him, placing a few feet between us.

"Oh, you have spunk," he said dryly. "You'll quickly learn to be careful in my presence. I am told I hold no such tolerance for misbehavior. Soon you, too, will learn to bow before me. No one stands before me." He grabbed my shoulder with a crushing grip and forced me to the ground, his vice-like fingers digging into my skin. As he released his hold, he stepped back, satisfied.

"You forget," I said, cocking my head to the side and narrowing my eyes, "that I bow to no one." I stood again and squared my shoulders. "You are no god, ruler, or master of mine, so I most definitely will not bow to you."

Nicholas looked shocked for a second, then his lips curled up into a devilish smile. "We'll see about that."

"Yes, we will. But in the meantime..." I found my voice was strong, my control firmly back in place. "Why am I here? What do you want?"

Nicholas looked confused before a smug expression flooded over his face.

"Why are you here?" He laughed. "As much as I'd love to take credit for this," he said, gesturing to the room around us, "I don't have the ability to summon you. These are your rendezvous, not mine. At the moment, I am on my throne."

I summoned him? How? The quizzical look on my face reflected in the crystal gloss of his eyes. His demeanor changed to relaxed as he looked at me in disappointment.

"Your friends have done an ill job of educating you. Your ability to connect with me is one-sided, it is only something that a mongrel can possess. My birthright and purity in blood prohibits me from such tasks. My throne—"

"Throne? You have no right to sit on a throne. The mere fact that you are breathing near it and pretending to be a king has tainted its authority," I said, shaking my head.

"Here's how I see it," Nicholas said, fighting to keep his temper in check. "You are worthless and lowly compared to my superiority, so if you want to save yourself and your friends, I suggest you listen to what I'm about to say." He raised his chin. "Granted, I can't say I see why they would mean so much to you. They are just dogs, insignificant mutts, but if they appeal to your interest," he shrugged, "well, whatever. If you want to see them live, then surrender yourself. Otherwise, they will die and so will you."

"How can I trust you to keep your word?" I asked as scenarios played out in my mind.

"You can't. It's like Russian roulette. Can you trust the villain to keep their word, or do you suspect they'll kill the victim anyway?" Nicholas was storming and burning inside as I stood my ground. I didn't balk. I didn't flinch. The steeliness of my inner demon took control and kept me in line.

"What will happen to me if I surrender?" I asked.

Of course, I already knew the answer. His men would bring me to his lair, his so-called castle. Nicholas would parade me around, bound and hobbled like an animal, just to humiliate me. Then, when he got bored of that, I would be tortured and bled until my strength was nil to none. Then, and only then, would he sacrifice me in front of his coven, making it out that I was the villain, and he would be the one to deliver them from…

My thoughts ended as Nicholas struck me, his hand landing on my face with such force that my teeth chattered and my ears popped.

"You will listen when I speak to you!" Nicholas yelled as he seized me by the neck. His skin burned and sizzled against mine, scorching my flesh.

As I yelled out in pain, my hands landed on his neck. I clawed and dug until he finally released me, grabbing his neck and hiding his pain behind anger and fury.

"You will regret that!" he said, as he lunged at me again. His face contorted with rage and hatred. As his hands touched my cheeks, I awoke, startled and in the confines of my own room.

I was awakened by the sound of my own screaming, the pain and burning still fresh on my skin. It didn't take me long to stumble out of bed and fall to my knees. Thankfully, it was only a dream, but the aching pain that weaved through my veins tortured me.

Practically crawling my way to the bathroom, I staggered to right myself against the doorframe. Looking at the woman in the mirror, I hardly recognized myself. Nothing about her resembled me. My brown hair was streaked with white. My eyes danced and swirled in Technicolor, like a whirlpool of red, green, brown, and gray rolling and spinning. My face was thinned and ageless, but it was the black circle blooming around my right eye and the line of burned skin under my chin and around my neck that caught my attention. Everywhere that Nicholas had touched me in my nightmare mimicked what I was now seeing. Horrified, I clasped my hand over my mouth to muffle my cry of fear. How did he do that? How is our mental link physical?

Ever since the disaster with Catherine and the Shadows, my vampire side had grown in strength. With each passing day, small pieces of my human side vanished behind a veil. That same veil opened to my vampire side. As I allowed it to flourish and grow, it gradually surfaced. Both sides fought to survive within me. Both sides were determined to win, but only one could be supreme. But which one am I? Human or vampire? To see the bruised mess reflected back at me, you wouldn't know I was either.

Although I appeared no older than eighteen and had powers that only superheroes possessed, I was, and felt, inferior against my one and only archenemy. If he could do this from a mere nightmare, then what could he do in person?

After I cleaned up and got ready for the day, I walked back to the bedroom, running my hand along the nightstand until my finger stopped. I picked up a frame that lay atop the table. The old porcelain was chipped from age, the color faded a bit, but the photo that lay inside was flawless, protected from the elements by glass.

My heart pounded. Three of the people in the photo were no longer with us. Out of eight of us, only five remained. One had been lost by blinded hate, the other two were taken from me because I was who I was. As I tilted the frame, my face reflected within the glass, shadowing the remaining people, and I stared at myself. Then it hit me—there was my answer. Me.

I had spent the last few years running and hiding from Nicholas, myself, my destiny, but not anymore. He said I'd declared war. He said I wanted to claim his throne.

Well, let's hope I don't disappoint him.

A smile curved my lips. The only way to beat him was to let him think he was winning. I changed out of my designer clothes into yoga pants and a tank top, clipped my hair up, and left for the hall.

SIXTEEN

With the fight Nicholas had promised on the horizon, I knew there had to be something I could do to help tip the scales of fate in my favor.

It was eerily quiet as I made my way down the hall. The doors to the dining room were open, but the room itself was empty. The library was barren except for the books that lined the shelves. The manor seemed deserted.

I wandered around the halls in search of the old gym that Michael had hidden behind closed doors. I kept my ears open for the sound of Michael's voice, but it wasn't his voice that called to me. I felt him. I followed my heart like a beacon of light until I stopped in front of a door.

"And what does Arri think of this plan?" I heard Terrish say. Rogan mumbled his approval.

"Arri will be privy to the plan, but right now, she needs to rest."

"I'm concerned for her, sire," Rogan said, speaking up over the mumblings of the coven at the mention of my name. "She shows a lot of promise, but still fears herself, almost like she doesn't know who she is yet." The room went quiet, waiting for Michael's response.

"Yes, you are right. She is still finding herself. But I have total faith that when she finds her motivation, she will be unbeatable," Michael said with trust and strength in his voice. "But as of now, I have a plan." He called out, "Colton?"

The focus of the room shifted.

"Yes, my lord?" Colton answered with a shaky voice.

"How many of your men do you trust beyond a shadow of a

doubt?" Michael's voice was businesslike and calculating. "Do you know who has infiltrated your coven and who has been corrupted?"

"Yes, sir. I also know who can be trusted in not only my coven, but also from those surrounding us."

"And your Coven Master? Can you trust her?"

"Yes. Amber can be trusted without fail. But it is Slone of the Kaw that cannot be trusted."

As Colton spoke of the disloyalty of one of his coven leaders, I could feel Michael bristle inside. The infiltration extending so far up the ladder—it was like Nicholas was just mocking him.

"Good. Here's what I want you to do." Michael made his way around the room, pacing as he spoke. When he stopped in front of the double doors, I could feel the exact moment he felt my presence.

With a smile on my lips, I went on my way. As much as I wanted to know what was going to happen and be in on the planning, I also knew that I was on my own mission. I had a debt to settle. After a few more lefts and a right, I found the door I wanted.

I pushed open the old and dusty wood, the hinges creaking in protest, and flipped on the switch. As I entered the room, I allowed the doors to close behind me. The smell of dirt, must, and old sweat filled the air. The towels lined up and rolled in the corner looked relatively new, but all in all, it would have to work.

Well, maybe. I was a little out of my league. The newer equipment was self-explanatory. Leg presses, bench presses, even treadmills littered the space. But as I stepped further into the room, I realized that there were some that were noticeably older and more worn.

As I explored the various forms of ancient fitness apparatuses, it became clear that they were more than machines to keep fit. They were tools and training devices for teaching and maintaining the ability for self-defense. Meandering further, I saw a padded mat surrounding a dummy-looking thing. It was an odd piece of equipment. Notches and gouges were taken out of the metal. Eight arms stuck out of its center, four high on each side.

A container filled with metal bars stood next to it; they were obviously used with this dummy. I picked one up and used it to touch one of the arms. As the top arm moved away from me, an arm near the bottom came at me with the same speed. Hitting another arm with the metal bar made yet another arm move. There was no rhyme or reason to the movements as far as I could tell, but it was easy to see what it was used for: self-defense. Because the piece of equipment was metal, I chose to stay out of reach of the arms, but when batting at them one at a time, I found myself hitting, then blocking, then hitting again, until the dummy and I had picked up a rather fast speed.

You will surrender, Nicholas's haunting voice whispered in my head.

Without thought, I hit harder, and the dummy moved faster, swinging violently.

You are a worthless cur, and as such, will die at my feet. Nicholas's voice haunted me again. His vial words seeping under my skin and angering me from deep down.

With another hit, the arm of the dummy swung at me hard and fast.

Accept your fate, and I will spare your agony and kill you quickly, Nicholas berated me.

My fate? The thought crossed my mind several times daily. The death I felt every time I saw my fate playing out before me hurt more and more. The pain and agony I felt as he tortured me and humiliated me, as he paraded me around in nothing but a plain, white, knee-length slip was about more than my failure—it was also about the safety of the coven.

I let lose another set of swings as the dummy fought back. With each whisper Nicholas breathed in my ear, I hit harder and faster.

Be careful; you know not whom you fight. I'm being polite by demanding your surrender. If I have to come and get you, you will regret it. Your death will not be the only fatality. At the time, his threat had only ignited a fire in me that made me want to strangle him. In retrospect, I can see that belittling his remarks would only prove that he is one to keep his word.

I am in way over my head. I slowed my attack on the inanimate object. In my emotional attack on the dummy, I realized I had drawn closer to the poor thing. I also realized that I was no longer alone in the room.

"How did you find me, Daddy?" I asked, my battle with the dummy turning slow and rhythmic.

"How did you know it was me?"

I blocked a hit near my knees, choosing not to answer.

"Now, I wonder," my dad continued, "why would a daughter of mine be hiding out in an old gym? What do you think it is that you have to prove?" Amusement filled his voice.

I grabbed one of the arms that swung at me, halting the onslaught.

"I know many men that can't do that," he said.

A smile curved my lips as my dad walked up behind me. Without turning around, I shook my head.

"What did that dummy ever do to you? I'm pretty sure it holds no ill will against you." My smile grew as my dad laughed at his own joke.

"These aren't all my nicks. I think most of these are from previous fighters," I said as I rubbed my finger along a few of the deep gouges.

"I believe those nicks are from Michael," my dad mused as he walked past me and stood facing me on the other side of the dummy. "What happened to you?" Dad yelled, pointing at my eye and neck.

"Nicholas. He paid me a little visit, or… I visited him. Last night in my nightmares."

"And he did this to you?"

"Yeah. It isn't the first time, but it is definitely the longest the bruises have lasted."

My dad looked at me and I knew that just below the surface he had countless questions, but when I rubbed and stretched my neck, he held back.

"Michael? What reason would he have to fight? He's a vampire," I asked, pointing out the obvious.

"Ah, but Michael was pretty upset when he found out what I did to him. I believe that dummy represented me at one point." My dad chuckled. "I'm glad I wasn't here to oppose him."

"Really? Michael did all this?" The fact that Michael just about killed the poor thing to let off some steam said a lot about his character. Michael may have been strong and silent, but I had felt the anger and rage he held in check, and this dummy played stand-in for anyone who dared to defy him.

"Yeah. He was pretty upset about what I did and took it out on this." My dad rested his forearms on the two upper arms of the dummy. "He reinforced it with lead and steel, but still, he managed to go through quite a few of them," Dad continued as he looked off to the side of the mat and gestured to many disfigured and disassembled dummy pieces.

"Wow. I knew Michael was upset with you for changing him, but I didn't see this in the memories," I said, shaking my head in amusement.

"See it?" my dad asked.

"Never mind." I smiled, dropping the metal bar and rocking my neck from side to side.

Dad must have figured out that I wasn't going to answer him, so he walked to another circular bin holding several wooden swords.

"Why are you here?" my dad asked, throwing one of the mock swords at me. He removed his shoes, then gestured for me to do the same. As I kicked off my shoes and socks, he rolled his shoulders as if loosening up for a match.

"I'm here because Jonathan and Alex are missing and it's my fault." I bent my knees and positioned myself for a fight.

"Oh, and how do you figure?" my dad asked, as he slowly lunged at me, like he was testing my responses rather than actually attacking. With a simple block, I tried not to show him what I was capable of.

"Nicholas took them because of me. He's after me, and every time he gets close, I slip away. Now, because of that, he has taken my best friends to even the score." I let out an exhausted sigh at the thought that Nicholas had yet again bested me.

I blocked another test attack as my dad got a little more daring.

"That is a good defense, pretending that you know nothing about fighting, but I have heard of your abilities, and I'm not fooled." With his confession, I smiled.

"He warned me, Daddy, but I didn't want to listen. Now he has taken them, and unless I surrender, he'll kill them." With tears in my eyes, I tried to avert my gaze from his.

My dad made his way in front of me. He raised my chin with a finger until I was looking at him.

"This is not your fault."

"Yes, it is!" I shouted, shaking my head. "Alex and Jonathan would be fine if it wasn't for me. Catherine would be alive and there would be no need for this war."

"Is that what you think?" my dad asked as he led me to a bench and sat me down.

Wordlessly, I nodded.

"Then you'd be wrong. This war started the day Nicholas became a vampire, and I should know." He eyed me carefully as if trying to convey his thoughts. "It was so long ago, I only wish I couldn't remember every little detail, but I have thought about it since the day you were born."

With withdrawn emotions, his memories rushed my mind. The images I saw were only small tidbits, but it was enough to piece together without words.

"The Old One warned me of this day and foretold your birth." His eyes stared at me intently, waiting for my fear to kick in. "I didn't mean to create him; I just didn't want him to suffer.

"The Old One knew of my makings. I was born, but when I almost died, something changed in me, and from then on, I am who you see today.

"When I ran into The Old One, I realized that who and what he and his Viking brothers were, fit me well. It was a lifestyle I didn't have to hide from. In one of our raids, The Old One hurt and maimed many men, leaving them to die, but with Nicholas, I felt bad for him. So, I went back and tried to help him. In doing so, I created the heartless man he is." My dad ran a hand through his hair, then stood and paced back and forth.

"Nicholas made it his life's mission to kill the one who created him, but he mistook The Old One for me. Before Nicholas came to our camp, The Old One told me of the visions he had seen: the coming of a man, Nicholas, and the coming of a great force, you. But the new force would be born from our blood."

As I saw his thoughts and memories, I wasn't surprised. I guessed that, deep down, I had already known, or at least expected, that he created Nicholas, but to be the first vampire was different.

"How does this affect me and Nicholas?"

"Ever since The Old One's death, and since Nicholas had read his visions, Nicholas knew who I was. I'm the first vampire, which negates his claim to the throne. Knowing that I had given life to his biggest and only threat, I was hoping that if I hid you from all this," he gestured to his world, "then you would be safe from his tyranny."

"It didn't work," I said, crossing my arms over my chest and bowing my head.

"No, it didn't. But the prophecy says, 'One who is one of us, but not governed by our rules, will defeat him.' That prophecy means you."

"Who wrote this prophecy?"

"The Old One wrote down every vision, everything he had ever seen, heard, and felt of the future, so that we will once again know peace."

"No disrespect to The Old One, but I'm not ready to fight a vampire who has been around long enough to know that I was coming before I knew it myself. I've had no time to prepare, learn to fight, or even come up with a plan to defeat him. He, on the other hand, has had a lifetime to prepare for me."

My voice was slightly raised as I stood and faced my dad. "I mean, exactly what do you want from me? What did you expect? It's not like you raised me to be Xena, Warrior Princess. You have hidden me behind the lies of normality. You've raised me far outside the reaches of this world. Granted, I've been through a lot these last few years, but it doesn't mean I am ready to fight your fight."

My dad's hurt and pain was reflected in his eyes. But I was right. This wasn't just my fight. This war started long before I was born, when my dad created Nicholas.

"I've defended myself against Nicholas, but he has still come out ahead. So, tell me, please… what do you want me to do?" I asked as I walked and paced the room.

My voice cracked as I spoke, but as close as the anger I held inside was to the surface, my hurt was stronger and closer still.

"I don't know. Fight with us, I guess," my dad answered as he shook his head, a resigned look crossing his features.

"No, Dad. You don't want me to fight; you want me to win. The whole coven is expecting me to win."

I took a deep breath. I stared at my dad with a calm exterior, fighting to hide the roaring storm that churned inside me. To hide the cowardly side of me that wanted, and begged, for me to quit.

"Well, I'll let you in on a little secret," I swallowed and cocked my head to the side like I was going uncover the world's biggest mystery, "I don't win."

When my dad stared at me with no emotional understanding, I snapped.

"I've seen it, Dad. I've lived it. I've even felt it. I don't win. There's no victory," I explained when he stared in confusion. "I lose, I fail, and I die."

As the last two words left my mouth, I physically cringed.

"No matter how many ways I spin it, Daddy, I die," I finished, my voice a straight-up yell.

My heart dropped as I said it. Although I knew my fate, I'd never admitted it to my dad.

"So, if you'll excuse me, I have some training to do. If I'm going to fight him, I want to at least scar him or something," I bit out as I walked past my dad toward the dummy. I picked up the metal bar and positioned myself for battle.

As I fought, my dad never left the room. His presence hung like a heavy fog over the coast.

With every tried and failed attempt to defeat a simple dummy,

I hit the ground with a discernable thud. My back, head, even knees hit the hardened mat with a striking force. A few times, I thought I was close, only for the dumb contraption to mock me by tripping me, a callous blow throwing me off my feet, flipping me on my back and knocking the air out of me.

Again, I would tell myself, as I lay on the mat, afraid to move only for me to be thrown down again. *Again, again, again*, I told myself over and over, like a mantra.

As the dummy and I took equal hits, my bruised and battered body screamed for a reprieve.

Hit, hit, duck, turn and jump, then block to the left—with each new move, came a new counter move from the fighting contraption. Then, wham! The top arm came at me from the side and swiped me across the face.

I hit the floor—blood sputtering from my mouth—curled up into the fetal position, and gathered courage to try again.

I could sense my dad and a few others hovering close by, but none dared to approach me.

Again, I said, but this time, my body didn't listen. The stone coldness of the white marble throne room felt icy, not like part of Michael's manor.

"Again? Twice in one day? To what do I owe the pleasure?" Nicholas's voice raked against my nerves.

I glared up at him.

"You think you've won?" I asked as I righted myself.

"I don't think it, my precious. I know it."

"Well, then, I guess you have it all figured out. You'll come for me, offer me a choice. But what if I chose to let them die?" I countered as Nicholas circled me like a mountain lion stalking its prey.

"You won't. You're too sweet and loving to be so heartless and callous. I'd bet your friends mean more to you than your own life. In fact, I am betting on it."

As Nicholas came to a stop in front of me, the dulled and muted rays of light touched his skin, showing me a new addition to the marks and scars marring his porcelain face. The claw marks I'd given him this morning glinted in the light. Tiny, thin scars lined his cheeks and neck where I'd tried to fight back.

"I may not be the monster you are, but I have no intention of going down without a fight," I bit out as Nicholas's fingers made a grab for me. Just as his nails barely touched my chin, I backed away. "Be careful, Nicholas. It looks like you are no more immune to my touch than I am to yours," I said, pointing to the scars I'd placed on his cheeks and neck. As Nicholas's face contorted into pure fury, his image disappeared, and I sat up with a start in the gym with Michael at my side.

"Again," I said as I tried to stand up.

"If you go again, there might not be much of you left to introduce as my mate at the ball tomorrow." Michael's teasing voice brought me back to the present.

My heart melted at his concern. Then, as if he'd read my mind, he helped me to my feet and handed me my bar.

"Again," he said, smiling at me, knowing I wasn't going to stop until I beat it.

As I stepped up to the dummy, I squared my shoulders and poised myself for more.

"For Alex and Jonathan," he said. He kissed me on the cheek and made his way back to the doorway, where I could feel several of the coven members watching me.

"Alex and Jonathan," I repeated out loud as I made the first move. Hit, block, hit, block, jump, and turn… the random hits kept on coming and felt like they went on forever.

"What are you doing? You were supposed to stop her, not encourage her," my mom said with anger.

"She wouldn't even if I tried. I felt in her what I felt in me many years past." Michael's attention shifted from me to my dad for a split second, then back to me.

"I won't apologize for what I've done," my dad said, never taking his eyes off me.

"You didn't have to; you gave me an even better gift." I heard the smile in Michael's voice as he watched me battle out my fears, emotions, and anger.

My human side weakened as my vampire side consumed me—emotionally, physically, and mentally. Tired and drained, I let my hits become slower and less steady.

Then a blow from nowhere struck and practically crippled me.

I spun around, but the room was split in two: the dummy and the gym on one side, and Nicholas's lair on the other, with me standing in the center.

"What gives her such strength?" I heard Nicholas growl as a new set of painful blows pounded me in my stomach.

"You'll have to kill us first," came Jonathan's melodic voice.

"Don't tempt me, mutt. I'd hate to disappoint Arri when I arrive at her front door without a gift," Nicholas's mocking tone rasped. "Now tell me, how do you expect a mere child to defeat me?" he yelled, losing his patience.

I stood still, mentally torn between the present and my dreams. Nicholas's thoughts and what he saw bore into my conscious mind, while physically, I played out my fight with the dummy.

"You will never be a match for her," Alex said, his voice ringing with pride and affection.

Then, as fast as the images came, they withered away into smoke.

With the added knowledge that they were both alive, and the renewed anger that sparked and roared inside, I harnessed my rage, my two sides becoming one, and took on the dummy bar none. My every move was as fluid as water, my strength was as strong as a freight train, and my skill was honed for accuracy. With valor, I raised the metal bar and swung. The blow was mighty, and without resistance, the dummy practically exploded as its arms flew from its frame and scattered throughout the room.

With a smile on my face, I let out a laughing sigh. I did it. I found my center.

With shaking hands and ragged breaths, I fell to my knees as a sense of victory washed over me. I might not beat Nicholas in the end, but if I can pull off anything close to what I just did here, then maybe, just maybe, I'd have a chance in real life.

My body shrieked and shouted out in pain when my vampire side retreated back into the hollows of my inner self. My human side, barely strong enough to resurface, brought me back to reality as it reminded me what happened when I let my vampire side take over.

My vision became blurry. My heart beat painfully fast, like a thunder of galloping horses racing inside, and my body relived every bruise, every hit, and every block I made without the bar's assistance. Although my vampire side could defeat Zeus, my human side was weaker than a wet paper bag.

My viewers were awestruck, but I was too weak to care. I saw Michael's smile, and that was all I needed. Even if I didn't win, I would fight for him.

SEVENTEEN

As I stared into the ancient, chipped mirror, I almost didn't recognize myself. In the last few years, I'd seen some minor changes in my body. My thinning face, my white-streaked hair, even my slimming waistline gave proof that I was half-vampire, but my physical appearance was not the only change. Mentally and internally, I felt different. My normal self had faded, and a new whirlwind of emotions, senses, and drive fueled who and what I was.

Instead of living in a house of my own, I was living in a castle nestled in the woods in the middle of nowhere. When I lived in society like a normal human, my vampire side had been suppressed by my humanity, but as I lived and associated with vampires, my human side had been the one to be slowly suppressed.

My strength was greater. My vision was sharper, my hearing was vastly keener beyond that of a human, but that was not all. When my dad spoke of adopting abilities, I had no idea how many, and how powerful, these abilities would be. While most people struggled with the ability to read minds, I struggled with suppressing the emotional and mental baggage people and vampires carried. This ability allowed me to not only read what they were feeling, but what they intended to do as well. It was like an inner voice whispering what they were going to do before they did it.

My ability to feel and sense where people were started out small. At first, I could sense them only when they were close, but with time, that ability grew as well. Instead of the muted senses, I could locate them like on a map, but could also place an emotional tag on each one. As my abilities intertwined with each other, so did the power they had on my inner self. It took me a while, but as my perspicacity grew, I found it was powered and controlled by my emotions. The more my emotions were out of balance through stress, fear, sadness, even joy and happiness, the more there was. Everything I felt, thought, and sensed fueled my powers.

I didn't know how or where it came from but bursting the streetlights on the day of Catherine's death had been nothing compared to what I did to the King of the Shadows. I'd held him at bay with nothing but swirling and skin-tingling air. But I had to be careful.

As my powers grew, and I found out what kind of destiny my future held, my emotional state was far from balanced. Finding out that I had to defeat and kill Nicholas, one of the oldest and most feared vampires to ever walk the planet, didn't help.

"Arri? Arri?" my mom's voice chanted as I stared at myself, unblinking, as my mom and Phoenix fiddled and fussed around me.

"Huh?" I asked as I finally pulled myself away from my thoughts.

"Are you okay, dear?"

"Huh? Oh, yeah. I'm fine."

My mom's brow furrowed. My heart warmed at the new look my mom and Phoenix had created for me.

"Oh, Mom, it looks great. I love it," I said, as I bobbed my head from side to side to get a good look at my hair. It had been a little choppy ever since the fight with Sarah—like a cleaner, less-oily grunge look. But now, my mom had cut my hair short and even. She even gave me a few highlights and lowlights to blend in the white streaks that never went away after I visited Nicholas in my nightmares. It was a spunkier and sassier me. Small, wispy bangs breathed over my forehead while the rest was styled into an untamed mess that looked amazing. A diamond-studded headband held back the majority of my unruly curls.

As my mom leaned over me for a maternal hug, she whispered in my ear, "A new look for a new beginning. You look every bit the princess you are and the leader you will be." Her smile was small, almost like she was reminiscing, but the twinkle in her eyes and the love and adoration in her heart, was proof of her pride.

As for Phoenix, tears glimmered in her eyes, which took me aback. Her heart twinged as she watched the exchange between us—mother and daughter.

I didn't know Phoenix's whole story. I only knew a small portion of it through hearsay. Her exact age differed dramatically from story to story, but a few things stayed the same. When she was about sixteen, sometime in the Middle Ages, her mother got really sick. Doctors were sketchy at best during those times, so to get the medication her mother needed, her father had gone as far as selling his daughter to the highest bidder. On the night before she was sold, a group of men trapped Phoenix in an alley and Ash came to her aid. He saved her life. When she woke the next day, she was in Ash's lair and her dad had been paid tenfold for her. The two had been inseparable ever since, but seeing the longing in her eyes now… that tore at my heart.

Phoenix then placed a hand on my shoulder and a shadow of the past fell across her face. Her mind wandered as she thought about her youth. I saw a few flashes of darkened, damp streets, and men watching her as she walked alone. I saw a few of the lascivious faces as they leered at exactly what they wanted. Just when one of the men stepped out of the shadows to obtain her, a man came out from the darkness. His white, unruly hair and his tattooed arms were a cover for his inner nature. After dealing with the men, he grabbed hold of Phoenix and took her from the streets. I could feel her fear as they entered a small house. His demeanor showed no ill will, but there was something dark and unnatural about this man. Then, as if she noticed I was watching, she shook her head, and chased the memory from her mind.

"What do you think? Is it too much?" Phoenix asked, sensing my appraising gaze on her.

I turned to the mirror to examine my makeup. It was nothing dramatic or overdone. I looked just like me. No enhancements or foundation covering my face like an iced-up cake, no blush brushing my cheeks. It was just plain ol' me: mascara and eye shadow with light, barely there, lipstick tinting my lips. That was it.

"There isn't anything that I could do to make you look better. Your beauty alone is enough." With Phoenix's compliment, I smiled. She was not one to hand out compliments very often, if ever.

"Thank you." I hugged her.

"Are you ready?" my mom asked.

I stood up and looked at myself in the full-length mirror. My dress was exquisite: see-through white lace overlayed a white pearlescent silk gown that lightly hugged my frame. Pear-shaped diamonds and pearls were sprinkled delicately throughout the floor-length lace dress. Small-capped sleeves covered my shoulders while white-satin gloves adorned three-quarters the way up my arms. I felt just like Audrey Hepburn in *My Fair Lady*, except with dark brown and white-streaked hair.

With a fortifying breath, I looked at the two women in front of me. My mom was straining with tentative anticipation, as she knew what I was about to do. She smiled at me as happy tears ran down her cheeks. I was going to face the coven and claim my title as Michael's mate.

"Are you ready to go out there and tell the coven who and what you are?" my mom asked, brushing a finger against my cheek.

As a smile curved my lips, I knew this was it. This was the moment where Michael and I would be official in the coven's eyes.

"Yes, I am," I said with confidence and poise. I raised my chin, let out a nervous breath, then turned to the door.

On the other side of that door was an entirely new future waiting for me. As Michael's girlfriend, the coven had given me a bit of a wide berth, but as his mate, I would be seen as a leader rather than a half-breed.

I opened the old wooden door and took a few tentative steps out into the hallway before stopping. The banister that separated me from the foyer danced in the candlelight of the chandelier. The room below was aglow in lights that somehow managed to make the space look warm and inviting rather than unappealing and harsh.

"Ahem." Michael cleared his throat.

I faced him. His tailored suit alone made my mouth water. In my eyes, Michael was and always would be handsome. His wavy brown hair, green eyes, and masculine build made me weak at the knees even in casual clothes. But put him in a suit and I was done for.

"I'm sorry, but your beauty has stolen all my words." Michael stared at me in amazement. His eyes were glazed over, and his smile showed he more than approved.

"You don't look too bad yourself." I attempted to stay calm and collected, but instead, my voice was soft and throaty.

A knowing smile curved his lips as he offered me an arm.

"Your escorts are awaiting you at the top of the stairs," Michael said as he gently took my hand in his. He kissed the back of my hand with a smile.

"You look stunning." His words were a soft caress of his affection. "Shall we?" he asked, gesturing to where my mom and Phoenix had just disappeared.

Phoenix's head descended below the banister, and strains of idle conversation whisked through the air as she made her grand entrance. The crowd clapped and commented on her beauty. Phoenix was wearing a floor-length dress in emerald-green silk that hugged her figure but complimented her wild side with the subtle lines of her signature black lace corset. Her hair was pinned up in silken curls. In short, she was beautiful.

Then there was Ash, and as always, Ash was Ash. Although he wore a black and green tailored suit to match Phoenix, the sleeves were torn out, with frayed edges leaving his tattoos visible. Only he and Phoenix could pull off the edgy look and still make it elegant and classy.

As the two of them neared the bottom of the stairs, a man with a staff stopped just in front of them. He raised his staff slightly and pounded it down twice with a thump, thump. At this, the coven quieted.

"Introducing Monsieur Ash and Lady Phoenix," he boomed throughout the large but packed foyer below. The crowd bowed to them.

Then, with a wink over her shoulder, my mom and dad started their descent. As my mom's red hair vanished below my eyeline and down the stairs, Michael and I edged up to the end of the hallway so I could see her, but not be seen myself. Her purple dress trailed behind her as she made her way down the last few stairs. My mom was beautiful beyond measure. Her beauty was more than physical. Internally, she was just as stunning, so her dress didn't need to compliment her. The easy flow of the purple silk outlined her in a flattering way. See-through glossy lace fell over the silk. No beads, just a design stitched in the lace, along with shimmering diamonds that shined when she moved. Just as with Phoenix, the room murmured at her beauty and applauded quietly.

"Introducing Lord Steven and Lady Ava," the maître d' said as he thumped his staff on the floor.

Michael turned to me. With a hopeful look on his face, he leaned in and kissed me gently but sensually. The kiss was just enough to dull the fear I had billowing inside.

"I know this is new for you, and I know you are terrified—I can feel it. But this is about more than presenting yourself to the coven. This is where your inner leader will start to shine, the one that has always been inside you."

With a simple kiss on my nose, Michael pulled away and smiled at me with encouragement and love. "Are you ready?" he asked, as he offered me his arm.

With a deep, fortifying breath, I nodded, and the two of us turned the corner.

I wasn't sure what I had been expecting when Michael said we were having a ball, but this was nothing compared to what I'd envisioned. I'd pictured a bright room lit to the fullest with large and gaudy floral arrangements scattered about. I'd imagined several tables off to the side, one with a gigantic punch bowl and enough finger foods and delectable desserts to feed a small country. Another would have an ice sculpture of two connecting swans and fruit and veggie platters lining the lace and silk tablecloths.

But as I stood at the top of the stairwell, my heart stopped.

This was far better than anything I ever could have imagined. Instead of harsh, bright lighting, what looked and felt like hundreds, if not thousands and thousands, of candles lit the manor. Chandeliers and sconces provided the quaint lighting. Not too bright, but beyond the normal brightness I saw on a day-to-day basis.

Small, quiet, and unobtrusive bouquets of white lilies, daisies, and wisteria were scattered throughout the room. The wood floor had been polished enough to show the reflection of each and every person who stood upon it.

Then there was the coven. Most were dressed in dark and obscure colors like black, navy blue, and red, with some in purple and gray. But the colors weren't what caught my attention. It was the time period in which they dressed. It was a menagerie with everyone dressed in whatever era made them happy, just like usual, except now, they were in elegant spins. Slick gowns curved over their shapes, accentuating their form. Others wore bushy dresses adorned with gaudy pearls. Every style of dress ever worn over time littered the rooms.

The men all wore suits, cummerbunds, and tuxes that complimented their mate's dresses. But most impressive of all was the number of coven members attending the ball. Normally, there were approximately sixty or seventy coven members that littered the halls and outer gardens, but here and now, members spilled from the foyer and into the adjoining rooms. The throne room doors were open, revealing the faint outlines of members as they strained to get a glimpse. The library, the ballroom… it looked like every room on the main floor had been stuffed to the brim.

For a moment, I paused at the top of the stairs, paralyzed. For some reason, I didn't think that this many people would attend, but here they were, all muted into a reverent silence. Gasps and awestruck faces all stared up at me in amazement. Light whispers and mummers of praise drifted through the room in hushed, low voices.

"Are you okay?" Michael asked. He patted the hand I had in

the crook of his arm with his free hand, in encouragement.

Not trusting my voice in the slightest, I took a calming breath, and gave him a warm and affectionate smile that I hoped conveyed what I felt.

There was no doubt that I was scared to death, but it was an exciting kind of scared. It was the kind of scared that put butterflies in your stomach, made your heart race, and lit you up with tingles of anticipation.

"Good," Michael said as he took the first step and guided me down along with him. With each step we took, the excitement grew until we reached the bottom where the maître d' stood awaiting our approach. After a low and respectful bow, he stood tall.

"Ladies and gentleman, it is my great privilege to introduce to you our Arch Leaders: Lord and Lady Michael London. Our District Leaders and Coven Masters." With his words, the entire coven took a knee. Men in tuxes, women in gowns, it didn't matter, everyone knelt on the floor.

There were no cheers. There were no gasps or opposing words. Everyone accepted us as their Arch Leaders with pride and honor. Then, when all were bowed, my dad rose and pinned a medal with Michael's crest and the covens coat of arms on Michael's suit coat showing his authority, and my mom placed a small silver diadem on me. My eyes welled up with tears—the good kind.

I stood at the base of the stairs, and as everyone knelt, a feeling of respect and dignity washed over me. At this very moment, I realized what it meant to be a leader. As each person bowed, they were entrusting us with their lives and safety, and in return, they were promising their loyalty to Michael and me.

I stood taller and raised my chin, pushing away any and all doubts, as the room got to its feet. With that, Michael and I joined the party.

As the two of us walked forward, the room parted like the Red Sea. Everyone stood aside.

"What are Arch leaders exactly?" I whispered.

Michael laughed lightly. "It's a fancy name for us because I serve as both District Leader and Coven Master." Michael leaned into me and kissed the top of my head.

I walked past a few of the guests and could hear a few comments and compliments on my dress, but when I saw one face in particular, I about started to cry.

The tired and worn eyes, the ashen skin, the wrinkles of age and wisdom, everything about this face broke my heart.

"My dear, Arri," the older woman said as I approached her. Her hand shook just about as bad as her voice.

"Nana," I gushed as I reached for her. Her frail and fragile body just about fell to pieces as I held her. Her light hugs tugged at my heart. "You're here. I didn't know if you'd come. You left so suddenly that I was afraid something terrible had happened," I said, looking deep into her eyes. The dark circles around them proved she was overtired and weary. I only wished I could do something to help her.

As concern creased my brow, her cold and icy grip on my hand tightened.

"He never returned," she whispered, trying to reassure me.

My mind spun back to the day that I had my first vision of Gavin using Nana as a food source. The anger and venom I felt helped fuel me the day I fought and killed him.

"Arri, dear. Are you with us?" Nana's voice shook with humor.

I smiled down at her and hugged her one more time. I knew a few coven members were waiting for a turn with Michael and me.

"Now go on, dear. Your future awaits you," Nana said, pushing me back toward the coven, but before she hurt herself trying to nudge me away, I looked at her one last time.

"Go," she encouraged. "You are the one being celebrated today. This wonderful party was thrown in your honor. I am very proud of you. I know I'm not one of you, but I pledge myself to you and your mate Arch Leaders Lord Michael and Lady Arri." Nana tried to bow, but in her brittle state, she almost fell to the floor. But as her knees gave out, she didn't have a chance to fall; Michael and I both braced ourselves against her and held her up.

"Come now, Nana. Please, let's find you a seat," Michael's endearing voice whispered as a slight pink hue crept up her neck and onto her cheeks.

As Michael walked the feeble woman out of the main crowd to a small niche in the corner of the room, the coven surrounded and closed in on me.

"Oh, Arri!" "Hello, my lady!" "Good evening, my lady!" People sang praises and rained compliments on my appearance, but when Lena and Tack made their way through the crowd, their words meant more to me than the ones telling me how great I looked.

"My dear, Lady Arri," the two of them said in unison as they bowed their heads. "It is my honor to serve you." As they raised their heads, I noticed the room had gone quiet, and all eyes were on me.

I smiled at them and spoke with a shaky voice.

"The honor is mine. There is no greater honor than the one bestowed by this coven in accepting me as a leader today. So thank you. The honor really is all mine." With a small bow of my head, I smiled up at the astounded crowd.

From the corner of my eye, I could see the pride in Michael for both the loyalty his coven had shown me and the way that I addressed the situation. I had told him once that a leader—was no better than his or her people, and today, I hoped I'd proven it.

For the next hour or so, I mingled among the covens. As I meandered around, meeting and greeting members and Coven Masters, the room had become more relaxed. It was good to talk to some of the members I hadn't met yet. Their take on adopting me as Michael's mate and new leader surprised me. Many were all for a change in leadership, claiming that Nicholas's reign was long overdue to end. Others were excited to hear that the new power had finally come, and to have me as Michael's mate and Arch Leader was just an added bonus.

"Oh, my dear." Nana's fragile voice barely carried over the muted murmuring of the coven. "I am so happy to have been present for such an event. I have no doubt that you will be the leader I know you are. I knew you were going to be a force to be reckoned with the moment you tried to stand your ground that first day. I knew then that you, my dear, would and could not only conquer the world, but conquer it with force and grace. Take care, my dear. You are destined for more than you give yourself credit for. Just remember, even fate needs a little nudge in the right direction to bring you to the heights beyond your destiny."

Accepting a few light pats on the cheek, Michael escorted her out of the front doors to a car waiting for her.

As she stepped into the car, I wanted to cry. Seeing her looking so old and frail killed me. The Nana I knew was strong, but the woman I'd just seen was nowhere near the stubborn woman of only a year ago. As her small, bony hand slipped from Michael's grip, I prayed that I would see her again.

I tore myself away from the sight and forced myself to join the rest of the party. Since the coronation, Michael and I had been inseparable. As we each took turns addressing the members who approached us to wish us happiness on the mating and luck as rulers, we fell into a mutual rhythm. But what I noticed most was the difference in the way the members felt. It wasn't anything negative, but their emotional state changed and differed from one member to the next. The members who Michael and I saw on a more frequent basis felt more comfortable around us, and notably more comfortable around me. As Michael introduced me to the Coven Masters and members from the outer rim of his territory, they seemed twitchy, quite agitated around the closed confines of Michael's castle. It was as if they felt the need to flee from me—or devour me. As if they couldn't make up their minds.

"Good evening, my lord, my lady," a member greeted us as we approached her.

"Good evening, Abby," Michael addressed her. "I assume your travels were pleasant?" he asked as she nervously glanced around. When she didn't answer, Michael smiled politely before greeting another.

"Who are you looking for?" I asked as I read her wants and emotions.

Abby stared at me with confusion.

"Oh, I didn't think I told you I was looking for anybody. I'm just admiring the wonderful decorations," she lied as her heart practically quaked with concern.

"You didn't. Let's just say that it is a small talent of mine. I sensed your concern. Who are you supposed to be meeting?" I asked with a smile.

Abby's shoulders fell, as she knew I was right.

"I'm sorry. I should be greeting and congratulating you as my lady instead of concerning you with my problems." Her eyes grew sad.

I leaned in toward the girl and whispered, "It's no problem. To be honest, I have been circling this room for hours and might have seen your friend."

With great hesitation, she sighed.

"I'm looking for Jonathan. He's a werewolf," she added. My heart fell to my toes.

I bit back tears, trying to stay strong for not only her, but for me, too. So far that night, I had pushed back the thoughts that had haunted me for the last two days. Knowing that they were at least alive was a big help. I knew they were. I had seen them in my visions. But how was I supposed to tell her that Jonathan had been captured by Nicholas and his men and was being tortured to find my weakness?

Just as I was about to open my mouth and tell her that I hadn't seen him, the room went quiet. No one moved. No one breathed. Members at the beverage table stood like statues with their wine glasses halfway to their mouths. The ones dancing stopped mid-stride as they stared at the doors to the throne room.

I glanced over my shoulder to what was causing everyone such panic, and then I relaxed, letting out a pent-up breath and dropping my guard. A smile spread across my face.

The way that everyone was acting, I had half-expected Nicholas to be standing in the doorway, but the person I saw was much better.

"Jakob," I said, making my way through the crowd to the rather large man standing just inside the throne room doors.

"Lady Arri," Jakob said, as he and his men bowed their heads slightly.

"Hi! I'm glad you came. Thank you for accepting my invitation," I said, smiling up at the man that just a few weeks or so ago saved my life by defeating his ruler Nizari.

When Nizari had attempted to kill me as a puppet of Nicholas's, Jakob stopped him by beheading him in front of all of Michael's coven.

As I looked around the room, I realized I had forgotten how the vampires saw the Shadows. Originally, they were assassins or contract killers, but as vampires evolved, so did they. Now, they were the secret keepers of the vampire world. The purpose of their existence was to clean up the messes and damage done by less careful and more aggressive vampires. They were said to hold no prejudices toward humans or vampires, and I tended to agree, because Jakob had saved my life.

"Is everything all right?" Michael asked as he came to my side.

"Yes. Everything is fine. Jakob and his men are here by invitation, and I am happy they could make it."

Michael's brows knit together as a small smile spread across his face.

"Yes, I remember. Arri was so concerned you wouldn't make it to the celebration." Michael squeezed my hand, but he was right. When I had first brought up the idea of us inviting them as friends, but also as a way to reach out to them in case we needed them to defeat Nicholas, Michael had been pretty hesitant. In the end, I sent the invitations regardless. Something told me that what Jakob did in the throne room that day had been more than just defending me. There was something more going on within the Shadows, and my defiance to Nizari had tipped the scale.

"If you'd prefer, we could leave," Jakob said without emotion. But truth be told, I wanted them to stay.

"No, of course not. Please, stay, eat, drink, and mingle. I invited you as guests. It would be an insult if you left," I said through a smile. For a moment, I thought I had offended him, but when he relaxed and smiled down at me, I knew all was well. Then he did something unfathomable. He hugged me. Then he and his men joined the party.

For the next half hour, I mingled under the close, watchful eye of Jakob. He was always close by, watching me connect with and appease members that floated by.

"Arri," Michael whispered in my ear. "It's time for one last announcement. Then the party will be over."

After leading me to the small platform stage at the far end of the room, the maître d' thrummed his staff on the hollow wooden floor of the platform.

"If I may have your attention," he announced as members stuffed and jammed themselves into the throne room. "It is my honor to introduce the Arch Leaders Lord and Lady Michael London one last time. Lord Michael and Lady Arri, Arch Leaders, District Leaders, and Coven Masters."

Michael and I took a step forward, and the coven bowed. As everyone rose, the Shadows made their way through the room.

"Yes?" Michael asked as they approached the platform and bowed their heads.

"If we may?" Jakob asked.

"You may," Michael agreed as they stood at our feet.

"As King of the Shadows, and on behalf of my brothers, we pledge our loyalty to you and your reign as Arch Leaders."

The room quieted.

Each Shadow took out his sword, held it by the hilt, and lowered himself to his knees. They pledged themselves to Michael and me—making it known, in front of everyone, that their allegiance was with us.

EIGHTEEN

I cried out in excruciating pain as the sword sunk into my chest. As if the metal sticking out from my back was not proof enough that he had killed me, Nicholas shoved the sword in further, until the tip of the blade hit the floor and the hilt pressed firmly against my spine. Nicholas held nothing back.

"You were born of a traitor, and you will die by my hand!" Nicholas's roar of triumph echoed through the silent room.

No one fought. No one moved. The room was quiet as they all stared at me in unbelieving reticence. I had failed. The pain ripping through me was proof.

As the room became blurry and the light that bathed the room in color faded, I struggled against the pain.

"Arri." Michael's concerned voice sounded just as panicked as I felt. "Arri." His voice rang with urgency.

My gaze fell to the red-stained marble floors, and I cried.

"I'm sorry," I whispered as my body went limp. The sword that had pierced me through the heart was yanked out and thrown just inches from me, my blood coating the blade.

Thump-thump… thump-thump…

I could hear the slowing of my heart as death seeped its way through me.

Thump…

Then there was nothing. There was no more beating of my heart. The sound of blood pumping through my veins ceased, and the tears that burned my eyes stopped falling as I lay there waiting for the sweet, merciful hands of death to lift me from my agony.

"I have won," Nicholas bellowed as his men cheered. "I have beaten

the chosen one, the prodigy. Now, no one stands between me and my throne!" he yelled, pride and egotistical satisfaction dripping from his words.

"Arri? Arri!" A firm hand rested on my shoulder. Then I felt as though I were in Michael's sweet embrace.

"Arri!" Michael's voice grew louder as I struggled against the pain of death.

The fact that I could still hear Michael's voice through all the chaos made my death bittersweet. What better way to die than to hear my love's voice echoing through my heart?

"Arri!" A sudden jolt woke me from my sleep. A piercing scream erupted out of me as I sat up,. The lingering pain of Nicholas's sword still cut through me as if it were fresh.

"Arri." Michael's hands gripped my cheeks as he struggled to get my attention.

I blinked against the bright light. The sun basked the room in the early light of dawn. Rainbows and stars floated around me as the rays of sun hit the stained-glass window.

"Are you okay?" Michael asked, wiping at the tears that streaked my cheeks.

I took a few calming breaths and nodded.

"What happened? Are you hurt?" Michael gestured to my hands, which were still clutching my chest. The pain and agony of the sword as it ripped through me still tainted me.

"I think I'm okay." I placed a hand to where the sword had pierced me. Even through my pajama shirt I could feel the raised and bruised mark it had left.

Michael looked me straight in the eyes. His gaze seemed to pierce my soul and read my every emotion.

I shook my head.

"No, I'm not okay. I don't like the feeling of carrying this burden alone."

"But you're not alone," he said. "We are all here for you."

"No, not really," I said. "Well, kind of."

"I don't understand. We are all training to fight alongside you." His heart was tinged with hurt.

"I know, and you are all so great, but I'll have to face him alone. I've seen it." I gestured to the bed where just a few minutes ago I lay down. My nightmare reminded me of my imminent death. "I've seen it. I've felt it. I think we both know that I have to face him alone."

Michael pressed my open palm to his chest, right over his heart.

"You will never be alone."

A smile spread across my face as I leaned my forehead against his. "I know. I'm just afraid."

"Afraid of what? You are the most powerful being I know."

"Yeah, but I'm still scared to death. I don't think I have the courage to defeat him." My heart broke. I was telling the truth. I didn't have the courage to face Nicholas. In my dreams, it was different. He was fictional, a projection. But in real life, I had felt the effects of what he was capable of and what he would do to kill me.

"You're mistaken." Michael tilted my chin up until I met his gaze. "Courage, bravery, and fearlessness—these are not the only makings of a hero. Heroism is also facing your enemy, especially when the odds are against you. It is standing up for what's right, no matter how many oppose you. As a human and a vampire, you are not beyond any of those emotions. Neither are your mom, your dad, or I. Ever since I met you, I have lived my life in fear."

I blinked in confusion. "I'd never hurt you."

"No, I know, but it is not the fear of you hurting me. It is the fear of losing you. In the many centuries I have lived, I have never coveted anything so special," leaning down, his lips brushed mine, "and I have no intention of losing you."

As he cradled me in his embrace, my nightmare became a thing of the past. I loved Michael with everything I was, and the fact that he was scared of losing me made me want to fight all the harder to keep my life.

"You know…" He paused when I looked up at him. "You've told me about your nightmares. I've seen how you die. But maybe, if I knew when, I could change it. Stop the outcome." Michael brushed a few stray hairs out of my face. "Can you tell me more about them? Maybe parts I haven't seen?" His eyes pleaded with me to trust him.

"Well, it all starts at the entrance of an old, abandoned mine shaft…"

As I told Michael what I had seen, he waited patiently, watching me as I talked and paced. The more I told him, the more I could feel his heart tighten in anger. When I told him of the torture, he all but came undone. Then, as the story came to my death, Michael was so furious that I knew his control was close to snapping.

During the whole thing, it was as if I were back in bed, having another nightmare. I saw everything, felt everything. With each piece I told, I closed my eyes and saw it as if it were real. The vivid lines of the corridors, the sounds of his men jeering, I saw it all, and I also knew it was just a matter of time before I saw it again when I closed my eyes and let my mental shield slip away as I slept.

"Come here, sweetheart." Michael held out his hand.

I stared at it for a moment. My emotions and visions were still so close to the surface. I didn't want to hurt him.

With a gentle smile, Michael coaxed me closer to him, but as my hand touched his, his body jerked, his eyes slipped closed, and he gasped as if I had shocked him. When I went to pull away, he gripped my hand tightly, frozen.

"Michael?" I whispered when his eyes finally opened and his grip loosened. "What's wrong? What happened? Did I hurt you?" I asked, panicked and scared.

"No, you didn't hurt me," Michael said as he pulled me into his arms.

"What happened?" I was so scared that I had hurt him. I tugged at my hand and wiggled to free myself, but it was no use against him. He only held me tighter as I fought.

"I saw it." Michael opened his mouth to say more, but nothing came out. He shook his head.

I stopped fighting and hung my head, but his hands never left me. He held onto me as if it would stop the fight from happening, like he was protecting me from it.

When I opened my eyes, Michael was staring back down at me. There were tears in his eyes and sadness and fear embedded in his heart.

"You don't have to hold this inside," Michael said as he tucked my hair behind my ear.

While I told him what I'd seen—the pain, the humiliation, and the fear—I felt everything come rushing back to the surface.

"You'll never have to go through it alone. Is this why you have been training in the gym and keeping me at arm's length?"

I nodded. I hadn't wanted him to know. He didn't want me to go through it alone, and I didn't want to burden him. Every day I carried around the knowledge that I would die. I didn't want him to carry around the same weight. He was Coven Master, and now he was also their Arch Leader. It didn't feel right adding my death to his never-ending list of responsibilities.

"I'm sorry. I don't want you to live with the fear that I do."

"You don't have to live in fear. I won't let it happen."

I tried to put on a brave face, but I knew the truth. Nothing was going to stop this from happening.

A soft knock at the door broke the silence.

"Enter," Michael's commanding tone barked.

"Excuse me, sire." A very nervous Lena poked her head in the room. "I'm sorry to interrupt you, but," Lena bowed her head in surrender, "there are a few men here to see Arri. They are not ours, sire." Lena rushed the news out as she physically cringed.

"Show them into the library. I'll be there shortly." Michael's emotionless tone sent chills down my spine.

"Yes, sire," Lena said. She closed the door behind her.

"Are you expecting company?" Michael asked with a smile in his voice.

"Not today," I said, playfully narrowing my eyes at him.

"I mean it, Arri. You don't have to go through this alone. I will always be there for you," Michael said as he placed his hand over my heart. "I'm always here."

"I know. I love you too."

"Well, then. Let's see who is so eager to see you."

As Michael and I walked hand in hand down the stairs and through the very large foyer, the coven bowed and curtsied before us.

"Your Majesty," Rogan and Terrish said as they approached us, kneeling on one knee.

"Rogan, Terrish," Michael greeted them as he nodded, giving them permission to stand.

"My lord, we respectfully ask to join you and Lady Arri into the library. I know these men, and although we have disarmed them, it will not stop them from trying to attack you or Arri." Terrish bowed his head then looked back up to us.

As I stared at the door behind Terrish and Rogan, I could sense a whole lot of anger and violent rage coming from the other side.

"Granted." Michael's simple one-word answer spoke volumes as he looked at me.

"Anger?" he questioned as my heart beat double time.

"No. Fear," I said, shaking my head and letting out a long, deep breath.

"No. Them, not you. I can already feel your fear."

"Your bond will strengthen you," I mumbled under my breath, remembering something I had once heard in relation to the texts of the prophecy.

"I beg your pardon?" Rogan paused at the doors.

A smile curved Michael's lips. He knew what I meant.

"Are you ready for this?" Michael asked as he squeezed my hand in reassurance.

"Ready," I said as Rogan and Terrish threw open the large doors. They clamored against the wall before slamming shut behind us. The two vampires standing front and center in the room looked unaffected and unamused.

"State your business," Michael demanded as he took a step forward and gently tugged me behind him.

As Michael read their emotions through me, he had already

anticipated their attack. The tall, dark one on the left folded his arms in front of him, and the other gradually rocked back and forth on the balls of his feet, like a caged wrestler waiting to be released. Then, with lightning speed, the one on the left grabbed the wrestler's arm and flung him at us. The attack couldn't have been premeditated, because as they launched their ambush, Rogan and Terrish were waiting for them.

In a heartbeat, Rogan had lunged at the wrestler and slammed him to the floor, forcing him to his knees. The tall, dark man growled and charged us, but he made it only a few steps before Terrish took him down. It wasn't much of a fight, but it was enough to make my heart skip a few beats.

As the two men were captured and forced to their knees, they glared at me in disgust, small daggers held firmly in their hands.

"I thought you had disarmed them?" Michael asked, shaking his head at Terrish.

"I thought I had," Terrish said as he rubbed his chin absently.

"The coat of arms," I said, pointing to where a shield hung as decoration on the wall. It had a bear painted on it with two real daggers crossed above it. "They must have improvised," I said, studying the two men kneeling at our feet.

"What made you think you were going to accomplish what every one of Nicholas's men so far have not?" Michael said, chuckling. "If the King of the Shadows couldn't kill her, what makes you think you could?"

The two men had the nerve to look insulted after pulling a stupid stunt like that.

"It was worth a try," the wrestler said, struggling under Rogan's sword.

"Since we both know you were not sent here to pull a lame stunt like trying to kill Lady Arri," the two men rolled their eyes at my title, "while she was guarded by her own coven with two of the best-known swordsmen at her side, then what are you here for?" Michael asked, still holding me partially behind him.

"Answer him!" Terrish bellowed after a long silence. Neither of the men wanted to talk.

"Traitor," the tall, dark one snorted as he glared up at Terrish.

"Brave words, considering we hold the swords," Michael said, taking Terrish's blade from him and pressing it harder against the vampire's skin. Small droplets of blood trickled down his neck.

"So, tell us. Why are you here?" Michael demanded as he returned the sword to Terrish.

"We're here to deliver the mutt a message." At the word mutt, Terrish growled and made a small gash across the wrestler's throat.

The wrestler clenched his jaw and howled out in pain.

"You will address her as my lady or Lady Arri, you mangy cretin," Terrish bit out.

"Thank you for your respect," I said to Terrish, resting a hand on his shoulder.

I turned back to the wrestler and glowered at him. "What is the message?"

"See, even she knows what she is," he said, trying to lean back and away from the vampire holding a sword to his throat. With the first strike being the attack, and the second being him calling me a mutt, I would have thought that he'd gotten the message, but apparently not.

"How many does it take to deliver a message?" Terrish asked Rogan.

"One," Rogan responded, a smile curving his lips.

"Wait, what?" the tall dark man asked as he eyed his friend.

"My lord?" Terrish asked Michael.

With a single nod, Michael turned around and faced me as Terrish carried out his orders.

The whistle of metal whisking through the air and the thud that followed told me what happened.

Michael spun around, trying to shield me from the mess that lay before me, but couldn't. My stomach turned, and I covered my mouth with my hand.

"So, what have you? Are you ready to talk?" Michael asked, his voice stern and cold.

The wrestler said nothing. The seconds ticked by slowly as we waited for his answer, but there wasn't one.

"So be it," Michael announced as he took my hand and escorted me to the library doors.

"Wait," the man pleaded, fear rocking through him. "I'll talk, but don't kill me."

"A little late to be making demands, isn't it?" Rogan snickered.

"If you kill me, you won't hear the message," he tried to bargain.

"Yes, but who is to say that you even made it here?" Rogan countered.

"Look, Nicholas's men are waiting for me. If I don't return with an answer, they will storm your castle."

"So what's the message?" I asked, turning around to face the fearful captive. My eyes were already burning knowing it had something to do with my surrender, as if it had worked in the past.

"It's Nicholas." He paused, choosing his words carefully.

"Yes, we know. What of him?" Michael yelled, losing his patience.

"He said to tell her that her time is up. He has already warned Lady Arri that he would come if she didn't surrender. I'm here now to accept her surrender or warn her of the consequences."

I chuckled and rolled my eyes. "I'm not surrendering," I stated, holding my head high and standing up straight.

"Then your friends will die. Do you really want their blood on your hands?"

"He won't kill them. They are the only leverage he has to make her come willingly," Michael said, not feeling too sure himself.

"Oh, but he can, and he will." The wrestler sounded so sure and cocky that I wanted to slap him.

"And why would I trust his word that he will release them once he has me?"

"What makes you think that he will not kill them if you don't surrender?"

It was the ultimate catch-22. With flashbacks of what I knew Nicholas had in store for me, I hung my head.

"She will make no decision now." Michael's nostrils flared as he felt and saw my flashbacks.

As long as we were touching, or holding each other, he was susceptible to feel and see what I did.

"There is no time," the wrestler barked. "If she doesn't surrender to me, then his men will come and get her."

"Then let them come!" Michael roared, his voice bouncing off the walls and shaking the picture frames.

NINETEEN

We drew the coven's attention when we left the library. As we stepped through the door, the wrestler realized that we were not coming back, and that there was a good possibility that he would be killed as soon as Michael turned his head. The wrestler's panicked voice echoed off the foyer walls as he tried to call out to Michael and me.

"Michael," I said, lowering my voice to a muted whisper, "he'll kill them."

Panic and fear rocked through me at the possibility that Jonathan's and Alex's deaths would be on my hands.

"No, he won't." Michael tried to reassure me as he placed a hand on my cheek. "He needs you, and in order to get you, he needs them."

"I don't know, Michael. Nicholas doesn't exactly play by the rules."

I knew that for a fact. Nicholas had proved that he would practically burn the planet down if it got him what he wanted.

"No, he doesn't, but that doesn't mean he's crazy. Nicholas knows what he's doing. I know his tactics may seem outrageous, but I assure you they're not. Everything Nicholas has done up to this point has been calculated and strategic. The attacks and the mishaps were planned in the knowledge that there was a possibility he would fail. In this, he has been methodical." His face contorted into anger as he spoke.

"Michael!" The wrestler's cry carried out of the library. "Michael!" His voice grew urgent and panicked as we ignored his pleas. "Mark my words. Nicholas holds no tolerance for insolence and arrogance. If your foul-blooded young mate doesn't surrender, then Nicholas will send his men out to retrieve her, and his orders are to kill anyone who gets in their way."

When he said "foul-blooded," Michael lost it. He ran back into the library, drew his sword, and gently slid it across the wrestler's neck.

"I will only warn you once; watch your speech. If one more offensive word, name, or gesture comes from you, I will mail your head back to your beloved leader. Am I clear?" Michael asked, his sword pressed firmly against the wrestler's skin. Blood dripped onto the floor.

"I am not in a gaming mood," Michael went on. "Your leader has declared war just so he might obtain a young vampire who threatens to overrule him. Arri may be the prodigy spoken of in the prophecy, but Nicholas created the threat she poses. So, tell me, what has this leader of yours promised? Freedom, glory and assurance as he sends you to your death, knowing that you won't live with the praises?" Michael asked, gesturing.

The wrestler's head bowed as two guards that he had no chance of beating held him, and Michael slid a sword against his neck.

"Is this the glory you had in mind? Is this the freedom you wanted?"

The wrestler lowered his head further as he looked away from Michael.

Michael dropped the sword tip at the wrestler's knees and shook his head.

"I thought so. Too bad no one will see the bravery you showed here today."

Michael faced me, and without looking back, he called to Rogan over his shoulder. "Take him to the basement. I don't want the coven to hear his poisonous words."

I was surprised to hear Michael tell Rogan to take him downstairs.

"Wait, we have a dungeon?"

I was curious. Was there a guillotine? Was Michael going to kill him, or keep him captive like Nicholas was keeping my friends?

Rogan smirked and shook his head as he dragged the struggling wrestler out of the library.

"Are you ready?" Michael asked. He took my hand and escorted me up the stairs.

Neither of us spoke as we ascended the grand staircase. The only sound was my hollow footsteps against the hardwood floors, each step sounding more and more haunted as we made our way up the stairwell.

As we came to a stop in front of Michael's door, Michael looked a little timid and apprehensive. With a shy smile, Michael opened his bedroom door and stepped back to let me through.

As I entered Michael's room, a smile crept across my face.

"I know we never really discussed you moving in with me, but… what do you think?" Michael's voice cracked with anxiety.

I stood still and silent as I looked around the room. Michael had thought of everything. He made me my own vanity in the corner near the bathroom. I had a little over half the closet, although I still didn't have that many clothes. My new wardrobe was definitely bolder and more daring, with the loose-fitting pants, pirate shirts, and corsets. But even with the new additions, I only took up a little under a quarter of the closet. Michael had the room painted and had moved his clothing into his section of the closet.

The longer I stood silently taking in the space that he had created for both of us, the more his heart tightened.

"If you don't like it, I can move everything back," he said, staring down at his shoes.

"No, it's great," I gushed as I closed the distance between us and kissed him long and deep. As the two of us embraced, I felt our bond grow profoundly intense. I could feel his deepest wants, his darkest secrets, and his most desired thoughts. We were one. With great difficulty, I felt Michael mentally inching away before he broke our bond. As he pulled away from me, Michael smiled. With honesty in his eyes, and hope in his heart, he gazed at me as if his soul was laid bare, waiting for me to answer.

"Is that a yes, you like it? Or is this a backwards way of saying you hate it?" Michael teased as he brushed his thumb over my cheek.

"It's a yes," I said, in a whisper, as I relished his touch. The softness as his thumb traced along my skin and the tenderness in the gesture told me everything without words. It told me he cherished me. It told me he loved me. It told me he'd never leave me. He was my trust, my wonderful, my safe. He was my… everything.

"You are beautiful beyond words, Arri. I am amazed. At each trial you face, and with Nicholas testing you at every turn, your inner beauty grows to match your outer beauty. I do love you, sweetheart," Michael said as he leaned down and kissed my forehead.

It was a simple but priceless gesture that meant the world to me.

With a shy smile, I blushed and looked away, embarrassed.

"Thank you. I love you too."

"Oh, here. I'll be right back, my love. I almost forgot." As Michael zipped out of the room, I sat on the bench next to one of the windows. I stared out over the expanse of his yard and chuckled.

Michael definitely had the best room in the house. He faced the north mountains, and as the sun touched the tree line, it lit up the branches like the boughs of a Christmas tree. Light bounced off the several gem-like stones in the walkway that remained invisible at ground level. The leaves swayed in the lightest of breezes and played with the rhythm of the shining and shimmering gems. It really was amazing. The same midday sun shone through the treetops, kissed the top of the stained-glass windows, and cast subtle but vibrant shapes and shadows throughout the room. As the light danced and swayed, the shadows rocked and darted out of the light's path, then, as the light chased back, the shadows grew and shifted until they engulfed the room entirely.

Shocked, I stood still in the darkness.

There was something off about what had just happened. For a moment, I debated whether or not I wanted to wait for Michael to return, or dare go out and find him, but then I heard a voice. It wasn't Michael's.

It was the foul, wretched, husky voice of Nicholas. His temper rippled through space and time in waves.

"I will ask you one more time. What is her weakness? How do I defeat the self-proclaimed prodigy?" Nicholas asked as his anger grew. "Answer me, you mutt," Nicholas growled.

A sizzling sound pierced the daunting silence and a man howled out in agony. His yell erupted through the empty caverns, bouncing off walls and echoing down the deserted chambers.

As the darkness weighed down on me, panic set in. The heavy, damp, and stale air choked me, and a deep horror settled on me. Nicholas was torturing the boys. It wasn't just sleep deprivation. By the sound and smell that permeated the room, he was branding them.

Tears welled up in my eyes and silent gasps and sobs broke through my strength and broke my heart.

As the room vaguely brightened, it looked blurred and distorted through my tears, but I knew exactly where I was. I was in Nicholas's lair. I've been here before in the many visions I've had.

I tried to take one step at a time toward the man screaming in pain, but my body froze. My feet wouldn't walk. I was scared stiff. It wasn't that I was scared because I didn't know where I was or what I was going to find. I was scared because I did know where I was and whom I was walking toward—but mostly because I knew exactly what I was going to find.

As I tried to quiet my uncontrollable sobbing, I felt Michael's arms snake their way around me.

"Arri?" Michael's faint words whispered in the background of my mind.

"Tell me!" Nicholas's voice raked against my skin as he yelled at Alex and Jonathan.

They were just a few doors down, but even so, I knew the boys were scared. I closed my eyes and tried to distance myself emotionally from their pain, but I wasn't fast enough. Their mental and physical suffering bled right through my defenses and killed me two times over. What I felt was disturbing. They were mentally begging for death. With every wound Nicholas inflicted, Alex and Jonathan's fight for life died.

"I'm here, Arri." Michael's voice whispered in my ear. "I'm right beside you." He squeezed my hand.

Physically, I was still safe and sound in Michael's and my room, but mentally, I was thousands of miles away. Most of Nicholas's lair was still a mystery to me. I didn't know if he was settled inside a mountain somewhere, hidden from the world at large, or if he was perched on a hilltop, living in riches as he pilfered off the village below him. Either way, he was a danger to everyone.

I breathed in deeply and released it slowly, trying to summon courage for what I was about to face. Nicholas is growing desperate, and I'll bet that his patience is just about gone. Which means, ready or not, we're closer to the war than we thought.

With a few more steps toward the stench of burning flesh, I paused in the doorway.

The partially closed door still gave a view of the room. Two bleak torches barely lit a small and damp cement cell. No windows, no cots, just Alex and Jonathan, withered and weak. With a feeble attempt at standing tall and proud, the two brothers stood side by side.

"There is nothing to tell you. Again, our allegiance isn't with you, and we would rather be tortured and die than tell you anything," Jonathan's graveled voice barely audible.

As the two boys stared at Nicholas with solid and resolute courage, I almost cried. The bags under their eyes, and the many brutal and unforgiving wounds they wore, tore at me. They were being tortured because of me. With a pained groan, I fought back the tears.

"Nicholas." I grimaced, as if his name alone left a bad taste in my mouth.

"Oh, well, well. Look at this. Here I was asking the mutts about you when you were here all the time."

Alex and Jonathan looked around the room for what or who Nicholas was talking to. Just like only I saw him in my mind, he saw me only in his.

"Enough with the pleasantries, Nicholas. Let them go!"

"No! Not until I get what I want," Nicholas spat.

"And what is that?"

"I thought it was obvious. I want you."

He growled as he poked me in the chest. His mere touch almost scorched me through my shirt.

"Speaking of which, have you made your decision?"

"What decision?" I asked, wishing I could push past him and comfort Jonathan and Alex. Their feeble bodies seemed as if they would break if I so much as looked in their direction.

"My couriers have delivered my message, I presume? Or do you no longer care about what happens to your two little friends now that you have your beloved Michael and are too busy pretending to be a leader and ruler?"

The way Nicholas spoke of Jonathan and Alex infuriated me.

"You and I both know that they need to live if you want me to surrender to you. You kill them and all bets are off."

"Is that so? You are hardly in a position to make such a presumptuous declaration. Your friends' lives are no longer in your care, and since I have them, I will do with them what I please. Now, what is your answer?"

"What makes you think that I would ever surrender to the likes of you?" I asked, feeling braver than I should have been considering two very precious lives were at stake.

"What makes you think you have a choice? Your defenses are being depleted daily, your alliances are growing restless with the knowledge that they are being ruled by a mere child, and I have your friends. It looks to me like I hold all the cards."

Nicholas's cockiness irked me.

"My alliances are ready and willing to rid you from the face of this planet," I said. "Our defenses are still strong and sturdy. You may have Jonathan and Alex, but not for long."

"It sounds to me like you have already seen where this is going," Nicholas mused.

"Yeah, but this," I gestured between the two of us, "is about more than you and me. The decisions we both make have a huge impact on the world around us. If I win—"

Nicholas shook his head. "You won't."

"Yes, but if I do, I take your throne. Then, if I lose—"

"And you will."

I ignored his comment and kept on talking.

"Then humanity dies. This war will never end. There will always be someone to contest your throne."

"Save your diplomacy for the humans. I don't care. I will deal with it when it comes, just as I have dealt with you."

"Dealt with me? You talk as if you have already won."

"I have already won. I have two werewolves right here to prove that I have won."

"You are mistaken. I am still standing. Taking Alex and Jonathan just proves that you play dirty, not that you have won."

"Now it is you who is mistaken. See, I know that these two canine mutts mean the world to you."

Nicholas turned around and grabbed Alex by the neck, holding him off the ground.

"I highly doubt that you will let them suffer any more than they already have, let alone die for you."

He had me there. I didn't want them to suffer anymore, but I also knew unless they were released before I surrendered, then they'd be dead anyway. That is, if I surrendered.

"What's wrong? Just now figuring out that I'm right? Afraid that I may know you better than you think? Well, don't get too comfortable on your high horse. From what I understand, there are more than a few who have died for your cause."

Nicholas let Alex drop to the ground and an unnatural crack came from his leg.

"Now, I am growing very tiresome with our little game of cat and mouse. Here's what I'm going to do. I'm going to send out some of my men to retrieve you. So, I hope you have decided whether you are going to cooperate and surrender like a good little girl or if you are going to force my hand. I suggest you come willingly unless you want the blood of half your coven on your hands. Not to mention that of your coveted canines." A mischievous grin spread across his face as he quirked a brow at me.

Nicholas was threatening the lives of my friends, and, after seeing his torture firsthand, the enmity I'd hidden deep down inside reared its ugly head. I clenched my jaw and focused all my anger on him. Beneath my feet, I felt the vibrations of the quaking floorboards as my control slipped. I couldn't keep it in. I couldn't contain the anger. Then it hit me. Although I could feel the power that flowed through me, as I looked past Nicholas and into the room beyond him, I saw nothing had changed. The pillars of the cell remained still, and the cement floors were untouched.

I realized that, no matter what Nicholas wanted, no matter how many he took, he needed to die.

As I focused back on the vermin that stood before me, Nicholas seemed to be staring at me. His eyes bored into mine as if he was trying to figure out what I was thinking. Then, Nicholas rubbed his chin absently as he opened his mouth to speak.

"I wouldn't—"

"Enough!" I yelled. I closed my eyes and pulled myself into the present, carrying my screaming voice along with me.

My hands shook with rage, my heart beat with fury, and my emotions churned and twisted inside me. My eyes burned with anger, and all the emotions I'd pushed down rose to the surface. The inner fire that I had tried to quench and suppress over the last few days boiled and poached the surface.

"Are you all right?" Michael asked as he held me tightly in his grip.

Slowly, he came into focus. The bright green of his eyes reflected concern as he watched me carefully.

As I strained to control my ragged breathing, all I could do was shake my head. If I spoke, then the control I had would slip.

Michael lifted me into his arms and brought me to the seating area in the corner of the room to set me in one of the chairs. The seat was similar to the one I had in my room. No, the softness of the fabric, the plushness… it was the same. It was the chair I had in my room.

Although it technically wasn't mine, I'd spent many sleepless nights sitting in this chair contemplating what I was going to do, what the future held for me, if what I'd seen in my visions was right, and if there was a way to change them. This chair helped me get through so many trials over the last few years that I've worn a groove in the center of the seat—where I've curled up and slept after learning of my death and so many things that have given me nightmares. In fact, I could say that about Michael too. I just wish that I knew what to do.

As I calmed down and pulled my powers back inside me, Michael held me close. I could feel his pain as he tore through the prickles I sent throughout the air. Everything I felt whisked and swirled around me, but Michael held me, feeling everything that I was feeling and bearing the weight of it all.

"Shh, I've got you, love," Michael whispered, pulling me in and nuzzling my neck.

"I think I'm okay," I said in a tear-filled voice.

"Are you sure?" Michael asked. He eyed me carefully, knowing Nicholas and I had had another one of our visits.

With a heavy sigh, I nodded, but things were far from okay.

I shifted in his lap so I could place my hands on either side of his face and look into his eyes. Then, a flash of a thought raced through my mind. What if Nicholas was right? What if the only option was to surrender?

For a fleeting moment, I tried to memorize Michael's features. His eyes were full of love and trust. The soft contours of his face showed me how gentle and forgiving he was. When I saw Michael, he was compassionate. The perfect lover.

"Do you want to talk about it?" Michael's concerned look almost broke me.

"What is there to talk about?" I said, averting my eyes. "Nicholas's demands still stand."

As Michael brushed his thumb across my cheekbone, Nicholas's threat, and the torture he'd inflicted, was still fresh in my mind. Michael placed a finger under my chin and lifted it so I could meet his eyes.

"Was there more than what I just saw?" Michael asked, his voice a whisper. "Please, Arri. I can't help you unless I know everything that happened. You've been there more than me. Only you know if there is something different," he pleaded.

"No, It's the same thing." I shrugged. "Nicholas wants me, and he will stop at nothing, and do anything to have me. Alex and Jonathan are suffering. The coven lives in a constant state of flux not knowing when Nicholas is going to try something, and now he is threatening a fight unless I yield to him. Only now, he is getting desperate."

I looked down at my shoes dangling off Michael's lap.

"What do I do?" I mumbled, feeling equal parts anger and helplessness.

If I surrendered, I would be betraying all of those who had fought and died to protect me from him. But if I didn't, then many more would die. The more I thought about it, the angrier I got. Nicholas was asking me to choose between the ones I loved and my own life. I didn't like being the center of Nicholas's wrath. All I had ever wanted was to just be me, and even now, I didn't call the shots. I wanted a life where I could come and go as I please, a life that I controlled. Instead of being controlled by my parents, now it was Nicholas who controlled me.

He had claimed my life as his, and nothing short of killing him would free me from the invisible cage that he had created to keep me within his grasp until he killed me.

The question was: am I going to fight, hoping that somehow we come up with a fantastic plan to draw Nicholas out of his lair long enough for us to kill him? Or do I surrender, pray he kills me swiftly so that I don't have to live with the knowledge of betraying everyone I ever loved and throwing away everything that Michael, my parents, and the rest of the vampire world hoped I would bring about—a free existence without the dictatorship and tyranny of an oppressive ruler?

"When?" Michael asked, snapping me out of my thoughts and back to him. "Nicholas is giving you until when? For what?" I could almost see Michael's mind racing as he thought of the many things he needed to do.

"I don't know. Tomorrow, I think. But if I don't give myself up, then many will die." I swallowed hard. "If I go willingly, then his men will spare you and the coven. If I fight, then he is going to kill everyone who stands in his way."

I scowled with the knowledge that my single-handed decision would and could potentially kill Alex and Jonathan—and anyone here who would fight for me. I felt tied and bound. There was no right decision.

"Hey," Michael's soft and velvety voice whispered in my ear. "Nothing is going to happen to you. I won't allow it. I have lived for centuries, and I never felt alive until I met you. The last thing I am going to do is allow you to slip through my fingers."

As Michael looked at me, I could feel how much he wished he knew what was going on in my head. Before I could think too hard, Michael kissed me on my forehead.

"I'm going to go talk to your father and tell him about Nicholas's new timeframe. Hopefully your dad knows a few tricks that can help us." As Michael rose to his feet, I grabbed his hand.

"What happens if we lose?" I asked, closing my eyes and taking a deep breath.

"We won't," Michael tried to assure me.

"If I don't go willingly, then his men will kill all of us," I said, letting go of his hand.

"Men? How many?" Michael asked, worried.

"I don't know, but I will not let the coven or anyone else get hurt at my expense."

Michael just shook his head.

"You're not seriously thinking of surrendering, are you?" Michael asked, practically glaring in my direction.

"I don't know. Maybe, if it saves Jonathan and Alex and the coven from Nicholas's wrath."

There was a stunned silence as Michael stared at me.

"Look, I don't know what I'm supposed to do, okay?" I said with a shaky voice. "I'm in way over my head. I mean, saving the vampire world? It just seems so big."

Michael mused for a moment.

"You're not saving the world, Arri. You are fighting to save your world, your family, your friends. They are your world. To save the whole world is too much for anyone, but to save your family, your friends, those who mean the most to you… that is within you. I know the concept is hard for you to grasp, but the boys are doing exactly what they are supposed to be doing."

"So, what—being tortured was part of the plan?" I interjected.

"No. Their circumstances are truly unfortunate, but they have protected you from day one, and to this day, they are still doing their job. We all have a job to do, and we all knew the price we would pay if Nicholas or any of his men were to lay hands on us. Don't you see it, Arri? You are not saving the world. You are fighting to save your world and avenging the death of your dearest friend."

As Michael grabbed my hands, he faced me.

"I know that you can't receive your visions when you please, but I want you to try. I want you to look into my mind and feel what Nicholas has done to the ones I care about, the ones who have died so that you could one day breathe."

Nodding, I looked Michael in the eyes and waited to feel his emotions. For a moment, there was a slight flicker of grief and fear. Then, as if a forceful wind hit me, images of torture camps flashed through my mind. I saw Nicholas and his men making people suffer because they refused to follow him. Then, one after another, came images of those who had died. Like a strobe light, their faces flashed before me, until it came to an end. And with each face I saw, I felt the impact each one had on Michael. The last few floated by a bit slower—two faces I had seen before. Catherine and Phillip. The memory of Catherine's death still weighed heavy on my heart, but seeing her death how Michael saw it felt different. His emotions were just as strong as mine. The feeling that he had failed her by not being able to help her, the feeling of uselessness as he saw me run to her, only to be inches from her and not being able to stop it. The emotions flooded me. Anger and fury churned inside me like a tornado.

Nicholas was responsible for all their deaths, and I would make him pay for it if it was the last thing I did. Many people had died because of Nicholas's obsession, some I knew, but many I didn't, and for each one, Nicholas would suffer. With a resolute foundation growing inside me, I finally blinked up at Michael.

"You're right," I said. "Saving the world is too big, but I am a leader now, and I will fight for every life Nicholas has taken, and for the lives of my coven."

TWENTY

When I saw the grief and heartbreak in Michael's eyes, I saw exactly whom I had to fight.

Nicholas was more than a tyrant; he was a murderer. He was responsible for far more than I had expected, and honestly, I'd thought that his obsession was merely with me. But as I looked through Michael's eyes, the world that I'd seen through rose-colored glasses was far from rosy. The deaths he'd caused, the torture he'd inflicted, and the torment that he'd wreaked just for the pleasure of it were all beyond words.

Dinner flew by in a blur, and to be honest, I didn't hear a word of conversation. There was something inside nagging at me, telling me something was wrong. Of course, something was always wrong. I was the—how did Nicholas put it—ah, yes, the self-proclaimed prodigy.

But I didn't proclaim anything. This was all his doing. It was Nicholas who created me as his nemesis—the hero to his villain. How had a life so easy and dull become so dangerous?

The moments slipped by as I thought back to everything I had seen and experienced, both myself and through others. Everything that had haunted my thoughts for the last three years shadowed me in every waking moment.

"Arri?" Michael's voice pierced my thoughts.

Michael had been by my side through everything. From the moment I stepped foot in Elsinore, Michael, like Nicholas, was drawn to me. When Nicholas was sizing me up, hatred and malice were his only intentions. With Michael, on the other hand, it was always about love and adoration.

I was caught in the center of a tug of war. Nicholas was on one end of the rope with animus and hostility and Michael was on the other with love and kindness. While my feet were planted firmly on one end with Michael, Nicholas mentally pulled me to and fro.

"Arri?" Michael called to me, a little more urgently.

I blinked up at him, vaguely aware that the rest of the coven was staring at me from across the table.

"Yes, I'm sorry." I smiled half-heartedly, shaking my head.

"We were just discussing…" Michael's words faded away as my thoughts drifted.

I closed my eyes and tried to concentrate.

There was something out there. I needed to focus.

I dropped my shoulders and raised my chin. Then it became clear. I saw at least a hundred men making their way through the trees. They were still several miles out, but that still gave us only moments to plan. Gazing past the trees and through the men, I saw Lyle and his Ravens.

I opened my eyes and looked at Michael.

"You'll want to answer that," I said, nodding to his phone.

For a half of a second, Michael looked at me, confused. Just as I felt it, Michael saw the fear in my eyes, the panic in my heart, and heard the uneasiness in my voice.

"But it's not—" Michael's words stopped short when his phone rang and cut through the awkward silence, stunning the room.

"—ringing," Michael finished as he picked up the phone.

"Yes?" he barked. "Where?" he asked. Silence. "Lyle!" Michael yelled.

I could physically see his anger rapidly growing. The set of his jaw tightened. His fingertips dug into his phone until, and with a loud crack, he crushed it in his hand and threw it, sending several of the coven members ducking. As the phone smashed against the wall, Michael let out a roar.

He eyed me cautiously.

"You saw it—" Michael paused, looking at me in pity, knowing that I saw what was coming for me. "You saw it, didn't you?"

I simply nodded. I'd have to admit that seeing the overwhelming number of people that Nicholas had sent to retrieve me was a little daunting.

I knew that Michael had a plan. Since Nicholas had given me the ultimatum, Michael had planned and orchestrated everything, knowing that this moment was coming.

"The phone went dead before I could get a sense of what we are up against. How does it look?" Michael asked with a heavy heart.

"There are at least a hundred of his men coming from the east and snaking around to the west. They are maybe ninety miles out and walking on foot."

The entire room focused on me, each one seeing me in a different light. Most, if not all, finally understood the power I held within. A power that I hoped would save me from my own death.

"Okay." Michael nodded, then looked thoughtful. As he collected himself, Michael changed his demeanor, transforming out of the sensitive man who coddled me when I was down. Michael turned his head, squared his shoulders, and readied himself to face the coven. Every move he made was minute and small, almost hidden and obscure, but to me, every move was obvious. Everything Michael did, and didn't do, was as plain as day because of the bond we shared.

Michael took in the room, categorizing each and every one of the members, making a list of who was here, who was absent, who was combat-ready and who wasn't. Mentally, I could see him calculate the odds of victory with fewer men than Nicholas.

"Here is what we have, ladies and gentlemen," Michael said, standing up, leaning forward, and eyeing the coven directly. "As Arri has said, about a hundred of Nicholas's men are on their way. They were spotted about ninety miles out and walking on foot." Michael paused, waiting for the news to sink in.

Before, when Nicholas's men had attacked, it had been only a few. For him to openly send so many was a little shocking to all of us. He had made multiple attempts to get me, and each attempt to gain my capture involved only a few men. Now that he had tried everything else and failed, he was sending in the numbers.

"Tack and Lena," Michael faced them, "sound the alarm. I want every vampire in the northern states activated. I want them using the tunnels. There is no need for Nicholas or his men knowing what we are doing."

"Steven." Michael looked at my dad as Lena and Tack left the room.

At his name, my dad stood, facing Michael with dignity and valor.

"You know what to do. It's time we brought them out of hiding and collect their debt." Without another word, my dad bowed his head to Michael, kissed my mom on the cheek, and darted out of the room.

"Ava, I'll need you here to protect your daughter."

Nodding, my mom stood from her chair and took her place behind me.

"It would be my pleasure, your majesty," my mom said as she placed her hands on my shoulders.

"The goal is simple: We are to protect Arri from Nicholas and his men."

"Is Nicholas here?" a tiny, scared voice squeaked.

I felt out as far as I could, but I couldn't detect his presence. Still, that didn't mean he wasn't out there somewhere.

I looked at Michael, shrugged, and shook my head.

"No, not as far as I can tell, but Nicholas isn't a fool. He will be seen only when he chooses," I said with my head held high.

There was a round of mumbling before Michael cleared his throat and drew the attention of the room.

"With three of the forty covens we had here for the ball now gone, it is up to us to improvise, stall, and fight until the rest get here. I have contacts around the entire world who are just biding their time until the occasion arises for them to stand alongside us and fight. They will be on their way. But until they arrive, it is up to us to keep Nicholas's men at bay."

Silence spread throughout the castle as if the walls themselves knew of the approaching war. Every man and woman in the room looked calm and collected on the outside, but inside, chaos was churning. Each member knew there was a chance of death, and each member willingly and freely readied for the fight.

"Arri is of the utmost importance. She alone is the key to Nicholas's demise. Everything that Nicholas has done, everything that Nicholas stands for ends with her. If we lose her, we lose the fight."

Michael pushed himself up off the table and stood tall. "We will not lose this fight. We will win this and save our world."

A round of applause erupted from the room as they all hooted and yelled out their enthusiasm.

"We will stand and face our enemy. Who will pledge their sword to mine?" Michael yelled.

The entire room stood, drew swords, and held the blades above their heads.

With determination in his eyes, Michael grabbed me by the hand and escorted me out of the room. As soon as we reached his room, he slowed his pace and opened the door for me.

"Why do I get the feeling that there is more on your mind than you are letting me know?" Michael asked after he closed the door. He placed his hands on my shoulders. He could see and feel the fear I was trying so hard to hide.

In the dining room, Michael had been gearing up his men for the epic battle. The battle between good and evil, light and dark, right and wrong, freedom and slavery. The battle of all battles. Only I was caught in the middle.

But contrary to what Michael wanted, I needed to fight. There was no other way. There was only so much that thirty-seven men could do to hold back a hundred—and that was our number including me fighting.

Only I wasn't ready. Physically and mentally, I knew that I could do it. My powers alone, no matter how untrained, could hold them off, but only for a short while. The more I relied on my powers to protect me, the more I used them, the weaker I got.

Michael's plan was to protect me. To make sure that Nicholas didn't get me. But there was one fatal flaw.

Nicholas wouldn't send so many men here unless he was sure that I would be coming back with him. As I mulled that information over, I knew that there was something missing from his full-on assault. It felt off.

"Arri?" Michael placed his finger under my chin. "I can feel your thoughts from here. What has you so scared? None of Nicholas's men will reach you. I will do my best to prevent you from even fighting, but there is more than fear that fuels your anxiety. Doubt and uncertainty also harbor within you."

"You're right. I'm scared of what is to come. I'm afraid of what I will have to do to keep my life, and who will have to suffer. I know this," I gestured out the window to the oncoming war, "will come regardless of my readiness. But am I ready to face it?"

My bottom lip quivered as I tried to hold back my tears and fears. My heart tightened as angst and terror billowed throughout my veins.

"I don't know..." I shook my head, unable to voice my greatest fear.

"You don't know what, my love?" Michael asked as he smoothed my hair out of my face.

"Anything," I said. "I don't know if this is where Nicholas wins, or if I win and the boys die, or if Nicholas is just playing some sick joke to see what our reaction would be. I can't see it. I can't see the result, the end, and the battle. I just don't know."

As Michael looked into my eyes, my own fears were reflected in his. He, too, feared the unknown. But within his fear there was hope, faith, and confidence that we would prevail. I only wished that I had that same confidence.

Did Michael know that he was placing the fate of his coven on someone—me— they had referred to as a child? A child who didn't even know that vampires existed until almost three years ago? A child who had powers beyond anyone else in this strange world? A child that didn't have confidence that she could defeat and conquer?

"Arri, I can see you are less than confident in your abilities to win this, but I know you can do it."

"With my powers?" I asked, interrupting him. "Powers that I can't always control? Powers that take and deplete any and all strength I have?"

"Shh. Hey, now. The prophecy didn't say anything about you winning with your powers. The prophecy didn't even mention that you would have them. You have them because Nicholas forced greatness upon you, and you adapted to uphold it."

"But what if it's wrong?"

"It's not. Look, I know you are scared. I know that this is overwhelming for you. But this is not the end." Michael placed both his palms on my cheeks and leaned down to look at me straight on. "You hold more strength than you know. It is up to you to tap into it. I saw it in you when you shared your memories and thoughts with me. I saw it when you said that saving the world is too big, but you are a leader now, and you will fight for every life Nicholas has taken and for the lives of your coven."

A flashback of Michael's memories flickered through my mind. Again, I saw what Nicholas had done.

When I opened my eyes, I knew that Michael was right. I was right to be scared of the unknown, but I couldn't let it control me and take over. I needed to fight it and find the resolute foundation that I would need to win this war.

"You're right. Courage isn't the absence of fear; it is action in the presence of fear. I can't run from my fears, but I can face them."

With an encouraging smile, Michael leaned his forehead against mine. I closed my eyes, feeling his strength run through me, before I saw and felt the approach of several men and women.

"I believe some of your company has arrived," I said.

Just then, a commotion came from downstairs. It was faint and hushed as each person came up from the tunnels and was given orders.

"So they have. Shall we?" Michael asked, offering me his arm.

"Yes, but first..." I looked over my shoulder to the writing desk and the bathroom door behind me.

"Of course." Michael kissed me on the forehead. "I'll be waiting for you at the stairs."

As Michael left the room, I turned to the desk. I didn't have much time, but I had to, just in case. Then I went to meet Michael.

"Your majesty," Rogan said as he and Terrish bowed to Michael and me. "They are approaching. They have breached the outer perimeter. With your permission, sir, I would like to take you and Arri to a safe location."

"No," I said. "We will fight alongside you."

"Arri is right. We will fight," Michael said as everyone faced us. "Rogan, deploy everyone to their defense stations, then wait for my command to engage. We are not all here, and I would like to have as many here as possible."

"Of course," Rogan said. As Rogan and Terrish delivered their orders, Michael and I looked to the front doors. It felt like we were facing a firing squad rather than heading into battle with our flags held high and courage on our sleeves.

"Are you ready?" Michael asked before he shoved open the doors.

Two by two, the remaining members of the coven filed out of the castle and formed a stronghold between the approaching men and us.

As dawn approached, and the sun lit the tips of the trees, a fog rose from the ground and covered the clearing in a wisp of smoke.

"Hold your ground," a man said as he held up his hand to signal his command.

"Sir, this is you and Lady Arri's last chance to get somewhere safe. Do you still wish to fight?"

"Yes," was all Michael said.

"They are here," a woman said, taking her mate's hand.

TWENTY-ONE

One by one, men and women took their mates' hands as they waited for Nicholas's army to appear through the trees. Looks of adoration and love were exchanged between the soulmates as each one took a stand. Their determination and bravery touched me, as did their concern for each other. No one wanted to lose a loved one; no one wanted to lose a friend, and this was a fight of life and death.

As they stood in front of me, each couple was prepared to fight for my life—and sacrifice their own—so that I might one day fulfill the prophecy.

One who is one of us, but not governed by our rules… that single phrase had changed my life in a way that I never would have imagined. It wasn't the fact that I was living among vampires—no, it was the fact that I was their living prophecy, and that every one of these men and women were willing to protect me just so that they could live without tyranny and despotism. I had always been a little different from your average Joe, but this was beyond even that: Here I was, standing in front of an army of men sent by my nemesis so that he could destroy me and rule uncontested.

"We have no quarrel with you or your men, Michael. Not yet, anyway," a woman's voice said. "We are here for the child. Hand her over and we will leave you and your coven alive." The woman approached the line Michael's coven had made to protect me.

"This child will not be going anywhere. She is one of us," Michael said in a condescending tone. "Each and every one of us will fight to the death if that's what's necessary."

"Fine. Have it your way," the woman said, showing us a toothy white smile. "But might I remind you that your coven is significantly smaller than ours, and that we outnumber you three to one. Given the odds, don't you think it wise to surrender the child? Really, she couldn't mean nearly as much to you as what she means to Nicholas."

"I can see your lips moving, Rebekah, but I don't hear anything worth listening to. You have always been, and will always be, nothing but a mouth. Nicholas is too cowardly and recreant to appear here and speak for himself, so he has sent you. So, tell me, are the words spilling from your mouth his, or do you actually have a brain beneath those black curls?" Michael asked.

"I was willing to leave here without shedding blood, but now you—and you alone—have signed death warrants for everyone," the woman growled. "Congratulations, Michael. You have slaughtered your own coven."

As the woman walked away, one of Michael's coven members in front of me—Nora—shook her head. Then, without warning, she drew her swords and attacked the woman.

As Rebekah's head hit the grass, no one from Nicholas's coven budged. No one moved. They simply stood there and watched as Nora killed the liaison.

As if realizing what she had done, Nora returned to her position.

"I'm sorry sir," she whispered, without looking back.

"You did me a great service. She was rather annoying, wasn't she?" a cold-hearted voice said, reaching out over the distance.

A man, matching the voice, stepped out from the ranks of his army. His eyes were so dark they were almost black. His almond-colored hair was oiled in place, and he stood straight up as if there were a board tied to his back.

"Sorry, but I don't dare take another step forward. Your," the man stopped and scanned our line, "I guess you call this a coven?" he asked. "Well, to each his own," he continued. "Your coven doesn't seem too keen on the idea of negotiation."

"Sparing our lives for hers isn't exactly negotiating," Michael bit out.

"Oh, sure it is," the oily man said with a snicker. "It's not as if the child's life is really worth anything."

"If her life is worthless, then why is it that Nicholas has gone through so much trouble to obtain her?"

"Touché. Well thought out, Michael. But you are missing one detail."

"Yes, I would agree, except that it is you who is missing out on one little detail. Nicholas made her into the threat he fears. His constant attacks are what made her into the power he dreads will overthrow him."

"Enough!" the man roared. "I was going to let you and your coven go, but now you have sealed your fate. Nicholas fears nothing!" the man said through his teeth.

"Except Arri, of course," Michael put in. "Otherwise, he wouldn't have sent out his minions. He would have come himself."

As Michael's words sank into the man's thoughts, his anger grew, his jaw clenched, and his hands coiled at his sides.

"My master fears nothing," he repeated. "He sent us because his time is better spent on more important details than wasted on some little ingrate."

Michael was unfazed. "The translation to your outburst is: he is a coward, and you were sent here because your lives are expendable. Hence, he sent you and your colleagues to do his dirty work—and to your slaughter."

At that, the man lost it. His nose flared as he hollered out in protest. "You will die!"

With speed and grace, Nicholas's men ran toward us, their swords drawn, their battle cries echoing off the mountains that surrounded us.

The sight itself horrified me. The bickering had been amusing, but when Nicholas's men ran through the yard, closing the distance between us with rapid speed, it wasn't so fun anymore.

"Michael?" I whispered, as fear rose within me.

"You are safe among us. We will protect you," Michael whispered, nudging me slightly behind him.

Nodding, I stepped back and watched as our coven slowly drew their swords. The sound of metal unsheathing resonated throughout the valley. The hypnotic rhythm of the coven as they each took a fighting position in perfect precision made Nicholas's men hesitate for a moment. Their momentarily unsteady gait as they paused wasn't unnoticed by any of us.

Although Nicholas's men had sheer numbers, we were better trained and excelled in technique.

Then, one of Nicholas's men took the first swing. Metal sparked, then again as one of his and one of ours made contact. Their attempts were fierce and bold, made up of nothing but power. The first two men were taken out as our side quickly blocked their hits and disarmed them before taking their lives.

As their attacks proceeded to come, our men were easily dismantling Nicholas's men, but some of them were quick enough to move past our perimeter defenses.

Like snow leopards chasing their prey, his men leapt over our line and right into the heart of the fight. With swords drawn and ready, Lena and Tack intercepted their attack.

As blood pumped rapidly through my system, I mentally readied myself for the fight. Michael said it wouldn't get to me, but with only one line of men standing between the enemy and me, it was inevitable. Nicholas's numbers were significantly more than ours, even with our men hidden in the trees, and behind them, his men seemed to multiply. For every one that we killed, two seemed to be standing in its place.

With our men making a smaller and smaller circle around me, encasing me, I knew that it was time. If I didn't do something, all of our men would die.

Not knowing how, I tried to push my powers away from me and through our men to Nicholas's army. I filled the air with needles and constricting winds, forcing some of his men to the ground. It wasn't a lot of them, just a few, but enough that the others started to wonder what was rendering them useless and making them scream out in pain. As I felt myself weaken, just a bit, I let them go and focused my depleting energy on one enemy at a time.

As each man broke through the inner circle that encased me in safety, I focused on them individually and only long enough for one of our own to behead them.

A rhythm and pattern flowed through me and the coven, and for a fraction of a moment, I felt as if we were all connected, like I could read and instruct them through thought.

Then it was gone.

One after another, Nicholas's men approached with caution and confusion, unsure what was stopping their brethren dead in their tracks before their gory beheadings.

Then his men retreated back into the safety of the trees, but we didn't follow. Although we knew the woods better than any of them, we had men out there ready for such a maneuver.

"Now!" Michael yelled over the expanse of the yard. His voice traveled through the distance and into the trees. Just as his words left his mouth, Lyle and his men stormed their back lines and brought them out into the open. It seemed to be a foolproof plan, but no matter how many men we killed, there were still a hundred more charging and fighting.

"Werewolves," I whispered to Michael as he forced me behind him.

"Where?" Michael asked as he searched the yard.

"About a mile out, coming up from behind us, but I can't keep it up until they reach us," I said as my legs almost gave way. I was so busy slowing down Nicholas's men that I didn't pay attention to how tired and drained I was until we got a break when they tried to retreat.

"What do you mean?" Michael asked as he fought off another attacker and beheaded him before a female attempted to beat him.

"My body, it can't keep up the demands my vampire side needs to use my powers. I can't slow them down anymore," I said, as I tried one last time. All I could do was make them hesitate for a second before they were charging again, and with more vigor than previously.

"Can you use a sword?" Michael asked as he fought with all his might to keep Nicholas's men away from me.

With Lyle and his men fighting from the back, and us from the front, it finally felt like his troops were dwindling—but then, so were ours.

"Yes, I think so. But not well."

"Then I suggest you use one. It looks like our defensive line just broke."

One of Nicholas's men charged through the circle and grabbed for me, only to be blocked by my sword.

"You think you can fight me?" a man asked. This wasn't just any man. It was the oily- haired man who had stepped forward before.

"No. I know I can," I said as I blocked another hit from him, then another and another.

As he swung and I blocked, his moves were getting more intense and more powerful, but with every power move he tried, I blocked him effortlessly and used his own moves against him.

"You will soon surrender to me, I assure you," he said as he blocked a swing from me.

Circling, he taunted me, but I blocked one blow after another.

"I will never surrender to you," I said as I felt a second wind energize me. But how? I can't just create energy out of nowhere. Then Mr. Oily thrust his sword in my direction again. I dodged it and grabbed his hilt over his hand, pulled his sword from him, and redirected it back toward him.

"As I said before, I will not be surrendering to you." Then, with a flick of my wrist, his head fell from his shoulders and onto the grass.

It wasn't but a second before I was fighting another. Even after the werewolves joined our forces, again and again I fought, killing Nicholas's men one after another.

What felt like hours of fighting were evidenced by the number of bruises and wounds I was accumulating. Although my healing abilities were off the charts, I couldn't heal a bruise fast enough before I got another one.

As I fought to keep Nicholas's men away from me, a feeling of fear and terror washed over me. Frantically looking around, I was shocked for a moment. We were winning. Nicholas's men were down to only a quarter of their original number, but then...why were they scared? I looked toward Michael, but he seemed to be holding his own, fighting off Nicholas's men like they were nothing. Ash was doing the same. I couldn't see Lena or Tack, but it wasn't them causing the fear, either. Michael's concern that my dad wouldn't make it in time grew, but that wasn't the source of the fear.

Mom! Where was Mom? As I went from frantic to panicked, I spun around, then froze.

With fear instilled in her heart, my mom was on her knees, a sword drawn across her neck. Panic and sadness filled her eyes before she closed them.

Phoenix, too, was on her knees with two swords across her neck. Blood dripped slowly down her neck and onto her shirt. I needed to help them.

"What will you choose? Their lives or yours?" a man said as he pressed the sword harder against my mom's neck.

With a sword held in each hand, I paused mid-stride.

"What you offer me is unfair. I have no assurance that my surrender will spare their lives." I tried to stall until I could think of an ingenious plan that would save them and me at the same time.

"Yes, I guess you're right. It isn't fair. But the choice remains. Their lives or yours."

I wanted nothing more than kill him right where he stood, but that would only make things worse.

"Arri, listen," my mom said. "I've lived my life, don't worry about me..."

"Enough," the man said as he pressed the sword harder against her already bleeding neck. "I'm not in the business of sweet sentiments. Now, make your choice."

A stream of tears spilled from my eyes as I found myself caught between a rock and a hard place. I wanted to save her, I did—but at what cost? Was my life any more important than hers? Was my life worth saving if I was willing to kill her so that I could live? My mom was a far better choice than me. So I possessed a few extra powers—

what good were those powers doing me now? I couldn't use them to save her. A premonition would only tell me she was going to die, but that didn't mean I could save her. My ability to stop them with air had been lost when I tried to stop Nicholas's brethren earlier. With little to no energy left, and with no faith that I could win, I wanted to surrender.

Phoenix's temper rose as she tried to fight back, pulling the sword away from her with her hands, but the man simply slid the sword slowly across her hands until Phoenix bit out a few Italian words—that I was sure promised him death—and a sword landed against her neck again.

"Time is ticking, and the longer you hesitate, the more blood they will lose," the first man said as he smiled at me maniacally.

I looked back to Michael, my heart shattering. I loved all three of them with all my heart, each in a different way—but whom do I save? My mom? She was one of my favorite people in the world. The person who brought me into this world and had been my guiding light. A friend? A person I knew had more courage in her little finger than I did in my whole being. Or a lover? A man who was just as much a part of me as I was of him. The choice was overwhelmingly difficult.

"Arri," Phoenix warned, "we are not meant to live. You are."

My shaking breaths became more and more quivery as I stared at the two women I would give my life for. That's it—I would gladly give my life to save theirs, and here was that chance.

Prophecy or no, there was no other way to save them without giving them mine.

Swallowing hard, I nodded. With uncontrollable sobs, I slowly let my swords fall to my sides. As I squared my shoulders, I felt Michael's attention shift toward me.

He knew exactly what I was doing.

"No!" he yelled. He thrust the man in front of him out of his way before making his way toward me, but it was too late. A new string of men came from nowhere and separated him and Ash from me like a wall.

I couldn't take it. My heart was broken and shattered. My family and my love were in danger. There was no other choice. I knew where this road led. I'd seen it in my dreams.

"You can have me," I said, as I dropped my swords to the ground.

As soon as they hit the grass, a similar sword came from behind me and was gently laid against my neck.

"We wouldn't want you to get any bright ideas, now, would we?" a man said.

As the men led me toward the side of the house, and the fight disappeared behind me, my heart sank. Michael's cries for me echoed off the walls and reminded me of what I had just done.

I hadn't just surrendered. I'd slapped Michael and his coven in the face. I was no different than Nicholas. I was a coward. I was afraid not to surrender. I would rather see myself die than sentence them on my behalf.

Even knowing that I had just betrayed everyone out on the field who was willing to fight for me, I was most ashamed to betray Michael.

As Nicholas's men pushed and shoved me in the direction that they wanted me to go, I thought of the letter I had left behind for Michael, and a small voice whispered in my head, "I'm sorry," pleading for his forgiveness.

TWENTY-TWO

As soon as I lost sight of the manor, the two goons detaining me were satisfied that we were far enough out of range and we slowed down.

Even with my lungs begging for air and the ache in my chest from panting, I felt numb—emotionally, anyway.

My heart shattered into a million pieces over and over again. I almost didn't care if I lived or died. I had betrayed Michael and had given myself over to my nemesis.

I had already done too much damage. Even if there was a fraction of a chance that I would survive this and live, life wouldn't be worth living without Michael, and after what I'd just done, Michael would never forgive me.

As the millions of pieces of my heart cried out to my parents for their understanding, deep down, I hoped that Michael would one day understand, too.

Silent sobs shook through me as Nicholas's goons pulled me farther and farther away from my home. I slumped, surrendering my soul to the abyss of grief and heartache of losing everyone I had ever loved, and turned one last time to see if I could glimpse the manor. I knew we were too far away, but it was more of a reminder of what I had left behind.

My inner turmoil and sorrow rocked through me as they led me to Nicholas, and ultimately, to my death. The two men said nothing, just pushed and pulled me to and fro, guiding me through the trees as I watched the forest floor. With each step I took away from home, my powers stretched and pushed for freedom. Even as I forced myself to suppress my abilities, the fallen leaves were blown aside and out of my way as I walked. It was like I had my own little secret bubble projected around me. Of course, this small but telling detail was unbeknownst to my captors.

"Turn around," one of the men snarled, yanking on my arm.

I hung my head and turned back, only to stop in surprise.

We had reached the edge of the woods that surrounded Michael's mansion, and there, waiting for us was a black Cadillac Escalade.

As the door flung open, a burly, clean-cut man stepped out and approached me with bold candor.

"So, you are the child who has given many of our men trouble," he said as he walked around me, appraising me. "You look harmless enough. With your small, and naturally submissive nature, it's a shame Nicholas wants to sacrifice you," the oaf continued as he ran his finger up one arm, across my collarbone, and down my other arm.

I pinned him with a murderous glare and let out a small burst of my pent-up power. The man's head flew back, and his body shot away from me, knocking him to the ground.

"Don't touch me!" I said through my teeth.

The two men at my sides quickly withdrew their hands and stepped back.

At that moment, I had the freedom to run. I could have easily released my energy and knocked or pinned them to the ground, but that would accomplish nothing. I had already betrayed my coven. To withdraw my surrender now would only make things worse.

As he recovered from my power surge, the man stood back up and grabbed my chin, forcing me to look at him.

"You are hardly in the position to make such demands," he growled.

I looked from side to side, realizing his own men had let go. I shook my head because he was an idiot. He and his men didn't have the power to hold me. It was my will to be captured that allowed them to feel in control.

"The only thing keeping me here is me. Your men cowered

away. Again, don't touch me," I said. Feeling my eyes burn with anger, I pierced him with a glare.

With his two goons keeping their distance, I was caught off guard and flinched as a fleeting shadow crossed before me. Then the lights went out.

As the ringing in my ears blared with gusto, and the pounding in my head hammered with brio, I winced at the pain. I dabbed at a gash above my left eye.

"Ouch," I cried as I tried to sit up. Blinking rapidly, I lifted my hand and shielded my eyes from the bright florescent tube lighting above me. The harsh, blazing light shone with brilliance.

"Hold it there, sport," a man said as he stabilized me. "With a wound like that, you're lucky to be sitting up at all."

"Where am I?" I asked as the room came into focus. The white, sterile ceiling and walls only magnified the intensity of the light.

"Ha, I don't think I need to tell you where you are." The man chuckled as he dabbed my cut with a wet white rag.

"Ouch," I cried again. I pushed him away from me with a little more force than I had anticipated.

"Oops. Sorry about that," I apologized as I helped him up.

"Don't know the power of your own strength?" he asked in a teasing tone.

"I'm sorry, really," I said, biting my bottom lip. "What was that, anyway?" I asked as I picked up the rag that flew from his hands and onto the floor. The smell of alcohol and antiseptic was strong, and it burned my nose.

"Just some ointment to clean out your wound. Here," the man said as he picked up another white rag from the tray sitting on a small table by the bed.

"It's okay. I'll be fine," I said, walking away from him to get a better look at the room.

The room was plain and simple and not too shabby. To be honest, I thought I'd be in a cell just like Alex and Jonathan's—cement walls, hard concrete floors, even a thick iron vault door—but Nicholas surprised me. A soft blue canopy draped over a white and pastel blue bedspread on a white four-poster bed was way more than I thought him capable of. Combined with the whitewash finish of the hardwood floors and the white metal door, the room had a quaint but bare look.

"Well then, if I'm not needed here, I'll just leave you to it," the man said as he walked to the door and knocked on it twice with a quick rap.

"What is this place?" I asked just as the door opened.

For a fleeting moment, the man's expression fell and sadness filled his eyes.

"It is with great regret that you should have to occupy this room. I hope you find peace in your remaining days, dear." With that, the man bowed slightly, then opened the door to leave the room.

"You are awake," another man said as he came in, nodded to the man, then closed the door behind him. "Sir Nicholas will be pleased to hear you are awake and coherent," he continued, stopping just a few feet from me.

I stepped back and considered the man standing before me. His eyes were harsh. His sturdy shoulders were firm and square. His feet were planted apart and his arms were behind his back.

As he reached for my arm, I stepped back a little further. He cocked his head, and the corner of his lips turned up into a smirk.

"Who are you?" I asked as I eyed him carefully.

"My name is Caleb. I am assigned to look after you." His answer was short and to the point.

As he took a step forward, I took a step of equal length back.

"Where are you going? Eventually you will hit the back wall and have nowhere else to go. Come now. Nicholas demands your attendance," Caleb said, with confidence and assurance as he grabbed my arm.

Nicholas—my situation was suddenly very real. In the confines of my dreams and visions, where I knew Nicholas couldn't actually kill me, I was full of vim and vigor. I had no fear of him. We were on an equal playing field. He may have been stronger, but I was more powerful, and it was me that created the link between us. At any moment, I could sever that link and end the fight. But here and now, I didn't have the protection allowed to me in my visions. I didn't have the courage to face him.

"You're scared," Caleb said as he approached me.

Snapping out of my thoughts, I faced him. My breathing was a bit shaky. My hands vibrated with nervousness, and my heart tightened in fear. Swallowing hard, I squared my shoulders.

"Come now. You can take comfort that Nicholas doesn't plan on killing you tonight."

"And that's supposed to make me feel better?" I said, as Caleb headed for the door, dragging me along beside him.

As I tried to pull my arm free, Caleb only held me tighter.

"There is no point in fighting. You will not win. Not today," he said, as he tugged to hurry me along.

"Don't touch me," I said through my teeth. Staring him down, I let small bits of my power go, and filled the air with sharp, pin-like prickles.

As Caleb let go of my arm and took a few involuntary steps back, I stopped the winds and took a few deep breaths.

"It was said that you possessed such powers, and I was foolish enough to doubt it," he said, righting himself and dusting off his clothes, "but this small show will not deter me from presenting you to our master."

"He is not my master. He is a self-proclaimed king and has no right to rule any more than a walrus has to fly," I said as I slowly allowed my powers to surround me.

"I am sad to hear that," a man said. His voice raked against my skin. The deep timbre sent shivers up my spine and made my skin prickle with awareness. It was Nicholas. I would know that voice anywhere. It haunted me in my sleep. It claimed to be my destiny. A destiny that he said was meant to show others what happened when anyone dared to cross or go against him—Nicholas, the king.

Closing my eyes, I turned around. When I opened them again, I came face-to-face with my own living nightmare. His pasty white skin looked powdered and smudged. His pristine white shirt, vest, and cloak paled his face. He blended into the white of the marble that surrounded him.

Nicholas turned away from me and walked toward a large chair that sat front and center at the end of a large open room. His throne, flanked by two heavy curtains on each side, was lined with gold and diamonds and had cushions of red velvet. Nicholas held a staff of gold with diamonds and a ruby perched on top.

"Nicholas," I said in disgust.

"If it isn't the renowned Arri, Arch Leader," Nicholas said with sarcasm, and before taking his seat on the throne, he bent at the waist and offered me a mocking bow.

With fear and courage both raging inside me, I followed him to his throne and stopped just short of an arm's length away.

"No one stands before the king," Nicholas said as he pointed to the ground in front of me.

"You are not my king," I said, holding on to as much courage as I could. I didn't want Nicholas to know that even if I'd showed courage and bravery in my visions, I was more afraid of him in real life.

"I said kneel!" Nicholas roared. He swept his staff forward and flipped my feet right out from under me.

As I fell onto my back, Nicholas's men laughed. Then I felt it. The same courage I had in my visions came to me. The rage that churned and whirled inside me, the power that begged for freedom, came to the surface.

As I stood, Nicholas's men stopped laughing. The room went quiet. Nothing moved, but as air swirled around me, my eyes burned, and my heart turned dark. When some of Nicholas's guards left the room, Caleb took a few steps in my direction.

"I will not kneel before a fraud!" I shouted. "You have no claim to this throne. You are a coward hiding behind your men. I will not kneel before you!" I yelled out as I slowly extended my powers away from me.

Caleb tightened his muscles as my first wave of powers soared around me. A few of his guards hit their knees and yelled out in pain. Now it was Nicholas's turn. As the edge of my powers hit him, he laughed at first.

"Is this the power everyone fears? It will take more than this to affect me." He grinned with brazenness.

I let him have it. I gently let the razor-sharp air surround him. I made the air slowly tighten before I reached out with my mind and squeezed him.

With his men incapacitated and yelling out in torment, a smile tugged at my lips.

Gasping, Nicholas grabbed his chest as the crushing air surrounded him.

"You may be able to kill me, but can you kill them?" Nicholas rasped pulling a cord hanging at his side as I tightened my hold on him and his men.

At that, two curtains opened beside Nicholas's throne. My heart tightened, and fear consumed me.

It was my mother and Phoenix.

Facing Nicholas was one thing. He had tormented me for the last three years. But to see my mother and Phoenix kneeling next to Nicholas's throne with four blades cutting across their necks—that was heartbreaking.

I thought I had saved them when I surrendered. I had done all this so that I could rescue them from death, and here I was putting them in danger again.

"What will it be, Arri? It's my life or theirs."

Nicholas's words, his voice, his cocky certainty that I would not sacrifice my loved ones just to satisfy my inner want—it all infuriated me.

I hated him for getting them. I hated him for attacking me. I hated him for making me choose between them or him. I wanted so badly to kill him, but I was smart enough to know that I couldn't sacrifice them.

I released my powers on Nicholas and shifted my focus to the men holding my mom and Phoenix.

"Let them go!" I demanded. As I mentally pulled the swords away from my mom's and Phoenix's necks, I pierced the men who held them with a few blasts of my powers. The men dropped their swords and relief flooded through me.

"Enough, Arri," Nicholas said, as he pointed his staff at me. "It is not just them that I hold captive. Your canine friends will suffer if you continue this," he roared over the vast expanse of his throne room.

As his voice echoed off the walls, more of his guards came running in, ready for a fight.

"You are lucky I value their lives," I said through my teeth as I lowered my powers.

"I knew you would see it my way," Nicholas said.

"Careful, my old friend," I said, reclaiming my courage as my mother and Phoenix were forced back to their knees. "I am willing to let you live only because they are alive. Kill them, and I will not show you mercy again." I pushed my powers in his direction. It was only enough to ruffle his cloak and shirt collar, but it was enough to prove my point.

As Nicholas's eyes grew large, he took a step back and resumed his seat as the false king of the vampires.

With a wave, Caleb walked up from behind me and placed a hand on my shoulder.

"Kneel," he said in a quiet but hard tone.

I knelt, forcing myself to keep my powers at bay. Nicholas's men had resumed their position with swords against my mom's and Phoenix's necks, but they kept their blades away from their skin. As I carefully watched to make sure there was no bloodshed or harm, I kept an eye out for Caleb as well.

There was no telling what Nicholas had planned for this little meeting, but whatever it was, I was sure he wasn't expecting me to display a portion of what I held inside.

"Now, as I was saying." Nicholas cleared his throat. "It is a shame that you should be sacrificed tomorrow. Imagine what we could do if you were to be my ally."

"I would never join forces with you," I said, narrowing my eyes at Nicholas.

"Nor would I give you the pleasure." Nicholas smiled. "The only reason I wanted to see you before I killed you tomorrow is so that I could see the child who is said to overthrow me. Take away your pesky little powers, and you would be no match for me, I assure you. Tomorrow, when the time comes, your friends will be there to watch. Any funny business, and they will be killed despite my death."

As Nicholas rose from his chair and walked toward me, I stood as well.

"Just between us," Nicholas whispered as he walked past me, "I will take great pleasure in your death."

I almost choked on his rank and foul breath. It was the stench of death itself.

As Nicholas left the room, my mom and Phoenix fought their captors to get to me, but it was no use. With the added guards, we were ten to one.

With a light touch behind my arm, Caleb escorted me to my room.

When I stepped into the room, Caleb flipped the switch and the fluorescent white lights felt like they were sucking the life right out of me.

"Caleb?" I called out as he closed the door.

"Yes?"

"How did Nicholas get you?" I asked. I had noticed a small bit of empathy was coming from him,. He pitied me when my mom was brought into the room.

"I owed Nicholas a favor. My servitude is payment for my debt," Caleb said as he backed out of the room. He didn't make eye contact with me, but I could feel that he hated it as much as I hated him for doing Nicholas's bidding.

Maybe there was a silver lining to all this. And maybe, just maybe, Caleb could become an ally.

TWENTY-THREE

As a man's scream echoed off the walls, my heart fearfully constricted. I wasn't scared for me; I was scared for the tortured man. His agonizing shrieks tugged at my soul. Over the last several hours, men and women alike had pierced the silence as Nicholas tortured them.

Suddenly, noises rang out from the other side of my door. Ominous ones—voices that were unkind and taunting as they gossiped. The details of their conversations were lost as I focused on their emotions.

As the yells of pain continued, panic trickled into my heart.

What if it's Alex or Jonathan? What if I'm next? Where is my mom and Phoenix?

Not only did my trepidation fall into a full-fledged panic attack, but the naysayers' words came into my head once again: *You will never amount to anything.*

Mark's words also came back to haunt me: *I was only with you so that I could bring you to Nicholas.*

Even my mother's words echoed from the past: *Are you sure they want her so soon? Do you think she is strong enough?*

These had been, and still were, very good questions.

Was I strong enough? Did I have the courage to die for my coven, and did I possess the qualities of a prodigy? Would I fulfill the destiny set forth for me?

In all the days and years of my life that I'd felt lost and confused, nothing compared to this.

Who was I, and if I wasn't who they all expected me to be, then could I fulfill someone else's destiny?

You are worthless. I cringed at the memory of Gavin's haunting voice. *You are a smudge, a stain on our name. It's a shame that you carry the mark of the prodigy. We are definitely doomed if you are to save us.*

His distain was nothing new. But did he have a point?

What was I to do? I was detained, captured somewhere in Nicholas's lair—which could be in London, China, who knows where—but I did know that there were at least four people here who were depending on me.

Do I surrender tomorrow, or do I fight back and hope for the best?

As my emotions soared and churned inside me, the temperature in the room plunged. The bed scratched and screeched along the floor as my powers pushed it out of my way. The bedside table rocked and vibrated against the wall, and the door to my room bounced and shook every time I passed by it.

I paced back and forth as the words of every naysayer echoed in my mind—my fear turned into anger.

Finally, I collapsed. When my knees hit the floor, it should have hurt. Yet I felt nothing. The air in the room froze, the bed stopped, and the table and door ceased to quake. I felt empty, hollow, and deflated. I had the world's powers at my fingertips, and I felt helpless to defend those who couldn't defend themselves.

For a brief moment, the guards on the other side of the door froze—not because my powers had restrained them, but because for the last several hours, I'd been pacing the room. After finding out that Nicholas was going to make my mother and friends watch him kill me, my powers whirled around me, and the room practically shook from the force.

Then, as my mind cleared, the voices disappeared like whisps of smoke in the winds. Silence filled my mind, and that's when I heard it.

Michael,

If you are reading this, then Nicholas and his men now have me.

I know you are upset with me for surrendering, but I didn't surrender. I chose to go so that I could save your life and the lives of our coven. I see the coven as my family, and I would never ask you or them to sacrifice themselves so that I might live. Their lives are no more or less important than mine, and if I can save you and them, I will.

You have been more to me than a mate. You are my one and only soulmate. Whether I live or die, you will always be a part of me, and I you. Thank you.

I love you, and please forgive me.

It was Michael's voice. He was reading my letter. The letter I wrote. He found it.

Pain and heartbreak consumed me. His heart shattered just like mine did when I wrote it. Confusion, anger, and sadness all wrapped up inside him.

Oh, Arri, what have you done? I heard as I listened to his thoughts. *I would have protected you. We could have fought this together.*

"I'm sorry," I whispered as I closed my eyes and lowered my head. "It was either I surrendered or I killed the coven, and in turn, everyone I loved. I may not be brave enough to fight Nicholas, but I am brave enough to die to save you."

As I focused on Michael, and I reached for him, he gradually appeared in my head. I saw Michael in his study, holding my letter like it was the last remaining memory of me. His heart was breaking, and he feared for me. He loved me.

"Michael," I whispered.

"Even now, with you so far away, I can hear your sweet voice, my dear, Arri. Please come home to me," he said as he held the letter over his heart.

"I'm here, Michael. I wish I could tell you that I will come home to you. I wish that I could say that it will all be okay, but I don't know. I don't know if I'm brave enough to fulfill the prophecy. I'm not even a true vampire. I am a half-breed. Do I even possess the power to stop Nicholas from killing my mom, Phoenix, Alex, and Jonathan before he kills me? Oh, Michael, I wish you could help me. I need you now more than ever." Then, as Michael's form froze, he slowly looked up.

He looked rough and ragged. His hair was mussed. His shirt collar was in disarray. He was a mess.

"Please tell me… Arri, is that really you?"

As Michael and I made eye contact, his heart thudded with relief.

I smiled and nodded as my eyes filled with burning tears. The hours of mental torture I went through, hoping that he would forgive me and hoping that he didn't hate me for my betrayal—it all faded away as his lips turned up in a relieved smile. Although he tried to hide it, faint traces of tears filled his eyes.

"Yes, Michael, it's me," I said in a tear-filled voice. "I'm sorry," I whispered.

"There is nothing to apologize for, my love. You are alive. That is all that matters right now. Are you hurt?"

"No, but he's going to kill me tomorrow at nightfall." My words may have been casual, but beneath the false calm, I was a nervous wreck. I wanted to reach out and hug him. I wanted to feel his warmth, feel like I still had hope. I needed to know he was real. That he was my Michael.

"Have you seen Nicholas?" Michael tried to hide the obvious. Like me, his hands itched to reach out, to comfort me.

"Yes. I started to kill him, but he brought in Mom and Phoenix." I wanted to tell him that I couldn't just kill them, but I had a feeling he understood.

"He's using them to rein you in. He knows that with your powers, he is no match for you," Michael said, deep in thought.

"But what should I do? As much as I know the outcome… I'm afraid," I said through a restrained sob. "I can't do this without you," I added, as I closed my eyes and tears leaked down my cheeks.

"Then we have until tomorrow," Michael said. He raised his hand to wipe the tears from my cheek only to stop and pull back. It was like we were both afraid to actually try and touch. After all, we were only images in each other's minds.

"But tomorrow is only hours away. We don't have enough time to plan." Even though I could see and feel Michael's pain, I felt oddly relieved that I could have this time together with him.

"Honey," Michael said with a smile on his lips. "Tomorrow is a lifetime away. You'd be surprised what I can accomplish by then." The old Michael was back. The man I knew to have a thousand and one plans, just in case one failed.

"Do you have a plan? Can you save me?" My hopeful words came out in a rush as I looked in his eyes and heart for something that could help me get through the day ahead.

"Not yet, my sweet. But I will," Michael said as he tried to reassure me, but as the vision faded, a small semblance of worry filled his heart, and concern was reflected in his smile.

Then our link was lost. With several deep breaths, I slammed my eyes shut and tried to call for him again, but there was nothing. Several times, I called out to him, asking him to come back, but I just couldn't reach him.

As my heart ached and cried, I fell forward until my fists hit the floor and sobbed myself to sleep.

"Come back," I cried out in my sleep as I searched for him. "Please."

"Who are you talking to, dear?" a woman asked, waking me up as she shut the door behind her.

At first glance, she looked about thirty years old. Her hair was pulled back into a bun. Her T-shirt and jeans seemed normal enough, but there was sadness in her eyes. Instead of standing tall and poised, she slouched and looked worn and tired.

"Who are you?" I shot to my feet and backed away. "What do you want?" I added, a little too urgently.

"Relax. I'm not here to hurt you. I was told to get you ready," the woman said as she tapped on the door behind her twice.

Without a word, Caleb carried in a small vanity. It was simple, really. A white wooden desk with a matching mirror on top and a small white stool accompanied it. After leaving the room for a few seconds, he returned with a large white bag that could easily double as a circus tent.

"Anything else you require?" Caleb asked.

"No, thank you. I have it from here," the woman said, eyeing me with uncertainty. She didn't trust me. She feared me.

"If there is anything you require, I'll be standing guard," Caleb said to the woman, though he was looking at me.

With a nod, the woman headed to the vanity that was placed in the center of the room and started to unload the tent-sized bag.

"What are you getting me ready for?" I asked as she placed perfume, mascara, and blush on the vanity.

"Nicholas wanted you looking your best for your execution."

"He's going to doll me up just so he can kill me?" I asked, as I backed up until my knees hit the bed. "That's sadistic!" I yelled.

"It's symbolic, nothing more. He says your blood must be shed if we are to remain true and pure." The woman's words were sharp and stabbing, but her voice held no tone. It was like she was reading a script, devoid of emotion and opinion.

I had no words. What was I going to say? He was psychotic. It was like dressing up the virgin to be sacrificed to the sea monster.

She pulled out a white, cloth-wrapped parcel. The silken fabric was almost translucent.

"Would you please put this on?" the woman asked as she handed me the white bundle.

As I glanced from the woman to the package and back again, my heart rate tripled, and I shook my head.

"It won't hurt you. I made it myself. It is sewn from the finest silk," the woman boasted.

"Silk or no, you're still asking me to dress up for a sacrifice," I said in a quivering voice.

"I'll give you a moment," she said with pity and compassion as she recognized my frazzled state.

As the door shut behind her, I started after her. Did she honestly expect me to put this on? With anger building up inside, I calmly placed the parcel on the edge of the bed and sat next to it.

A knock came moments later.

"Are you ready, Lady Arri?" the woman said as she entered the room.

Without a word, I stood, picked up the package, and gingerly placed it on the vanity.

"I will not dress up for the slaughter. If Nicholas wants to kill me, he will have to do it in my regular clothes. I am not going to be a symbol. He is killing me out of fear, and I will not become a willing participant in his push to make my execution a symbol of his false power."

As the woman stared at me in disbelief, she stumbled through her nod and backed toward the door. With two knocks, the door opened and she exited. I didn't know if her fearful expression was reserved for me or for her fear of me, but as I turned around and headed for the bed, I noticed that the vanity shook, the drawers in the bedside table rattled, and the blanket and sheets on the bed rippled.

She was afraid of and for me. She knew that my refusal to go along with Nicholas's wish would result in force and pain, but she also feared me. The power I accidentally released in the room was only a smidgen, but it was enough.

As I sat on the bed and placed my hands in my lap, I tried to hold my powers in and rein in my emotions.

"Put it on," a man yelled as he barged through the door. His husky build, tight jaw, and dark and unforgiving eyes had me scared for a moment. That fear quickly turned into anger, and with that, my control started to slip.

"I said put it on," the man yelled again, as he picked up the packet of clothes and threw it at me.

The fabric satchel hit me in the face and broke open. As the two-piece outfit hit the floor, the man walked toward me.

"I've heard about your stubbornness and your obstinacy, but here, you will do as you're told," he snarled, as he picked up the two pieces and handed them to me.

I clenched my jaw and held on to as much control as I could. With a deep breath, I folded my arms.

"You are insubordinate and defiant, but I'm sure after I'm done with you, you will be a little more willing to oblige."

With a quick move, he struck my face with the back of his hand.

Immediately, it felt like my eye was going to explode. He hit me again. This time, it was on the other side, across my jaw. With my breath quaking in pain, anger, and fear, I clenched my fists and held my ground, but it wasn't for long. The next strike hit my stomach, and while I was hunched over, his hand flew up and knocked me in the nose.

With blood falling to the floor, and with my head in splitting pain, I cried out.

"Now put it on," he growled as he handed the clothes to the woman and walked back out of the room.

With gentle hands, the woman offered to help me up.

"No," I said, piercing her with a glare and jerking my shoulder away from her. "I can get up myself," I snarled.

I stood, squared my shoulders and closed my eyes.

"Here," the woman said as she handed me a clean white cloth.

I grabbed the rag from her and held it against my nose until the bleeding stopped, then dabbed at the cut under my eye.

After I was all cleaned up, the woman handed me the clothes and offered to step out again.

"Please, Lady Arri. Kennan will be back if you don't, and I'm afraid your friends will suffer as well." I noticed that she called me Lady Arri, not child, girl, or ma'am. She referred to me as my title.

As the woman left the room, it gave me hope to think that not all that serve under Nicholas are loyal to him and maybe, just maybe, they could help me. I debated the chances of me winning this war without help, but my odds were slim. I might be able to hold it off for a bit. Even if I used my powers, I highly doubted they would stop until I was subdued or knocked out, and it was hard to fight back when you were unconscious.

As I looked at myself in the mirror, the white shirt, the white pants, and the bare feet made me appear every bit the sacrifice I was meant to be.

"You're dressed," the man called Kennan said as he walked toward me. "I knew you would see things my way." He planted a hand on my shoulder, guided me to the vanity chair, and forced me to sit.

"I am going to step out, but if you give any trouble to Gena, then I will be back here to teach you the manners you obviously lack." With a curt nod, Kennan exited the room, and I was left alone with Gena.

"You have such beautiful hair," Gena said as she combed and smoothed my hair to perfection.

I sat for what felt like hours while she tried and retried many styles. With short shoulder-length hair, there was not much she could do, but Gena managed to pull half of it up and braid it down the back, leaving the rest to fall around my shoulders.

Next, she turned the chair around, opened the blush, and applied it to my cheekbones, then mascara to my eyelashes, then perfume spritzed all over.

"You are naturally beautiful. I only added some color." Staring at my nose and eye, she looked puzzled.

"Your cut, it's…" Gena shook her head.

"Gone," I finished, as I nodded. "I know."

"Well, I guess you're ready then."

Gena stood back and appraised me from head to foot, then brushed, smoothed, and tugged at my clothes to make sure they were perfect.

Seeing myself in the mirror, all dressed in white, made up like a doll, and forced to appear as a symbol of Nicholas's power, made my insides cry. My heart broke, and the fear that controlled me was bleeding through my shield of will.

I wasn't ready to be ready. I felt like messing up my hair and smearing my makeup to prolong the inevitable, but my efforts would be wasted. Either Kennan would come back in, or Nicholas would just bypass the ceremony all together.

"Michael, please, if you can hear me. Help me. I need you," I pleaded as the door opened, and Nicholas stood in the threshold.

TWENTY-FOUR

As I walked down the marble-lined hallway, my bare footsteps echoed off the barren walls.

The faint but rhythmic pulsing of my heart seemed eerily calm as I walked to my death.

"I must say, with the powers and strength you possess, I expected more of a fight." Nicholas's unearthly voice grated against my nerves.

"I'm sorry to disappoint you," I said, toneless and detached.

As I put one foot in front of the other, the reality of my future weighed heavily on my heart. When I'd surrendered, it had been out of love for my mom and Phoenix. Love gave me the courage to do it. But as I walked one step behind my adversary, I saw the error in my decision.

"You don't mind, do you?" Nicholas asked, holding up a pair of ruby-red shackles and handcuffs as we reached the door to the throne room.

"What for? Haven't you won already? You have my mom and my three best friends as captives to make sure that I cooperate. What more could you possibly want?"

"Until your blood stains the foot of my throne, I will settle for nothing."

"So, you intend on parading me through that door as if you had actually captured the horrible Arri yourself? You want to keep them from knowing that I surrendered?"

As Nicholas narrowed his eyes at me, I wanted to smile. He knew I was right. If I walked out there on my own, it would seem that I was not as threatening as Nicholas had made me out to be.

But in shackles and handcuffs, I became the demon.

With careful and gentle hands, Caleb fastened the iron shackles around my ankles, making sure that the metal was placed over my pant leg and not against my skin. With a weary smile, he held out his hands for mine.

"Your wrists, please," Caleb said in a curt tone.

I held out my wrists. Caleb locked the cold, hard metal cuffs against my bare skin.

"Seeing you like this," Nicholas said as he took hold of the chain that bound my hands together, "gives me an extreme amount of pleasure."

"The only reason I am letting you do this is because I value my family's and my coven's lives. Otherwise, I would have killed you yesterday when I had the chance. Do you honestly think that a simple pair of cuffs and chains would stop me from killing you if I really wanted to? No. This little charade of parading me around, chaining me, and belittling me, is only because I am allowing it," I said as I stared at the doors to the throne room.

I didn't have to look at him to understand that he was seething on the inside, and that if he let even a smidgen of his control slip, it would tell more than he cared for his coven to know. Deep down, Nicholas was scared that the prophecy might have been right. If it hadn't been for him bringing in my mom and Phoenix, he knew I would have killed him. On the outside, he talked a lot of talk—he might even flex his authority—but he feared me. I could feel it.

"You're rather cocky, given you are the one in chains," Nicholas said with arrogance as he mentally shook off his uncertainty.

"I'm not cocky. I know how this is going to end. I have seen it. I have felt it, and I have even lived it. I also know that without their lives holding me back, you wouldn't have had a chance."

"Be careful. I'm going to kill you tonight, no matter what," Nicholas said as he placed his open palm on the heavy marble doors.

"Then why do I need to be careful?" I sneered.

With a hearty push, the doors swung open. As they hit the wall, a loud and thunderous boom resonated throughout the cavern.

Voices hushed. The stirring of men and women quieted. Nicholas made his grand entrance.

In one hand, Nicholas held my chains in a death-defying grip. In the other, he pounded his staff on the hard marble floor. As the sound resonated throughout the cold chamber halls, it might as well have resonated throughout the entire vampire world as a symbol of his obsession with power.

I stepped out from the shadows and into the brightness of his throne room. White columns and marble floors extended beyond what I could see, and thick white arches lined the eight-story ceiling in a hall that was filled in a never-ending sea of Nicholas's men.

Nicholas stood at the entrance until everyone bowed to him. Every member of his coven did without question or thought as they saw him as their leader, their god.

"Rise," Nicholas commanded. His voice boomed and carried as he made it known that he was the ultimate power.

As everyone rose to their feet, Nicholas stood tall, towering over them.

"I promised you years ago that the prophecy was a ruse, a hoax to deter me from claiming my rightful place as ruler. For years we have waited, biding our time until the so-called prodigy that the prophecy foretold arose. Men and women have been spared, sacrificed, and killed so that when the alleged child came to be, we would be ready to conquer and crush it, and for this, our patience has been rewarded. May I present to you, the *soi-disant*, the *ideo-dicitur*, the so-called prodigy, Arri," Nicholas said as he faced me.

With an evil and sinister look, Nicholas offered me a nefarious smirk. Then, without warning, Nicholas's grip on my chains tightened before he yanked me through the doorway.

Hobbling and stumbling through the limitations of the chains, I fell into Nicholas's throne room. As he pulled and dragged me to the center of the platform, the metal handcuffs dug into my wrists. The shackles around my ankles felt like vices as the chains tripped me. Pain and fear rocked through me as I hit the floor. Then, as Nicholas threw me forward, my knees stung and burned as I tumbled and fell onto all fours.

The roaring laughter and snide sniggering of Nicholas's coven echoed and oscillated throughout the vast hall.

"I give you the destined child," Nicholas said as he placed his foot on my back and pushed me down until I was flat on my stomach.

As I struggled and fought to get up, Nicholas pushed harder until it felt like he was standing right on top of me, and my ribs were going to snap.

"This child, this abomination, was said to overthrow me. The prophecy may have foretold of a new upcoming power that was supposed to defeat me, but as you can see, I have defeated the child, the prodigy!" Nicholas roared. He yanked me up off the floor and lifted me into midair by my chains.

As I hung, the handcuffs carved into my wrists until blood dripped down my arms. Pain cut through me as I yelled out in agony.

Nicholas howled out in laughter and his coven roared in amusement as I screamed.

"Please," I whimpered as Nicholas dropped me to the floor.

As I landed on my knees, I wanted him to just kill me and get it over with. Postponing the inevitable and delaying the relief of death was torture as he toyed and dangled me in front of his coven.

"By removing and destroying Arri, we are removing all hope from our opposition. We are making their past, present, and future endeavors fruitless, thereby cutting a path for us to take our rightful place as evolution would have it: to rule the world. Nothing was ever going to stop it; this is simply our destiny."

With fear pulsing through me, and my heart screaming out in pain, a stifled cry escaped my lips.

I was terrified. I squared my shoulders, trying to stand tall and brave, but pretenses weren't enough. I wasn't brave; I was scared to death. My hands shook, my breaths came out in quivering gasps, and I fought with all my might to hide the tears that ran down my cheeks. With fear and terror building inside, my inner demon was rearing up. As I took my worst nightmares and turned them into strength, the air around me chilled.

For the first time, I noticed I was alone. My mom, Phoenix, Jonathan, and Alex weren't here. With a deep breath, I grabbed the chains that bound me and slowly pulled.

"To aid us in our conquest," Nicholas said, as several of his men escorted ten people up onto the platform. Each one was dressed the same as me with shackles and cuffs, and two double bladed swords crossed against their necks.

The first four I knew—Alex, Jonathan, Mom, and Phoenix—but the other six I didn't. They could be anyone: members of Nicholas's coven, spies, infiltrators who had been caught, or, knowing Nicholas, they could be random members—even humans. Either way, I felt sympathy for each and every one of them. It was because of me that they were here. They knew their fate was close to follow mine.

As my eyes met Phoenix's, I could see a fear that I'd never seen in her before. I wanted to reach out and hug her.

I let my powers die down and pulled them back inside me. Nicholas's light chuckle sounded softly; he knew he had won again. He knew I wouldn't kill them.

Alex stood next to Phoenix. His strong and easy disposition was broken. His soft, pale skin had been mauled and beaten until there wasn't much left of him. His heart was shattered as his sad eyes met mine.

"I'm sorry," I mouthed. As he gave a sad shake of his head, I could feel his regret, his understanding of what I thought I had to do.

Jonathan looked just as bad as Alex did—maybe worse. As Jonathan's strength and cockiness shone through, I knew that he would have pushed and fought back as much as possible, but now, he was beaten and tortured down to nothing. His will to live was gone, and even though he knew I was there, he was too afraid to look at me. His guilt over his failure was too much.

Then there was Mom. As our eyes met, I couldn't contain my sobs any longer. Looking into her eyes, I saw fear, disappointment in herself, and pain as she had to watch her daughter die. As much as I tried to push her away when she first came back, I saw now that it was her love for me that had kept me alive. Her love for me had made me into the woman I was today. Without her guidance and sacrifice, I never would have lived at all.

"I love you," she said, just above a whisper. Her voice was strained and choked as she cried uncontrollably.

As I saw each of their faces, I expected anger, maybe even pleading looks to fight back, but acceptance filled their eyes. New and restored anger grew within me, but I was useless against such odds.

As my fear faded, the moment felt bittersweet, sort of surreal. It was like walking in a daze, or through a dream, as I saw Nicholas's coven all staring at me. The looks of pure disdain, the sneers of vile and vulgar words passed right through me, and I felt nothing.

My fear of death vanished, and the sadness of my betrayal of Michael and my coven dulled.

My coven. That was a phrase I thought I'd never say. My coven—and they were. Not because I had pledged my life and myself to protect them, but because I knew that with all great things, sacrifice was often necessary. In the last two days, I had gone from calling the coven Michael's, to ours, then mine—and they were mine.

As I stepped up next to the slate table, Nicholas immediately pushed me down to my knees. My heart was racing with the knowledge that the time was growing near. It made me nervous, but I understood and knew what I was doing.

"Arri!" my mom yelled as she tried to step toward me, only for Nicholas's men to push her to her knees. They held her head back by the hair, forcing her to watch as Nicholas stepped up behind me.

"Behold the prodigy!" Nicholas's voice boomed across the vast expanse of the room as he pushed me over the table.

The emptiness that echoed off the corridors instilled finality in my heart. This was it. The moment of truth; the moment that I hoped would never come.

Three years ago, my biggest worry was work. Now I was

hunched over a stone slab after I'd surrendered to my archnemesis, about to be killed in a show of his power. Wow, how things have changed.

I looked over to my mom. Her tear-streaked cheeks glistened in the light. The fear in her heart pained me to no end.

"I love you, and I'm sorry," I said, as I wept. I turned away from her shattered look, trying to hide my fear from her. To die was one thing, but to see the pain and misery it inflicted upon my mother and friends was more than I could bear.

As I cried, I waited for the final moment. Tears pooled at the base of the altar, and I watched my reflection ripple. In my visions, I saw myself in this exact moment. I saw Nicholas raise his sword. I saw his men jeering and mocking me from the crowd. Then, I felt piercing pain as Nicholas drove the sword into my back.

Then, as movement in my pooled tears caught my eye, I saw Nicholas standing behind me. As he drew his sword, the sound of the metal scraping against the sheath made my heart tighten in fear. I could feel the stir of air as he swung the sword around before he pulled it up and poised it above me.

"No!" my mom yelled as she fought and tugged to free herself. The sound of Nicholas's men struggling to hold her back drowned out the sound of his coven.

"Arri, no! Fight back! Let us die, but save yourself!" she pleaded, as tears and sobs choked out her words.

The more she tried to free herself, the more I wanted to fight and run to her, to hold her one last time before I died. But Nicholas's men managed to subdue her, and her sobs were deafening as I felt her pain.

Can I do this? I wondered. I want to save my coven, I want to save my family, but again, at what cost? Why should I have to die? But if my family died because of my selfish act, then what kind of leader would I be? The battle raging inside me between fighting to live, and surrendering to save my family, pushed and pulled at me. What do I do?

The moment of my death flittered on the horizon as I

contemplated my dilemma, but to sacrifice my coven would make me no better than Nicholas.

With a pained heart, I bowed my head and accepted my death. Nicholas yelled out in victory as he swung the sword down toward my back. I slammed my eyes shut as I waited for the final blow, the pain that I knew would signify my death, but as air passed by, a heavy thump resounded throughout the room. Nicholas's coven hushed and froze as he grunted out in pain.

A small but sharp sting grazed my ear. Then I heard the clatter of metal as it hit the marble floor beside me.

I opened my eyes. The glittering gold of Nicholas's sword lay on the floor next to the altar.

For one startled moment, I stared at it, confused, but faint rustling from where my mom once kneeled drew my attention. I was afraid to look. What if Nicholas's men had killed them?

As if everything was in slow motion, I turned my head and cringed, but instead of my mother and the rest of the hostages kneeling, they were free. Some of my old friends, the Shadows, had Nicholas's men kneeling before them.

With shock and confusion running through my veins, I saw a titanium sword sticking out of Nicholas's right shoulder.

I didn't understand, but without hesitation, and with his attention drawn to the sword, new and resolute strength seeped into my heart.

This was it. I was free. As my heart took a chance and soared with exhilaration, I scrambled away from the stone table. With a few determined breaths, I gathered my courage and power. I grabbed the chains that bound me and pulled until the chink of metal vibrated the air around me, and my hands and ankles were free.

With lightning speed, my mom ran up beside me and pulled me into her arms. Fresh tears sprang into my eyes as we embraced.

Prying myself from her arms, I scanned the room to see who threw the sword. I saw Nicholas's men carving a path as Michael and Ash weaved their way through the crowd.

At first glance, it looked as if Nicholas's men were going to stop and fight the two, but with a closer inspection, my dad stood tall and proud as he followed right after them. At my dad's appearance, Nicholas's men stood back out of fear.

"It's Steven," one said, and bounced between bowing to my dad and standing up straight.

"I thought Nicholas said he was dead," another said, as he took a few steps away from my dad.

As my dad, Michael, and Ash carved a way to the altar, what looked like hundreds, if not thousands, of Michael's men filtered in behind them. It was an army.

"We are ready to fight, Nicholas," Michael announced as the three of them got to the steps.

"There will be no fight," Nicholas said, as he flicked up his sword with the tip of his foot. Then, with frightening speed, Nicholas caught the hilt. As I reached inside, and called on everything I had to fight him, it all surged forth: the power rising, the strength climbing, and the courage growing. With one last fortifying breath, I set my shoulders, then gasped out in pain.

I wasn't fast enough.

"No!" I heard Michael yell as my vision blurred. The agonizing pain ripping through me took every bit of air I had left. I struggled to breathe through it, and after staggering a few steps toward Michael, I fell to my knees, then felt Michael's arms wrap around me. Nicholas had done it. He had stabbed me through the back as I had foreseen. As I looked down at the tip of his blade sticking through me, fear chilled me.

"Michael… Mi…" I tried to speak, but it was no use. As Michael's lips touched mine, I felt the constriction of my heart as I heard the final beats.

Thump-thump… thump-thump… thump… thum… thu…

The sound of my own heart ceased, and silence filled the air. No one in either coven moved, breathed, or fought; they all were watching me.

As time stood still, the faces of my coven reflected my own shock and horror. Pain ripped through me, tidal waves of fear, panic, and despair crashing everywhere. My family's faces flashed, reflections of my life flooding my mind. The family dinners, the protectiveness, everything that they had done to ensure that I lived, had been lost. I had failed them. They sacrificed their lives so that I would have a chance at life, a chance to love, to grieve, to experience my hopes and dreams, and I repaid them by sacrificing myself so that my coven, my family, and my love may live.

I thought I knew what the prophecy meant when it said that with my death, their lives would be spared, but I had no clue. I had taken my life, my love for Michael, and my mortality for granted, and now I was going to lose it. I was going to lose my family, my friends, and Michael. If I could tell them just one more thing before I died, it would be that I was sorry.

"Arri," Michael yelled, but even as the world went black, I could still feel the coolness of the marble beneath my body, and the warmth of Michael's touch as he stroked my bare skin.

As the shadows of doubt and fear consumed me, the blackness that surrounded me fogged, then brightened, until the face of an old man looked back at me. With his rugged and leathery features, his kind and forgiving eyes seemed familiar, like I had seen them before. It was like I had known him forever. I had felt his presence, I had heard his voice, and I had even felt his guiding hand as I wandered through life with half-opened eyes. He was The Old One.

"*Styrkur minn mun koma með dauða*," the old man said as he nodded at me. "*Styrkur minn mun koma með dauða*," he repeated as he placed his hand over my heart.

"I don't understand," I said, trying to recall where I'd heard that ancient language before, but he kept repeating the same thing over and over again until his words became more than words—they became a feeling.

"My strength will come with death?" I asked. He smiled from ear to ear. "Please, I don't understand," I pleaded, but he just shook his head.

"Þú munt ráða." He smiled.

"I will rule?"

"*Berjast,*" he said. His form faded, and darkness took over.

"Fight?" How? I was dead, right? The faint, unarticulated sounds of mumbles and rumbles grew.

Nicholas. Nicholas. Nicholas.

The chanting of Nicholas's name was the first thing I heard before the chink of metal hitting metal.

"Ahhh!" Michael yelled, and the familiar sound of sword fighting took over.

As the cold and unforgiving marble floors pressed against my face, I swallowed. The pain that had pierced me, the unbearable agony as Nicholas slid his sword through my heart, had ceased.

Was I dead?

Carefully and slowly, I dared a glimpse of the world around me. Through cracked lids, I could see Nicholas's men and our own fighting in an artful war. Swords swung in heavy battle as Nicholas's men fought for their lives. With me dead, they felt they had already won. The prodigy was dead, Michael and Nicholas were in one-on-one combat, and our coven had been beaten badly. Through this heavy war, both Nicholas's men and ours had taken great casualties. I could feel it.

I could feel their deaths as if they were my own.

As our covens fought, I could feel the deception, the anger, and the hatred running through Nicholas's coven's blood. In ours, I could feel the glimmer of hope in some, and the dying optimism and faith in others.

As each sword swung, and as each person fought showing their loyalty, I began to see through their thoughts and into their soul. This war wasn't over freedom; it was over dominance. Nicholas's men held no thoughts or feelings on freedom. It was Nicholas's words, his thoughts, that fought. Not his men.

Somehow, I found the courage to open my eyes. I took a deep breath. A river of blood ran off the marble steps. A pool of red spilled where I had fallen. But I wasn't dead. *Strength will come with death.* The prophecy was right. I was alive. I could feel the strength building within me. My heart, though unbeating, was full of life.

I took a cautious, relieved breath and braced my arms on either side of me to lift myself. With great difficulty, I pushed the blade through my chest and out of my back before I managed to reach behind me and pull the cold steel the rest of the way out.

As I pulled the metal from my heart, the scraping and grinding of the sword against my bones vibrated throughout the entire hall.

Everyone froze.

Inhaling sharply, I opened my eyes wide and looked out over the vast and boundless hall. As everyone stood in awe, I held the jewel-lined gold sword out in front of me.

As the crimson-stained blade shone in the light, apprehension and doubt seeped into every soul.

"No!" I heard Nicholas yell.

As I turned around, Nicholas picked up Michael and threw him against the sidewall before he charged toward me.

"You are a corruption to our blood," he roared. "I am the rightful ruler, and I will not be beaten by a mere child!"

Just as he reached me, Michael stood between us with his sword drawn. Restored faith and hope thundered through his veins as his heart leapt and danced with relief that I was alive.

With total and complete ignorance, Nicholas's sword came toward Michael's neck with fierce and brutal speed. I could feel the acceptance in Michael's heart as he stood to die for his love.

"I love you," he whispered as he took my hand in his.

"No!" I yelled. I threw my hand out and spread my fingers wide, letting the power I held within proliferate throughout the small space that divided Nicholas and me. I let my power tighten until he was immobile, frozen in mid-stride and mid-swing. "There will be no more deaths tonight," I stated. As my power soared and pounded through me, I could feel the air lick and caress each and every stunned member of our covens.

Nicholas's fury only doubled as he fought and struggled against the crushing and constricting air that I whirled around him. As he gritted his teeth and cursed beneath his breath, a smile twitched in the corner of my mouth.

"You will rule no longer. The age of Nicholas is over."

"I will never surrender to you," Nicholas spat as he narrowed his eyes at me.

Rounding Michael, I stood face-to-face with my arch nemesis.

"I am not asking you to surrender. I am taking your throne from you. You cannot and you will not stop me."

"You will have to kill me if you think you are going to take my throne. My men will protect it," Nicholas said as his eyes searched out his most loyal minions.

I turned to the crowd of men and women that stood stock-still in absolute awe.

"Do any of you wish to protect Nicholas's throne and challenge me for it?" I cried, taking a few steps toward the edge of the stairs. I let an icy and biting charge slip and move between them, letting it be known that I was now the absolute power.

There was no way for me to suppress it. As the Old One had said, my strength will come with death. As my human side died, my vampire side took over. I had no mortal weaknesses. I had no energy to lose. My powers were woven and derived from my vampire side, and it was my human side that had weakened. But now, as I stood facing my adversary and his coven, I found myself completely and totally fearless. I had died by the hands of my archenemy, and now, because of him, I was immortal.

I waited for the men that Nicholas claimed would protect his so-called throne, but no one came forward.

"You are cowards!" Nicholas yelled as he eyed each and every one of his most trusted minions.

As I turned around to face Nicholas, I held out an open hand, then slowly closed my fingers. With each centimeter they closed, Nicholas's sword drifted between us until it flew into my palm, and I closed my fingers around it.

I looked down at the sword I had dropped after pulling it out of my back, then flipped the tip of the hilt with my toe until it, too, flew into the air. I grabbed it.

With a sword in each hand, I walked to Nicholas, and released my hold on him. As he dropped to his knees, he clutched his chest.

"I am not done with you, you cretin," Nicholas yelled, but as he struggled to stand up, he froze. "Is that how you are going to do it? You are going to behead me without the dignity of a proper duel?" Nicholas said in a low and husky tone.

"I'm giving you as much of a duel as you offered me when you bullied me into surrendering. When you tortured my friends and family to keep me from using my abilities, and when you used them as pawns when I let you live on your throne last night, you lost the right to a proper duel."

As Nicholas's coven whispered and muttered over his deceit, a small part of me smiled within.

I looked at Nicholas, a sinister smirk tracing my lips.

"You promised them years ago that the prophecy was a ruse, a hoax to deter you from claiming your rightful place as ruler. Well, may I present to you, the *soi-disant*, the *ideo-dicitur*, the so-called prodigy, Arri," I said with a mocking bow.

"This child," I went on with sarcasm, as I cocked my head to the side, "this abomination, overthrew you. You cut a path for evolution, but it wasn't to rule the world. It was for freedom, and the right to live. That was our destiny."

As I threw his own words back at him, he trembled with anger. Nicholas squared his shoulders and dared to try to stand.

I crossed my two swords against his neck, shaking my head.

"I don't want to kill you. I'm not a murderer. The war is over." With a saddened heart that it had to come to this, I let my swords drop and Nicholas stood tall and proud.

"The war isn't over until you are dead," Nicholas said as he picked up a discarded sword from the ground and swung it in my direction. With an effortless flick of my wrist, I swung my own weapon. As the blade slid through his throat, I could feel his life slip from space and time as Nicholas's head hit the floor.

He was dead.

With my sword in midair, I glanced down at the blood-stained blade.

A single tear fell down my cheek as I realized what I had done. My breaths came out in shaky gasps as my shoulders quivered. It was never easy to kill a man, especially when there had already been so much death, even if he left you no choice. But what he had taken from me would never make up for his death.

As I laid the swords down across his chest, finality and completeness filled me. It was over.

Although we had won, as I looked over at his coven, they felt lost.

"Your debts have been paid. Your services as Nicholas's servants are no longer needed. But in this, you still have each other. It is up to you to keep this from happening again. I hope that you will be able to find it in yourself to become families and covens, not under dictatorship, but under loyalty to your covens and Coven Masters." I didn't know what to say, but I hoped that they would be able to make it into civilization as vampires, not enemies.

As the room quieted, and all eyes landed on me, I saw hope in each and every face. With a pledge of their hands over their hearts, the entire room, both covens, fell to their knees before me.

I turned around and reached for Michael. As we joined hands, Alex, Phoenix, Jonathan, my parents, and Ash all bowed. Behind them, the Shadows took to their knees. Michael and I were the only ones standing. We had become the king and queen, the ultimate leaders, the supreme Coven Masters.

As everyone looked up at Michael and me, I felt what they wanted. They were asking us for our acceptance.

Michael and I looked at each other, then back out at our coven, and we bowed our heads as we accepted our roles.

Alex, Jonathan, Phoenix, and Ash beamed with pride and honor as they smiled back at me. My mother had tears in her eyes and my dad bowed to me with respect.

Then there was Michael, standing right beside me. I had felt his presence and strength helping me along the way.

"Are you all right?" I asked as I smiled at Michael.

"Me? I'm fine," Michael said as he took my hands in his. He

flipped them over and traced the two tiny scars where the metal handcuffs had ripped into my skin, then pulled me into his arms and hugged me as if we had been apart for centuries rather than forty-eight hours.

As his breath grazed my neck, and his palms stretched out along my back, I felt at home.

"How are you?" Michael asked, pulling me in for a kiss.

"Me? I'm fine," I said, smiling.

It felt surreal, almost like one of my dreams. I half expected to wake up and realize that Nicholas was just playing with me, and I would awaken with scars and burns like before. Except for this time, I wouldn't sit up in a panic because it was not imagined through our thoughts. The blood on Nicholas's floor, the red-stained blade in my hand, and the white marble room that haunted my every waking moment until this point was real and absolute. While both covens stood in silent reverence and the Shadows behind me, all eyes were on me. The attention of the room had shifted from two separate covens to one. Feeling throughout the room, I felt no ill-harbored emotions for Nicholas's death, my authority, or even the union of Nicholas's coven.

Could this be real? Could it be as easy as cutting off the snake's head, and the rest will follow? For three years, I have ducked and dodged Nicholas's demand for my death, and just like that, all is forgiven. Then it hit me. Nicholas's claim was that I was a half-breed, a mongrel, an abomination, but by his own hand, he has made me powerful and as pure as himself. For him to be a pure vampire, his human side had to die, and now, so has mine. Nicholas had created me from fear, and now, I take my rightful place as his successor.

Three years ago, I was afraid of my own shadow, wishing for adventure but too scared to face it when it came. Now I stand before my adventure with courage and excitement to face the future, whether it be smooth sailing or fierce and dangerous. I am ready.

THE END

THANK YOU

Thank you for reading the *Paradox Trilogy*. I hope you enjoyed reading it as much as I enjoyed writing it. Don't forget to sign up for my Newsletter to receive my exclusive bonus chapter Forgotten Journal, new releases, and more fun. Ascendance is the last book in the Paradox Trilogy, but my new saga the **Last Turning** will be available soon. I hope you enjoy.

Dear Reader

Hello Readers,

Thank you for reading Ascendance, I'm happy you got to read the Paradox Trilogy.

I'd love to hear from you.
If you enjoyed Ascendance, please consider leaving a review.
Every review helps, even if it's only a sentence or two. You know us author types, we just love that sort of thing!

For reviews!
Amazon
Goodreads

For new release updates and to follow me:
Facebook
jamieripp.com

Thank You and Happy Reading,
Jamie Ripp

ABOUT THE AUTHOR

Jamie Ripp is the author behind the Paradox Trilogy. She has lived a full and adventurous life as a hostage negotiator, a referee, and a monster slayer. Jamie is the main character of her own personal safari as she fights off mountain lions, has standoffs with bears, and contains flightless aviaries and herds of hoofed wildlife. She has studied battle strategy, visited the rainforest, battled vampires, demons, and courted death with nothing more than a pen and caffeine.

Actually, while living in the mountains of Montana, Jamie has come face to face with a mountain lion, slept in a tent alongside a bear, and enjoys feeding her chickens and deer while trekking through three feet of snow. As for a referee and monster slayer, well, she is married and the mother of three.

While Jamie has never been in a hostage situation, she has been part of a group chat and has been a prisoner of war within the battalion of three teenagers.

While writing, Jamie has played the part of writer and character. She has defeated coven masters, found love among the trees, and courted the Grimm Reaper.

In short, she is Super Woman with an imagination, also known as an author and a mother.

BOOKS BY JAMIE:

Paradox Trilogy

Paradox
Revelation
Ascendance

Exclusive Bonus Chapter:

Forgotten Journal

www.ingramcontent.com/pod-product-compliance
Lightning Source LLC
Chambersburg PA
CBHW020306030826
48979CB00029B/2190/J